THE RIGHT THING

TERRY PERSUN

WILD BLUE
PRESS

WildBluePress.com

THE RIGHT THING published by:
WILDBLUE PRESS
P.O. Box 102440
Denver, Colorado 80250

Publisher Disclaimer: Any opinions, statements of fact or fiction, descriptions, dialogue, and citations found in this book were provided by the author, and are solely those of the author. The publisher makes no claim as to their veracity or accuracy, and assumes no liability for the content.

WILDBLUE PRESS is registered at the U.S. Patent and Trademark Offices.

ISBN 978-1-952225-94-9 Trade Paperback

ISBN 978-1-952225-93-2 eBook

Cover design © 2021 WildBlue Press. All rights reserved.

Book Cover Design / Interior Formatting by Elijah Toten
www.totencreative.com

THE
RIGHT
THING

CHAPTER 1

The blade penetrated deeper as Ten pushed the tip of the paring knife into his shoulder. He didn't stop until he could feel it. Really feel it. By the time that happened, his other pain, the one that had tormented him all evening, the monumental loss of his wife and unborn child, brought tears to his eyes.

The lights blinked. *Not that too.* The storm had rumbled its way toward his street since early afternoon. Now, after midnight, it arrived. He let the knife drop into the kitchen sink.

He still couldn't sleep well, even after a few years. Haunted, he walked around in the evenings by nightlight, more zombie than man.

Blood ran down his arm. He plucked the hand towel from where it had been slung over the oven handle and put pressure over the wound he'd just created to sop the blood. The lights blinked again immediately before a loud thunderclap shook the windows. He squeezed the hand towel, and his skin burned underneath.

The pain proved he was alive.

He ran water over the bloody blade of the knife for a second before placing it into the dishwasher. Neatness was a habit. He threw the hand towel into the washer on his way back toward his bedroom. A bright light cracked outside— or would soon crack—as lightning jagged across his room, illuminating the rumpled sheets, clean dresser top, and open closet door. Then the thunderclap he expected shook the windows again, just before the bathroom nightlight went out. He glanced outside. No street lights. The complete darkness of the outside world now matched his inside world as he collapsed into the bed, praying that his exhaustion would bring sleep.

Ten awakened to light streaming through his bedroom window. Clear skies opened beyond the sheer curtains. He rolled and the top sheet came with him, stuck to the dried blood on his arm. He pulled the sheet loose and saw his wound had bled more than he'd expected. And it hurt. "Fuck." He stood in his boxers and stripped the bed, walked down the hall, threw the soiled sheets into the washer, poured in detergent, and pulled the knob on. He stripped and showered, the shower nozzle delivering cold and hot water at intervals from the washer pulling hot water. He didn't care.

After dressing, Ten set the clock in his bedroom to match his cell phone, then set the microwave clock before heading toward the front door. He opened the door and saw Maria's car parked in his driveway and her leaning against the driver's side door with her arms crossed.

She pushed off and walked toward him. "You forgot, didn't you?"

"Breakfast. It must be Sunday."

"You really need to get a regular job." She took his arm and tugged him forward.

He flinched, then acted as though he was checking for his house keys to hide the reaction. "You're right. I had forgotten."

"I could tell by the way you looked at me. I take it you were going out for breakfast anyway."

"Going to get coffee at least," he said.

"We can do better than that."

He had met Maria soon after the murder of his family. The government had chosen to get rid of every scientist and their families involved in a particularly dangerous, secret nanobot technology. Maria's partner was killed too, while attempting to protect them for as long as he could. He died in her arms.

Now she worked for the same outfit that tried to kill them at that time. That same government group was now headed by Jacob Sempter, one of the scientists involved with the first secret nanobot technology group. *Oh, the tangled web.* The whole government operation had been wiped clean of the in-house monsters who had ordered the mass murder. Jacob now made sure the group did the job it was supposed to do in the first place—protect the people.

Ten worked for the group, ISTI (International Security for Technological Innovations), as a freelancer, but it had been over a year since they'd called him. Maria's interest in having breakfast probably meant Jacob had sent her to sway Ten into another job. He wouldn't need much convincing this time. He was running low on money and could see the future pretty clearly if he didn't do something soon. Yet perhaps Maria was right and he should just get a regular job.

She let go of his arm so he could step around the car and get in on the other side. "Denny's," she said. "Which side of town?"

"We don't have to go to Denny's."

"I know you like it," she said.

"I do."

"So, I'll decide. It's a nice morning to drive across town. The scenic route."

"Did Jacob talk with you about this morning?"

She gave him a sideways glance. "Is that what you think? It's our every-other-Sunday breakfast, that's all."

"I'm sorry. You seemed different is all."

"I like to check on you occasionally," she said with a slight smirk. "Why'd you ask about Jacob?"

"No reason."

"You know," she started, "I sent you to my therapist because I thought she could help. But if you don't try—"

The comment seemed to come out of the blue. He looked down at his own feet. Maria didn't waste time with small talk. "Did Carol tell you I wasn't trying?"

"No, she doesn't talk about you when I'm with her. Hippocratic oath and all that." She quieted as she turned toward town, passing the Denny's they could have gone to had they chosen the closest one. "You flinched when I grabbed your arm."

"Is that why you grabbed it? To check?"

"Jesus, Ten. Not everything is thought through. You're the only one who does that. That big brain of yours won't stop analyzing. It won't even let you sleep." She winked at him playfully. "That observation is from those bags under your eyes."

"You observe too well," he said. "Talk about a big brain."

"You wouldn't want me to be any other way."

"So, how about that storm last night. Did your lights go out?" he asked.

"Change the subject all you want. I worry about you."

"I know. You don't have to," he said.

"You won't. Someone has to."

"Did your lights go out?" he asked again.

Maria nodded. "All right. Yes, for a while in the middle of the night. I woke up and the clock was blinking, or I wouldn't have known."

"Mine went out about 12:30."

"I was fast asleep by then. Not even the thunder and lightning could wake me."

"I wish I could sleep even half that well," he admitted.

"Carol can help."

"I won't take pills."

She laughed as she swung the car around a corner. "That's not what I meant. Does she give you exercises to do? Ways to think differently? Observations to make? That's what she does with me. I've even started meditating, not that I'm good at it. But the world is still here, it's still beautiful, and you still have a place in it."

"I'm glad she's able to help you," he said.

"Did you even notice how beautiful the day was this morning?"

"Yeah." He turned his head away.

"You need to do something with that big brain of yours. I'll talk with Jacob. You wouldn't consider joining us, would you?"

"I like my independence, my freedom. Besides…" He let the sentence slip away and noticed Maria didn't finish the sentence either.

Once she pulled into the parking lot, Ten exited the car almost before it stopped all the way. The engine was still running. He made his way to her side of the car and opened the door.

"Thank you. For a moment there, I thought you were going to run away."

He took a deep breath. "You're right. It's a beautiful day, and I need to notice that."

She took his other arm this time. "If Carol isn't helping, I have to consider it's because you don't want to be helped."

"I didn't say she wasn't helping. As she tells me when I ask if she expects to see any progress, 'Only time will tell.'"

"So you haven't given up?"

Ten slowed and turned toward Maria, looked her in the eye. "Amy was the love of my life. At the time, I couldn't imagine living without her. We were going to have a daughter." He shook his head slightly but kept his eyes on Maria's. "Now I am without her. And I'm not living without her. I'm not living at all. I'm existing."

Maria brushed the corner of her eye. "I know. And I'm sorry."

"I know you know. You lost Ben. I don't know how you do it."

"You will. Keep at it. Keep seeing Carol." She gave him a quick smile. "Okay, my friend, you may have been right to avoid this conversation. Tell me what you've been doing with yourself and I'll tell you all the boring details about my past couple of months working with those girls who were involved in the Humanzee experiments."

"The girls who were trafficked. I thought that ended months ago."

"I'm still very much involved with a few of them."

"Good. They need someone with your compassion."

"I'm no expert."

"You're better. You care. Sometimes all an expert offers is knowledge. Those girls need more than that."

A waitress showed them to a table near a window overlooking the parking lot. Maria sat facing the front door. Ten hesitated for a moment, then sat across from her as another waitress, wandering around with a coffee pot, stopped by and filled their cups and asked if they'd like to order. Ten knew what he wanted. Bacon and eggs, hash browns. Coffee. A simple breakfast. He quickly glanced around the diner, noticing other guests either talking or bent over plates of food. The coffee smelled good, strong.

Maria ordered a Belgian waffle with mixed berries and whipped cream.

Ten fidgeted with his coffee cup and glanced over his shoulder. He asked if Maria was still on full time with ISTI.

"Jacob has managed to keep me busy with small projects where my biological training is useful." She winked. "He could do the same for you."

"I've considered it, but like I already said on the drive over—"

"You're afraid of what they'll ask you to do," she suggested.

"I'm afraid," he said and left it there.

Ten's arm hurt when he moved it the wrong way, so he tried to keep it still. He must have driven the knife in pretty deep, and for a moment, he wondered if he'd damaged anything important. He had an urge to touch the wound but held back, not wanting Maria to think it was worse than it really was. He could inspect the wound later. Besides, he'd find out more tomorrow when he went to his Taekwondo practice and had to use the arm. If it wasn't for those practices and the gym, he'd be worse off, and he knew it. He had told Carol the same thing. But he didn't say that to Maria.

She went on to explain about the girls she'd been working with, trying to get them over the horrible insemination they had gone through, the birthing of inhuman children, the shame they felt for themselves and their families. "It was a complete horror show," she admitted. "I did everything I could to help before the professionals took over."

"Were you okay about that?" he asked as he looked around behind him again.

"Yes. It was best for the girls. I think I did my part. And like I said, I'm still involved with a few of them peripherally." She reached toward him and tapped the table. "You want to swap places?"

Ten had to laugh. "Would you mind? I like to see whose coming in."

"Facing the door. You're still on duty." She slid from her seat and let him swap over to her side. She sat down and dragged her coffee cup in front of her. "Feel better?"

"Much."

"Maybe this isn't what you want, but you're a natural. You're always on alert. You evaluate everything." She looked around the room. "I bet you know which of these couples are arguing and which aren't."

"Maybe," he said. "But I also know our breakfast is coming."

Maria leaned back as the waitress got closer. "You need to work."

"You may be right, but who would trust me other than Jacob?"

CHAPTER 2

Valeria stood behind Ken, her hands pressed on to the back of his chair as she leaned over his shoulder and watched his progress. He smelled her sweet breath next to his cheek. Part of him wanted her to leave and another part wanted to impress her. But that wasn't what his actions were about at the moment.

"I'm not sure this is such a good idea," she said, "but if you're serious..." She reached over and punched a few keys.

"Brilliant," he said.

Valeria was a cute Mexican girl who went to school with him. She got her interest in computers from her uncle and cousin who had helped get her and her family to Pennsylvania in the first place. Her dad was a mechanic, a great one. He could fix anything. But she had never been interested in engines. She did love computers though, and Ken knew she was a near genius when it came to programming.

"I *know* it's not a good idea," Craig said. He sat on the edge of Ken's bed. They were in Ken's bedroom, had been for hours. Craig rubbed his hands together, and his feet bounced on the threadbare carpet. A slight breeze of cold air pushed through the slightly open window. The desk lamp held back the moonlight, keeping it outside.

"I'm almost there. At least I hope so." Ken gave a nervous laugh, his fingers flying over the keys of the laptop.

"I can't believe this," Valeria said. "I wouldn't have imagined."

Craig stood and paced. "Please don't. Ken, really. This isn't a good idea."

"I know, but I have to do something. He was innocent and now he has a record."

"I don't want to get into trouble," Craig said.

"No need," Ken said. "We get it. Really, we do. I don't want any of my friends to get into trouble." He glanced at Valeria again. "Not that I even expect to get into trouble."

"You're too good at this," she said.

Ken felt blood rush to his face.

Craig thanked them again and left the room. Valeria turned back to where she stood before and watched as Ken attacked his laptop keyboard as though time were running out.

"You really shouldn't be here either," Ken said again. "I worry about you."

"I can take care of myself. I've been doing it long enough."

"Sorry, I didn't mean anything."

"I know. Just keep working."

After a few more minutes, he grimaced.

"What's wrong?" she asked.

"I don't know, something doesn't feel right. But I'm almost there. I can do this."

"I know you can," she said.

Blood rushed to his face for the second time that night. Her support felt good. He kept going, even though it didn't feel the same all of a sudden. A few more steps that seemed maybe too easy, and he was in. He sat back for only a second.

Valeria put a hand on his shoulder. "That's so cool."

He went back to the keyboard. "You helped."

"You going to change his record now?"

"I'm going to remove him from the record completely. Maybe that'll help him get a job. At least make it easier."

"I can't believe you're doing this," she said, "but I love it."

"It's scary," he said as he searched for all the places his dad's record could be hidden. There must be a central location that, if he deleted it, his dad's name wouldn't appear anywhere else. Or maybe it was simply that the record was only in one place. He deleted as much as he could, did another search, and pulled out, blocking how he got into the system. "Let's hope," he said while opening his browser to do a search. He typed in his dad's name and came up with some general information but nothing about his arrests or the time he spent in prison. Even he was shocked that he could do it. He smiled and turned in his chair.

Valeria smiled back at him, then bent down and hugged him quickly. "I've never seen anything like that. You are so good at this."

"We can't say anything. Even to Craig," Ken said. "We can't tell him it worked. He would never lie about anything and I don't want to put him into that situation."

"I know."

"What about you?"

"I won't tell anyone," she said. "We could both get into a lot of trouble."

CHAPTER 3

Josh Hobart burst into the room like there was a fire in the hallway. The five students jumped from their huddle of conversation and stared at him as he halted in front of his desk and dropped his computer onto it, making a loud clap. He quickly focused his attention on Kenneth Hemming.

"What?" Ken said.

Hobart's lips tightened. He shook his head violently. He was pissed. "You most likely know why I am late to Computer Club?"

Ken produced a tentative smile. The other kids stepped back from him, except for Valeria, who reached for his hand but only tapped it with her fingers.

"Don't solace him," Hobart said, not even looking at Valeria.

She pulled her hand away but still didn't step away.

"It's okay," Ken said to her. "I don't know what happened, but I know what I did."

"And what did you do? Please, tell the rest of us," Mr. Hobart said.

"I hacked the FBI records."

"They came to my house. I just spent an hour with them. They weren't happy."

"You didn't do anything," Ken said.

"No, but I'm your teacher. I run Computer Club. They wanted to know why I'm teaching my students how to hack government servers. Which, as you all know, including you,

Mr. Hemming, that I do not teach any such thing here. In fact, any such activity is off limits. There are rules. Everyone else sticks to them." Then he let out a long breath as though he'd been holding it since he'd entered the classroom. He finally took his eyes from Ken. He couldn't help the kid. His defeat, he was afraid, was showing. "I have to kick you out of the club," he said to the wide-eyed group.

"I understand," Ken said smoothly.

"No," Roger said in Ken's defense. "He won't do it again." He glanced back and forth between their teacher and Ken. "Come on."

"We won't let him," Valeria said.

"I'm afraid it's the rules," Hobart said. "I don't want to do this either. It bothers the hell out of me, to be honest." He pointed toward Ken. "You are good at this. You just have to watch how you use it. I know you know that. I know this was just thrilling to see if you could." He nodded. "And you probably had a reason," he admitted. "But your actions could cost my job and have you thrown in juvie." He shook his head. Fighting with his own decision. But he had to make it. There had to be limits. "I'm sorry," he said again. And he meant it.

"It's okay, Mr. Hobart. I understand. It was my choice. If I stay clean for a month—"

"Maybe the beginning of next year. After summer break. That's the best I can do." He looked to the other students, then back at Ken. "This was a warning. They could have come for you right away. It's their way of giving you a break. And, I suppose, their way of telling me that I have to watch you guys a lot closer. Either way, they won't do that again. The next time, we'll both be in big trouble."

"I didn't think you'd get into trouble. That makes no sense. I'm the one who did it."

Hobart ignored his apology and looked to the others. "You guys can keep him up to date on what we're doing. Just don't get involved in anything illegal." A part of him admired Ken, but that wasn't the part who taught the class. "Get your things together." He walked over and put a hand on Ken's shoulder. "I'm sorry."

"I get it," Ken said as he stuffed his laptop into his backpack and threw it over his shoulder. "I'll see you guys later." He gave them all a slight wave before leaving.

Once he was gone, Mr. Hobart walked back to his desk and sat on the edge, his eyes planted on the darkening sky out the window. "Maybe we go over the rules again before we start."

"We know the rules," Roger said.

"Maybe you can give Ken a break," Craig said.

Valeria gave Craig a quick stare, then turned away.

"The FBI gave him one already. They gave us both a break. They won't do it again, and I can't let this go by. I just can't. For now, this is how it has to be. It won't last forever as long as he stays clean." He looked at the small group of kids. "He'll listen to you guys. You know that. Maybe you keep him clean while you keep him up to date." Mr. Hobart paused. "I'm sure a few of you were with him at the time." He shook his head quickly. "I'm not asking. I don't want to know. Just keep him straight, okay?"

"It's because of his dad," Valeria said.

Mr. Hobart blew out another breath. He needed to breathe more often. He wasn't going to tell them what the FBI had discovered, but now that Valeria had said it directly... "His dad did something wrong. That's why he was in prison for a while. Tax evasion. Doesn't sound like much, but if you get caught, well. But he did his time. Ken was trying to clear his record, deleted a lot of files so it wouldn't show up when his dad went on job interviews. I can only imagine how tough it's been over there. For my part, I didn't want the FBI thinking the apple fell too close to the tree. That doing illegal things was easy for the whole family. I think they knew that wasn't true either. Maybe that's why they came to see me instead of arresting Ken in the first place, to get a line on what kind of kid he is. I'm sure they checked with the school and found he'd never been in trouble. I don't know. Maybe they knew it was out of desperation." He stopped for a moment.

"I need you guys to help me keep him safe. They won't be so flexible next time. I think I convinced them that Ken is a good kid. He's a kid. Just pushing the envelope." He talked through a lot of his explanation to the FBI while staring out the window, repeating what they'd told him as he tried to get it all straight himself. Once he finished, he turned back to them. "Some of you have more reason to hate the government than he does." He stood. "I don't know." He looked around the room. "Okay. Let's talk about what the rest of you have been up to. How's the assignment going?"

The students spread out and took their usual seats. Valeria, the only girl in the class, sat next to Craig, the only young Black man in the class, while Bill and Roger sat behind them. The group was tight, and both Bill and Roger reached out and tapped the person in front of them to let each know that they were still in this together. At least that's how Mr. Hobart saw it.

These were some of the smartest kids at Milton High School. They'd each had their share of time as an outcast. This time together seemed precious to them. He often felt he had saved one or two of them by bringing them together. He hated to have to be the one to push any one of them away. Like Ken.

Before they left later that evening, he pulled Roger aside for a moment. "I know you and Ken are pretty close."

"We all are," Roger said.

"I'd like you to let me know what's going on with him. That he's doing okay with this. That he's staying clean. If the FBI comes by again, I need to know the truth or I can't help keep him out of trouble."

Roger nodded. "Thanks. I didn't even know he was going to do anything. He never told me."

"I wasn't suggesting that."

"I know. I just wanted you to know. From now on, if I do find anything out, I'll tell you."

"I appreciate it."

"We know you're on our side."

"Thank you. Tell the others I said thank you too."

Roger walked out the door and Mr. Hobart stepped back into the room to collect his things. He hoped they would watch over Ken. He hoped they didn't get tied up in any of it. They'd all end up in juvie. As he turned to leave, Valeria stood at the door. "Did you forget something?" he asked.

"You were talking about me, weren't you? When you said some of us have more reason to hate the government," she said.

"Not just you," he said. "I suppose we all have our reasons." He smiled. "I wasn't an angel all through college. That's why I want you guys to know what not to do. Luckily, I never ended up in jail for anything."

"You weren't caught," Valeria said.

He shook his head and smiled at her. "Oh no you don't. We don't go into the teacher's past." He steadied his gaze. "Don't do anything that will jeopardize yourself or your father. Trust in the legal system. You can tell your friends that too."

"I could get in trouble," she said.

"We all could. You know that now. Take Ken as a warning." He tucked his laptop under his arm and headed toward the door with her beside him. "Is that all you wanted?"

"I just stayed back to let you know you don't have to worry about the rest of us," she said.

"I'm glad to hear it. Now, if you can keep Ken clean as well, we'll have a great year next year."

"Plan on it," she said as she walked down the hall ahead of him.

He turned off the room lights and locked the door. She was gone when he turned around. He wanted to believe her but there was something in the way she responded that caused him doubt.

CHAPTER 4

In the middle of the night, Sarah Andrews heard the clunk. Her eyes popped open, and she waited to see if it was real. It could have been a dream, that just-before-sleep shock to her system. She slid from bed and walked toward the barred cell door.

Had anyone else heard what she heard?

She approached the cell door cautiously. Something about the way it hung on its hinges told her she had been right. She pushed against it with her fingertips, and the door opened. She peered out. Two other women were looking out their doors as well. She smiled at them.

A glitch in the system?

Sarah waved for Sue and Emma to follow her. If they tried to wake those still asleep, it could cause too much of a fuss. Take the women who were already awake and forget the rest. The only thing to do next was check the door leading to the guardroom. If that was open…

***

For once, Ten had fallen asleep early. When he heard his cell phone playing "Owner of a Lonely Heart," it shocked him into full alertness. He had left the phone on the kitchen counter. By the time he got to it, he thought he'd missed the call. That it had gone into voicemail. But he answered anyway. "Yeah."

"I figured you'd be awake."

"Jacob. Actually, I was fast asleep and had to run for the phone. Why do you call me in the middle of the night anyway? When do you sleep?"

"Sleep?" Jacob laughed.

"Not important," Ten said. "You wanted something?"

Jacob laughed again. "Awake and grumpy." Ten could hear the fatigue in his voice. "I called because I have something for you, the two of you."

"Maria put you up to this," Ten suggested.

"There's been a prison escape. Women's prison in Pennsylvania. I can't allocate anyone, and I don't want to send her alone." He paused for a moment, probably waiting for Ten to respond. When he didn't, Jacob went on. "She may have mentioned you could use something to do, but I'm serious about not wanting her to check this out by herself."

"I'll only work as a contractor," Ten said.

"Whatever way you'd like to do it. You know that." Jacob's voice had trailed as though he was reconsidering his call.

"Did it just happen? The breakout."

"Earlier this evening. They're not exactly sure when it happened. They're investigating. I got the call a half hour ago."

"Are the escapees dangerous?"

"I don't have the full report, but I will email it to Maria's secure line as soon as it comes in. At the least, let's assume they don't want to go back to prison and might do anything not to get caught. Stolen cars. Hostages."

"Not sure what I can do to help. I'm not a policeman, not the FBI. I have to wonder why ISTI is even involved." He paused but not long enough for Jacob to respond. "But I'll go with her." He needed something to do. Some money.

"Great. That's what I wanted to hear. Can you meet her at Dulles in an hour? Tickets will be waiting for you."

"I can do that." Ten hung up as Jacob was saying thank you. He set the phone down and headed for the shower.

He'd forgotten to look at the time. Before he even turned on the water, the phone kicked in again and he answered faster this time. "Hi, Maria."

"You heard from Jacob then."

"Just got off the phone and was headed for the shower."

"Pick me up on your way. No need to pay parking for two cars."

"I'll be there in twenty. And thank you."

"You'll earn it," she said.

It didn't take long for Ten to shower, dress, pack, and drive over to Maria's place. She was already outside. She wore navy slacks and a green blouse. It looked emerald green under the streetlights. She wore pumps. Always practical. He pulled up behind her car in the driveway. She held her key fob up and the trunk popped open. She removed a case and nodded toward Ten.

He rolled his window down and opened the door. "I have a case for my gun."

"We can put them both in here. Efficient."

Ten pulled his gun case from his duffle and opened it before handing his Glock 17 and two full magazines to Maria.

"Still using that, I see."

"Sentimental."

"You have a strange idea of what's sentimental."

"Let's go." He jerked his head toward the car. Maria walked around the side and put her small suitcase on the seat behind the passenger seat of the car and set the gun case on the floor in front of it.

He dropped into the driver's seat. "Did you get more information from Jacob?"

"Something came through while I was getting ready, but I didn't look at it yet. We can read through it together on the flight to Montoursville. We have to fly through Charlotte to change planes. It'll be a while."

"Charlotte? How long is it going to be?"

"Four or five hours, I think," she said.

"What the fuck is Jacob thinking? We could drive it in that amount of time. Up Route 15 probably."

"Let me check that." Maria took out her phone. "The prison is only about a half hour or so from the Williamsport Airport." She tapped away as Ten drove toward Dulles. "We might save an hour, not counting the time we have to park and wait for our flight, then the time it'll take to rent a car once we get there." She laughed. "I'll let Jacob know we're driving."

Ten pulled his phone from his pocket and asked for directions to Williamsport. While he waited for his phone's GPS to kick in, he dropped it into his cup holder. "I think we can take 267 to 15. It'll be a pretty drive too."

"We get to watch the sunrise," she said.

"It'll be worth it." The phone responded. He glanced down. He was right.

"You're not too tired to drive?" Maria asked. "We can switch whenever you want."

"I got some solid sleep before Jacob called."

"I think this will be fun," she said.

"*Fun* isn't what I'd call it. We don't even know what we're supposed to do once we get there. Check it out? Help find the women who escaped? I'm sure the local police will just love to see us show up."

"We're supposed to figure out how they escaped. The electronics unlocked a bunch of doors in the middle of the night."

"Hackers?"

"Probably. But who would do that?"

Ten sped onto the highway. "I guess we're supposed to figure that out. Can't ISTI's software guys do that? It's not really our expertise."

"I think everyone is allocated to other jobs," she said.

"We're low on the totem pole, then."

"You have work, don't you? Besides, maybe this will teach us something."

"Like?"

"Like how some people have it worse than we do."

He gave her a sideways look. "I don't need to learn that. I get it. I'm not in prison. I'm not dead."

"I don't think you get it at all sometimes. All that aside, you're guessing about what may have happened. It could have been mechanical, an inside job, pretty much anything at this point."

"Can't figure it out until we get there." Ten turned on the radio. "Classic rock or classic rock?"

"Either one." She reached behind her and unzipped the side of her suitcase. "I'll check my email and see what Jacob sent over. Maybe they have a lead already. I can read it to you as you drive."

He pointed toward the radio. "Background music, then," he said as he turned the sound down.

Maria opened her email and pulled up a PDF report that Jacob had sent over. "It's longer than I thought. Maybe I'll just read it and give you the CliffsNotes."

"Deal. Can you read with the radio up?"

"Sure, if it keeps you awake."

He turned up the radio and opened his window. The cold morning blew in as he drove. Before long, they were driving through the country, and the temperature turned cooler and the air moister. He raised the window halfway, hummed with Lynyrd Skynyrd, and enjoyed the drive.

After a short while, Maria closed her computer and glanced out the window. "Sun's coming up. Going to be a beautiful morning. Carol told me to try to see the beauty in things. That it would help."

"Has it?"

She turned the radio down. "Truthfully? Not always." She gave him a forced smile. "I miss him. Never had a real boyfriend, for the most part. Men are nervous around smart women." She reached over and touched his arm. "I don't mean you. Anyway, he was good to me. Funny. Would listen even when he didn't understand what I was talking about." She laughed.

"Amy was like that."

"You had the same thing I did. The perfect person for an oddball. We're oddballs."

"You know you're not helping."

She sighed then took another deep breath. "Sometimes I think I'm trying to help you because if I can, then it proves we can get through this."

"So you don't feel better?"

"I do." She swung her head to look out her window. "Shit, Ten. It comes and goes. It's getting better. But is it time passing or Carol helping? My attitude changing or my memory slipping? I do all the things she says to do, like admire the sunrise, treat myself to a good breakfast—every other Sunday—spend time with friends. Sometimes I feel good about being alive, and sometimes I feel bad that Ben is dead. I understand what you're going through. I want it to stop. For both of us."

Ten nodded. "You're a good friend."

She stared at him for a moment, then laughed loudly. "We have some strange shit in common."

"On top of being oddballs?"

"Way on top of that," she said. "Do you think the others are as fucked up as we are?"

"No. Not Jacob, for sure. But I think he found his place, his moral place."

"You trust him."

"I do. And I know he's trying to do the best job he can. I just can't be tied up with the government in any committed way. Not after what happened. There are too many people with their own agendas involved. Not Jacob, which is why it's nice to have him on the inside. But others. I don't trust most of them."

"We're off topic," she said. "How about that sunrise?"

Ten laughed. "Thinking... and talking about all of this keeps my mind busy too. I have to thank you again. Work is good for me."

"But you won't join ISTI."

"I'm not ready."

"When you are—"

"I know. And I appreciate that. In the meantime, did you get anything from the report?"

"Not a lot. Some of the guards weren't around, and the one who was there had fallen asleep."

"Not around?"

"On break or something."

"Did they fire them?"

"I suspect there are not a lot of people in the area who want those jobs," she said.

"So no. Did they at least put them on some kind of probation?"

"They have to attend a night class."

"What the hell are we getting ourselves into?"

The eastern clouds bloomed with sunlight and pushed orange across the trees in the distance. Ten lowered the car's visor to block the glare.

Maria stared out her side window. "Ben would have loved to see this."

Amy would too.

***

Maria eventually napped for a half hour and awakened with a snort. "Oh God, sorry."

"It's okay," Ten said. "You didn't snore at all."

"Except when I just woke up. God, you get to see the worst of me all the time. Lucky you."

"It's mutual," he said.

She turned the radio off and asked how close they were.

"Getting there." He glanced at his phone's GPS. "Says twelve minutes."

"It's still early. You think we can stop somewhere."

"Breakfast or bathroom?"

"Both and then some. I need to wake up and regroup, don't you?" She took out her phone and asked for the nearest restaurant. The phone answered, and she pushed a button, then held the phone toward him with directions.

"Not too far out of our way. We'll have to backtrack a little." In a few miles, Ten turned off the highway and found a Cracker Barrel on Lycoming Mall Road. They parked and walked inside.

Maria stopped at the gift shelves for a moment, then told Ten to order her bacon and eggs. "And coffee. Lots of coffee." Then she walked into the restroom.

Ten was led to a table by an older woman with a newly washed apron. She must have just gotten on duty because the other waitresses didn't look so crisp. Soon after he sat down and ordered, Maria walked in from the lobby and took a chair opposite him.

Ten pointed and said, "Got you coffee."

"Good."

He held up his cup. "Cheers."

"You ordered?"

"Yep." He looked across at her. "What are we looking for, really?"

"The report was vague," she said.

He laughed. "Usually, we're working on some top secret, strange science-y thing. Now we're looking into a prison break. What has ISTI turned into?"

"You're complaining about getting work again," she said. "Besides, the last job wasn't so science-y, as you put it. I mean, artificial insemination to create monsters is a little, but we weren't involved in the actual science part of it. In fact, I don't even know what happened to the equipment after the whole thing broke loose."

"I'll bet it's in some warehouse like they show in *Indiana Jones*," he said. "Long aisles of secret stuff, alien weapons, high-tech black hole producers." He laughed. "Back to this case. What do you think we're supposed to find? If it's just a hack, it's probably a one-time deal. If it's an inside job, can't the locals take care of it?"

"I suppose we'll find out." She leaned back as their breakfasts were delivered. "I think it's something deeper than we might imagine. I don't think this is the end of it, and I don't think Jacob believes that either or we wouldn't be here."

"You make it sound ominous."

"It usually is."

CHAPTER 5

The scent of newly fertilized fields brought tears to their eyes as they drove toward Muncy. "Cow manure," Ten said as he raised the windows. He glanced at the temperature gauge on his dash. "It's already 76 out there." He flicked the air conditioner on. "And I thought DC was a swamp."

"Does it always smell like this?" Maria said with a wrinkled nose.

"This time of year, I suspect. It's going to get hot today too, I'll bet."

"Maybe the gaining cloud cover over those hills will bring some cool rain."

"With tons of humidity first." He shook his head. "I'll pray for rain."

Maria said, "Turn right to get back onto 405. We have to cross the Susquehanna River pretty soon. Then we're right there." She wrinkled her nose again. "You think it'll smell like this inside? If so, no wonder the prisoners want to escape. I couldn't work somewhere like this."

"It's not like this year round, you know. Only during fertilizing season. On your other note, where are they escaping to?" Ten asked before answering his own question. "Fields and fields of that terrible odor unless they head for the hills."

"One of the women who escaped is pretty dangerous. Killed two men. Mentally unstable. The others aren't much better," Maria said as though she forgot about the smell.

"What makes people—"

"Don't even go there," she said. "These women have been so abused. It's insane. Everything from getting beaten regularly to being pimped out by their own fathers. Or mothers. All for drugs or booze or money. God knows there is way too much crazy in this world. I'm surprised more people aren't killing each other."

"It happens enough."

"Wide river," Maria said as they entered the bridge. "Looks high."

"Spring runoff, maybe."

"I wouldn't want to be in there." She pushed her head against the window. "You think they might try for the river? Float downstream? The current looks wicked."

"I wouldn't, but then I'm not trying to escape something that's potentially worse."

They crossed the bridge and were back in a space of open fields and a few farmhouses and businesses. "Here we are," Maria said as Ten turned toward the Muncy Correctional Institute.

He drove the long drive between fields of grass. A few trees, newly leafed and green in the early summer heat, stood on either side.

They had called ahead, so there were three people waiting near the gate when they arrived. Two men, one in a police uniform, and a woman approached once they parked, got out of the car, and walked toward the entrance. It was humid enough that Ten's upper lip and forehead beaded sweat before they reached the others.

The woman stepped forward with her hand out. "Hi, I'm Superintendent Cooke." She shook each of their hands with a huge, fake smile plastered across her face. Then she stepped back and motioned toward the suited man. "This is Dr. Paton. He heads up the Psych Ward." He also shook their hands but without the fake smile. They were both very stiff in their movements, as though they were trying way too hard.

The man in the police uniform didn't wait for her to introduce him. He reached toward Ten. "I'm Jake Carney, police chief around here." He shook Maria's hand too.

Ten and Maria were all *nice to meet you* as well. Then Maria introduced herself. "Maria Tanner," she said before turning toward Ten. "My associate, Tempest Nesbit."

Ten hoped that he and Maria didn't appear quite as tight-assed.

"Beautiful grounds," Maria said, making Ten throw her a quizzical glance.

"Except that it stinks around this time of year," Superintendent Cooke said. "And it's getting humid already. Let's go inside."

Cooke and Paton dressed similarly in dark slacks and light-colored shirts, Cooke in light blue and Paton in light green. Chief Carney's uniform looked stiff with starch. His hair was cut short, and he sported meaty fingers. Geared up the way he was, Ten expected him to look hotter, but his brow was cool in all that baggage.

Ten wore a plain navy t-shirt and jeans. Maria's emerald blouse didn't appear to fit in.

Ahead of them stood the main building. They walked to the right of a flagpole that stood in the middle of the sidewalk. The brick building looked old, its architecture more like a state building than a prison. The other buildings that housed the prisoners were separate from the office building and looked like warehouses from a distance. That's probably what they were. A bell tower rose up from the center of the building in front of them. Four sets of windows looked out from either side of the central entrance, first and second floor. And half windows opened onto the lawn from what must have been the basement offices. As could be expected, Cooke and Paton led them up to the second story and to a conference room that overlooked the front lawn.

Best views for the top brass. The conference room was all very well-appointed with a long oak table and oak chairs.

Ten turned to the wall where photos of prisoners were hung, all of them smiling as though they were at an amusement park and not in a prison. He noticed that there were photos of some of the cell blocks but only one or two of actual cells. He got closer to one of the photos and saw it was decorated with kids' drawings on the wall. It seemed obvious that the kids' mother lived in that room. A thin, young figure sat on the bunk with her back toward the camera, slumped-over shoulders, head down. Regardless of the happy drawings of a sun and stick people with their arms out in celebration, the photo gave off a depressing feeling. In the cell, there was a tiny, one-person desk with an open notebook on top, and the skinny bunk where the girl sat defeated. The room looked unbearably tiny to Ten. Just getting so close to it made him claustrophobic, and he had to step back and turn toward the window to regain his equilibrium. He noticed Dr. Paton staring at him when he turned around. "They look awfully happy for being imprisoned," Ten said.

"We try," the super said. "But I suppose you're not here to talk about the happy ones." Her head jerked back defiantly, and Ten noticed a tinge of cockiness from the way her chin rose. That was just before the fake smile stretched across her face again. "Before we start, do you mind showing us your credentials?" Her eyes widened.

"Not at all," Maria said. She pulled her ID from a small pocket in her slacks and held it toward the superintendent, who leaned over to glance at it.

"And you," she said to Ten.

"He's with me," Maria said. "My technical consultant."

Superintendent Cooke glanced at the police chief, and he nodded.

"Please, sit down." She looked at Maria before turning her head toward Ten. "Maria here said you drove up from

DC. So you may not have heard that we caught two of the three women." She nodded her head as though agreeing with herself. "And I'm confident our local police will find the last before long." She smiled at Chief Carney, who had remained standing near the window.

"Soon, I suspect," Chief Carney plugged in.

"As you probably noticed, there are not many places to hide at this time of year." She shuffled in her seat and glanced at Dr. Paton before driving her eyes into Maria for a long pause before speaking again. "I'm not sure why you're here at all. We have this under control. We've done nothing wrong."

"We're not concerned about your ability to find the escapees," Ten said.

Maria leaned forward then. "We are from ISTI, not Homeland Security."

"I saw that on your ID. I don't even know what that is," the superintendent said.

"International Security for Technological Innovations," Ten said.

She laughed and looked at her colleagues with amusement. "Innovation? You've got to be kidding me."

"We're not," Ten said.

"We suspect a hacker, which means there has to be some way to get into your systems," Maria said. "The very reason Ten is here with me."

"Have you had any recent upgrades, any breaches of your technology at all?" Ten asked.

Dr. Paton said, "Wasn't there some new equipment installed recently?"

The superintendent looked annoyed, as though she wanted this to be over with quickly. "Hardware upgrades. We're in the middle of it now. It's still really old equipment. Trust me, there is nothing new being used in this building." She huffed.

"I would like to have access to it, if you don't mind," Ten said.

Cooke appeared slightly flustered. "Well. Hmm. Well, I guess I can't see why not."

"We won't be long," Maria said.

"Someone has to go with you."

"I'll wander down with them," Chief Carney said.

Cooke nodded. "You know where we keep most of the equipment downstairs."

"I may want to check the hardware at the buildings, the interconnections, and the cameras." Ten waited for a response.

"Sounds like it'll take longer than a short while."

"We'll be quick," Maria said, "but we'll also be back."

Ten wasn't sure why she said that unless she was establishing territorial rights with this uptight super. He rather liked the way Cooke's face muscles tightened when Maria announced her authority. Shifty-eyed Dr. Paton hadn't said a thing but stared at the two of them as though trying to evaluate what was before him. Maybe that's why Cooke had him there.

"You ready?" Chief Carney asked as he headed around the table.

Maria smiled at the superintendent and pushed back in her chair. "Ten."

He followed the two of them out and could feel the eyes boring into his back. They walked all the way down two flights of stairs into the basement offices. They entered one room where a rack of electronics with blinking lights and cables stretched between them were mounted against the wall.

"Only part of the stuff, as you can imagine," Carney said. "There are observation rooms several places, and Wi-Fi routers around."

"You sound like you know your way around this equipment," Ten said politely.

"Kind of a buff," he said. "Look, I don't know what this ISTI group is or what it has to do with this, but it's got to be more than a few escaped prisoners. I didn't want to say anything around Elizabeth, but I would like to know what's going on."

"Elizabeth?" Maria asked.

"Cooke," he said. "She can be a bit of a—"

"Bitch," Maria said.

Carney laughed at that. Then he got more serious. "It's a tough job. Things like this happen and everything opens up. One door opens and it makes it look like things are out of control—even when they're not. I'm sure she doesn't need a lot of people snooping around."

"If she's done nothing wrong?" Ten asked as he pulled at wires and looked to see what type of equipment was plugged into what.

"A huge disruption, no matter what," Carney said.

"We're not here to make her life difficult," Maria said.

"I'll let her know that. And that you two are okay." He took in a deep breath. "Look, if I can help in any way. Or at least keep me informed."

"We might need your help," Maria said. "Once Ten figures this all out."

"I could use some tools. I have a meter in my duffle. But I'd like to take a walk-through and familiarize myself first." He nodded toward Chief Carney. "Okay with you?"

"I'll have to talk with Cooke. She'll want her IT person to go with us."

"Great. He can explain everything."

"She," Carney said. "Wait here and I'll get her. Her office is just around the corner."

In a moment, Chief Carney came back into the room with a young woman about twenty-five years old with short, cropped blonde hair, fair skin, and a slight body. She didn't look anything like an IT person.

"Hi, I'm Nancy," she said, but didn't hold out her hand to shake or anything. In fact, she held back, slightly behind Carney.

"You look pretty young," Ten said.

"Seriously?" Maria said. She stepped forward and reached toward Nancy. "He's an idiot. Pay no attention. We're glad to meet you."

They shook and Nancy glanced at Ten before saying to Maria, "Got my degree a year and a half ago. Top of my class. I only chose this because I felt morally obligated."

"I'm sorry." Ten stepped next to Maria. "I'm Tempest Nesbit. I didn't mean anything. I should know better. I graduated early and worked on some pretty unbelievable jobs right out of school." He nodded toward Maria. "But as you probably guessed, she's the real genius in this room."

Nancy smiled authentically then. "I'll take that as an apology." She walked further into the room and pointed at the rack of equipment. "That's all new stuff, but it's not all online yet. We're phasing it in. I can show you around if you want."

"Let's wait until I have my tools," Ten said. "I just wanted to get an idea what was going on. Do you happen to have installation manuals available that I could look over?"

"Give me your email and I'll send you a PDF of the brochure, the install guide, and the troubleshooting guide. I'd send the catalog but it's just specs you can find in the brochure for the most part."

"That would be fantastic." He read off his email address and she entered it into her phone.

Maria said, "Well, Ten, are we good to go for now? Or you want to take a walk around after all?"

"Later is good. Once I have a chance to check out the equipment guides."

"So, is it Ten or Tem?" Nancy asked.

"Ten," he answered. "Acronym for Tempest Eugene Nesbit." He was impressed with her focus on details. Probably good at her job.

"Clever," she said.

"Not really. I have to explain it more than I'd like."

She laughed. Her demeanor was friendly and relaxed, almost too relaxed, unlike everyone else they met so far. Although Chief Carney relaxed more as they got to know him and he got to know them. "I'll send that stuff to you. I'd better get back to work now." She smiled and walked away, just like that.

"Nice kid," Carney said. "Known her family since forever."

"Do we need to check out before leaving?" Maria asked.

"I can take care of that," Carney said. "Remember, I'd like to help if I can."

"Oh, we'll be calling," Maria assured him. "But for now, Ten's got some reading to do."

Ten smiled at him before he turned and they filed out of the room, up the stairs, and outside. Jake Carney stopped at the front gate and shook each of their hands again.

"Let her know we'll call before coming over," Maria told him, referring to Superintendent Cooke.

"Will do."

As they walked toward their car, Maria asked out the corner of her mouth, "Any idea what's going on here?"

"I have no idea whatsoever. But I plan to figure it out."

CHAPTER 6

"Every fucking thing in the damned universe is connected to the fucking internet these days," Ten said while Maria sat across from him nibbling at her salad.

They sat in the snug sitting area off the lobby of the Holiday Inn Express in New Columbia where they'd checked in. Ten's duffle and Maria's suitcase sat next to their chairs. Their pistol case sat on the wide coffee table in front of them. Ten had his laptop across his knees and was hunched over it while reading.

They had picked up a sub for Ten and mixed salad for Maria from a local quick-stop sandwich shop on their way. He hadn't noticed the name of the shop, but there was a line at the counter when they walked in, which was a good sign, especially in a small town. They figured they could get water in their rooms but didn't make it that far. By the time Maria checked in for two rooms, Ten had taken one bite of his sandwich and had opened his computer. He was skimming the PDFs Nancy had sent over to him. He shook his head.

"You should eat," Maria said.

He looked up. "Yeah. We should probably head to our rooms pretty soon too. I just wanted to take a quick look."

"I *did* check us in," she said. A loud rumble like a train passing just outside the doors interrupted their conversation. "I love thunder."

"Maybe the shift to negative ions," Ten said.

"I like the rain too. It's finally coming. Maybe it'll cool down."

"Let me close down here." Ten logged out and lowered his laptop lid. "I need a few hours to look this over."

"Want company? I can't do much, but if you can chit chat while skimming those specs? We need to discuss what's going on here anyway. Make a game plan. I'm suddenly not sure why we're here either. Not sure why Cooke and her buddy are so nervous and why Chief Carney wants to stick close."

Ten looked up at her. "A lot to talk about. I get it. Okay." He stuffed the laptop into his duffle and stood. He reached for the pistol case.

"I'll get our food."

"Great. Thanks." He headed toward the elevators.

Maria wrapped his sandwich up and closed the lid to her salad container, then juggled them into one hand before picking up the handle of her suitcase with her other hand and dragging it along. "Right behind you."

In the elevator, Ten tucked the case under his arm and reached toward his sandwich. "Let me help you."

Maria pulled away. "I got it. Don't mess with my balancing act."

He laughed and leaned against the back wall as the elevator doors closed. "It's nice to be working together again."

"We'll see," she said, that slight smirk crossing her lips again.

"What's that supposed to mean?"

"You get grumpy when you're focused."

"How so?"

She poked him with her elbow. "*Fucking internet is connected to everything*," she said, repeating his words from downstairs.

"Well, it is."

"We're to the right." She followed him.

The case still tucked under his arm, Ten unlocked his door using the key card and walked in. Maria walked past him and set the food on the desk that sat against one wall, then took two steps to the window and pulled the sheer curtain back. "Nice view of the parking lot."

"It didn't look busy, so why do they always do that?"

"You want me to ask for a better view?"

"I'll be working anyway." The sky had darkened, and another round of thunder shook the area. "It's going to pour all afternoon."

Maria grabbed her salad from the table. "I'm going to my room next door and freshen up while you get settled here. I'll be back in a few."

"You can leave that if you like. If you're coming back anyway," Ten said.

"Good idea. Give me ten."

After she left the room, Ten pulled out his computer and set it on the corner of the desk and opened it up to read through the PDFs where he had left off. Fairly simple control software and hardware in general. He wanted to see the actual operations at the prison, check how many fail safes they had in place, and maybe talk with Nancy about what might have happened. He could have asked her earlier but didn't want to open up any conversation he might want to shut down with Chief Carney standing right there.

In a few moments, his phone rang, and he picked it up. "Change your mind?"

"Jacob emailed me. There's been another breakout," Maria said. "Something's up."

"In Muncy?"

"Some small town I've never heard of in Texas."

"He's not sending us out there now, is he? We just got here."

"Not yet. But several people were killed during that breakout. He thinks it's going to happen again. Anything we can learn here will help. He sounded frustrated. In a hurry." She hung up in his ear.

In a moment, there was a knock at his door. Ten ran over and opened the door so Maria could scoot in. "I don't like this," he said. "How do we know where this is coming from? This first one might have been a wild goose chase."

"Jacob thinks that it started here. He must have his reasons for thinking that. He believes this is as good a place as any to trace things back."

"Why didn't he just contact me?"

"You're not part of ISTI, idiot. I keep trying to get you onboard. He uses a secure account to get to me. We could always upgrade your system, connect you two."

"No thanks. I like keeping my distance."

She sat down in the chair where Ten had been sitting a few minutes before. She opened her salad container. "Maybe it's some international, anti-government group we haven't heard of yet."

"I don't think so. This feels less organized than that."

"There have only been two so far. How can you tell how organized that is?"

"Just a feeling."

"Okay, then, what do you think?"

"Find out if this town in Texas is installing the same equipment as here," Ten said.

"I hadn't thought of that. Good idea. I'll check in with Jacob. But let's eat first."

Ten picked up his sandwich and sat on the corner of the bed. "You're not in a hurry." He unwrapped his sub.

"I just think it's coming a little quickly and we might want to think things through before we fly to conclusions."

"Checking on something is not a conclusion," Ten said.

"Eat," she said.

He was only halfway through his sandwich when another knock came to his door. He glanced over at Maria and she shrugged. "Yes?" he yelled.

"Jake Carney. Got a moment?"

"Shit." Ten set the rest of his sub aside and walked over to let Carney into the room.

"Didn't mean to interrupt your lunch." He looked at his watch as though making sure he was right about the time. The shoulders of his shirt were soaked and his hair, what little there was of it, lay flat over his head. He wiped rainwater from the side of his head.

"Come in. Come in." Ten sat on the bed again and waited. "You wanted something?"

"Elizabeth Cooke is dead." The chief turned his head away as though trying not to get emotional. "Shot herself."

Maria jumped from her chair. "The superintendent? What? Why?"

"She didn't leave a note. I picked up Dr. Paton and Nancy Wilmoth. Have them down at the station. I thought you'd want to talk with them."

Ten said, "That's nice of you, but I'm not sure—"

"Yes," Maria interrupted. "It might help if we understood more of what's going on."

Ten shook his head. "We're not investigators. I do technology, not people." He glanced at Chief Carney. "Isn't this a local police matter?"

He looked surprised by Ten's response. "I was trying to help. Thought that whatever you were here for might be part of the reason... shit, I don't know."

"And there's been another break," Maria said.

"There has?" the chief asked. "Here?"

"Texas."

"What's that got to do with this?"

"You're right," Ten said to Maria.

Chief Carney gave him a quizzical glance, then looked at Maria.

She said, "It's all connected somehow. We'd might as well find out how."

Ten wrapped the last two bites of his sub into a ball of paper and set the package on the desk next to Maria's salad, which he closed the lid on. "You need anything from your room?"

She stared at Ten for a moment. "My phone and our case."

"Just the phone." He pointed to Chief Carney. "We have protection." The chief's chest puffed out enough to notice.

"If you're sure," she said.

"Meet us downstairs."

Maria left to go to her room while Ten and Carney headed for the elevator. By the time the elevator doors opened, Maria stood beside them. She held the case with their pistols inside. After exiting the elevator and walking toward the front doors, a man in a dark suit approached them as another man stood back.

Chief Carney's eyes went wide. "Munson? Are you involved in this?"

The man in the dark suit turned toward Ten and held out his hand. "You must be from ISTI."

Maria stepped forward. "Actually, I'm from ISTI. Ten here is my assistant."

A surprised look crossed Munson's face for a second. He swung his outstretched hand toward Maria. "Agent Munson, FBI."

"Maria Tanner." She shook his hand, then gave a nod toward Ten. "This is my assistant and tech expert, Ten."

Munson turned his head as though he hadn't heard her correctly.

"A nickname. T-E-N," Ten said.

"I thought that's what I heard." Munson stood back. "We're here to help. It appears a lot is going on." He raised his eyebrows toward Chief Carney.

"And you don't think the local police can handle it," Carney said.

"You know that's not what I think. I'm just following orders."

The two of them stood and stared at each other for a long moment. Maria stepped between them to head out the doors. "All right, that's enough, boys. We have work to do."

Ten followed behind her, figuring the others would be along soon enough.

She stopped at the edge of the hotel awning. Rain poured from the sky and splashed onto the pavement and parked cars loudly. "Well, it is cooler," she said.

Ten felt the presence of the others behind him. "We're going to make a run for it. We'll meet you at the station." Then he took off into the pouring rain and headed for his car with his key fob out, unlocking the doors as he ran. He popped inside and slammed his door closed. A second later, Maria sat beside him. They both stared out the windshield, the trees and other cars blurred by the rain. The loud pounding somehow relaxed Ten. He turned toward Maria before starting the car. "I wish I knew what the hell we were doing."

"Do we ever know?"

CHAPTER 7

The rain had slowed by the time they reached 14 North Washington Street in Muncy. "Looks like someone's house," Maria said as Ten parked near the front of the building. A small sign nailed to a porch post read MUNCY BOROUGH OFFICE. A Dollar General sat across the street, its parking lot half full, an older woman running from her car to the store with a light jacket pulled over her head. Noticing, Maria said, "That's got to be hot. Who would wear a jacket in this heat?"

"Someone more afraid of the rain," Ten said.

Before long, Chief Carney's police vehicle turned onto a side street toward the back parking lot. A dark sedan followed, the windows too tinted to see into.

Ten and Maria sat quietly listening to the rain for a few seconds.

"I love that sound. Soothing," Maria said.

Ten gave her a quick smile and slight nod. "And now we have to go in there and talk about a suicide. What the hell?"

"I know. But we're helping."

"Are we? And who exactly are we helping? Surely not ourselves. After what we've been through, you'd think we'd try to find a peaceful place to sit and hide. Maybe a job that didn't throw more dead bodies into our faces." Maria lifted the gun case that sat between her legs and pivoted so she could transfer it onto the floor of the backseat area. "We probably don't even need those."

She narrowed her eyes toward him while she settled the case flat on the floor. "I heard you the first time. At the hotel. We're investigating a prison, after all. I'd rather be safe."

"If that's true, we're not safe with our weapons in the car."

Before twisting all the way back around she put her hand on Ten's shoulder. "I think we'll be okay in the police station. As for what we're up to in general, I think we are where we're meant to be, where we can do the most good."

"If you say so." He opened his door and stepped into the rain. The street was wet. Water ran along the gutter toward a grate a few parking spots beyond where they were. The humidity had shot up, of course, and it was pretty warm. Ten didn't mind the rain though. The rain was the only cool thing about the weather. He locked the car and they walked onto the porch and into the offices.

Carney met them at the door, Munson and his silent buddy behind the chief. "Come in. We have a small interrogation room in the back. I'll bring them in one at a time. You have a preference?"

Maria said, "Let's try the good doctor, shall we?"

"Those two going to be there too?" Ten asked about the FBI agents.

"All five of us," the chief said.

"You think the guy will talk with a room full of people?"

The chief didn't answer. He walked down the brightly lit hallway, passing between the two FBI agents, while Ten and Maria took up the rear. Once in the interrogation room, he motioned for Maria to sit in a chair that was settled center across from a single chair on the opposite side of the table. The others sat on either side of her—the two FBI on one side and Carney and Ten on the other.

Carney tapped the tabletop and leaned way over to get everyone's attention. "Here's how this will go. Maria here is in the lead and will do all the questioning unless she relinquishes to one of us. You can raise a finger if you have something to say." He stared at Munson. "ISTI is in charge of this investigation. Understand?" Everyone nodded. "Okay, then. I'll go get Blake Paton."

In a few minutes, he walked into the room leading Dr. Paton in handcuffs. Carney unlocked and removed the cuffs, then backed over and leaned against the door instead of taking his seat next to Ten.

Dr. Paton rubbed his wrists and sat in front of Maria. He then put his hands between his legs and lowered his eyes as though looking at the floor for something he dropped.

The man's eyes were red and puffy.

Maria leaned on her elbows. "I know there are a lot of people here but focus on me for now. I just want to know what you know so we can try to figure out if this has anything to do with the breakout."

Dr. Paton didn't look up. His voice cracked as he spoke. "Of course it does. But not in the way you think."

Maria glanced at Ten. "And how do I think?"

"Elizabeth didn't spring them. She's not guilty of that."

"And you know this how?"

Dr. Paton didn't say anything.

"Can you tell us how she is involved?"

Still nothing.

"Dr. Paton. Do you have any idea how much trouble you could be in if you hold back information? Would you like to be inside a prison like the one you're involved with?" Maria's voice got rougher as she pushed each word out. "We can have you charged—"

"She was having an affair," Paton blurted. "Nancy knows more than I do. Talk with her. That's all I know. It's sick."

"An affair with one of the escapees?" Maria said incredulously.

"Sarah Andrews."

Maria shot a look toward Carney.

"On it." He opened the door and walked into the hallway. "Carson!"

Ten heard Carney walking down the hall in a rush. Orders to an Officer Carson trailed into mumbles.

"How long have you known Superintendent Cooke?"

"Twenty years. We both grew up here."

"And you didn't know about her," Maria seemed to struggle with the next word and abandoned it altogether, "dealings with Sarah Andrews?"

"It's not like we hang out together. I do my job and she does hers." For the first time, he looked up and into Maria's eyes. "She was always nice to me."

Dr. Paton was a small and meek man. His demeanor was soft-spoken, quiet, almost invisible. Ten had noticed those features when they were at the prison the first time. But now the reason had become clear. Blake Paton had had eyes on Elizabeth Cooke and, at this very moment, was heartbroken. He knew of her escapades. He would have denied them even if he had been exposed to them, except for this violent act. Ten felt certain about that. He could see it in the man's eyes. Paton was sad and shocked and understanding all at once. Twenty years. How could the man have missed the truth? Is that what they were all doing—failing to face what was right in front of them? Ten took a breath, and Maria glanced over at him in question.

"It's hot," he whispered. "Humid." He wiped at his forehead, pushing his hair back.

She turned to look toward Dr. Paton again. Munson raised a finger and Maria nodded for him to speak.

"Would the superintendent have access to the control system? Knowledge that would allow her to help Sarah escape?"

Paton gave Munson a dirty look. "I told you she had nothing to do with that. Besides, why would she even want to? Don't you get it? Elizabeth had Sarah right where she wanted her. She couldn't get away, couldn't go anywhere, do anything, be with anyone else. She owned Sarah."

Ten pushed back from the table and sat farther back in his chair. *Yikes.* All of a sudden, another side of Paton was showing, and Ten didn't know what to do with that.

Maria seemed annoyed at his movement. She leaned closer toward Paton, like she was trying to get him in focus and everyone else out of her peripheral vision. She wanted to feel like they were the only two in the room. "You think she took her own life because she was afraid she'd get caught?"

His head shook and his shoulders shivered but no sound came from him. His chin sat against his chest.

Carney stepped back into the room. Everyone looked up as he backed against the closed door again. "I sent some people over to the super's house. I'll bet we find Sarah Andrews there."

"Can I go? I don't know anything more." Dr. Paton stared at Chief Carney. "You know me, Chief. If I had more information, I'd tell you. Talk with Nancy. Ms. Wilmoth. She obviously knows a lot more about this than I do."

Carney glanced at Maria, who nodded her approval. Then the chief put cuffs back on Blake Paton and led him out of the room.

"Jesus," Munson said the moment Carney and Paton were gone. The other agent just looked into his folded hands sitting on the table in front of him.

Maria patted Ten on the knee. "You doing okay?"

"That guy was distraught," Ten said. "Not easy to handle at such close range."

Maria smiled at her partner. "You ready for what's coming next?"

"Why can't it just be technology?"

"People are involved in everything, I suppose." She looked past him when Carney brought Nancy into the room, uncuffed her, and let her sit down across from Maria.

If anything, Nancy was the polar opposite of Dr. Paton. She looked stern, confident, practically emotionless. She wasn't ruffled at all. No sooner did she sit down and square herself in her seat, she began to talk. "I've known about Superintendent Cooke and Sarah Andrews for a while. Well, soon after starting work a year ago. She threatened my job and physical harm unless I kept silent. I hated what that woman was doing but I didn't expect this. I wouldn't wish this on anyone."

"We have a lot of questions," Maria said.

"Shoot away," Nancy said, then caught herself and turned her head. "I'm so sorry."

Maria jumped right in then in a way that Ten had never seen before, aggressive and deep, seemingly pushing Nancy's buttons whenever she could. Almost as though she was angry at the young woman for knowing what she knew.

The details were sordid. Nancy had seen some videos, and when she approached the superintendent about them, she was asked to delete those parts from the records. "At first, she wanted me to tamper with the files or lose them somehow. But that wasn't good enough." Nancy tightened her lips in her own anger even as Maria drove questions at her as though she were the perpetrator. "Cooke ordered me to transfer some of the camera feeds into a separate file and deliver it to her later for private viewing. At least that's what I assumed."

"And you did that? That was okay with you?" Maria asked forcefully. "I can't believe anyone could let such a thing go on."

"It was horrible!" Nancy yelled back. "You don't know. You judge me now, but you don't know. I was scared of her, what she might do, what she *could* do."

"And you had to watch this on video in order to save it? Are you sure it was so horrible?" Maria asked in a disgusted tone.

Munson and his partner had their faces turned. Ten stared more unbelievably at Maria than at Nancy. Occasionally, he heard Carney grunt or mumble something from his post against the door. Ten didn't want to hear any details.

"I didn't watch." Nancy turned her head from Maria's onslaught of energy. "I tried not to. But I had to see enough to know when it started and ended. I jumped back and forth or fast-forwarded with my eyes averted the best I could. Who wants to see anything like that? It was rough. Violent. Elizabeth was violent, and so was Sarah. God!" Her cheeks tightened as though she were going to cry but no tears came.

Munson raised his finger and pushed his hand forward to get Maria's attention.

It took her a moment, but she nodded reluctantly for him to speak.

He swallowed loudly before asking Nancy, "Did you get any type of alarm signal about what had happened during the breakout?"

Ten was happy that Munson got the conversation back on track.

"No. I was home. There is an app, but I hadn't implemented it yet." Nancy's tone was softer, yet she stared at Agent Munson with some intensity. She was getting tired, looked exhausted, and she had only been sitting there for half an hour.

Ten felt exhausted too, and hoped this would end soon.

Maria pulled out a few more questions concerning who else might have access to the new control system they were still in the process of installing, then looked around to see if any of the others had additional questions. No one held up a finger to talk. She'd covered it. Too well.

Carney walked over and cuffed Nancy again. He helped her get out of the chair, then halted to look at Maria.

Maria's eyes narrowed. "Can you hold her for a few more days while we check out the electronics and see if she's telling the truth?"

"I'm telling the truth," Nancy blurted. She shook her head angrily at Maria. "I hated it." She went silent and started to walk toward the door, pulling Chief Carney along behind her. He still held her arm.

After Carney returned, he asked, "Should we talk about all this?"

Maria stood. "Not yet." She indicated Ten. "We have to evaluate the system and go over our thoughts. Let us know when you find Sarah Andrews, if she's at Cooke's house. We'll be at the hotel for a few hours. Oh, and we'll want to go to the prison first thing in the morning."

"I have a lot of paperwork. How about ten?"

"Who's taking over for Cooke?" Maria still didn't call her superintendent. Of course, she wasn't the superintendent anymore.

"I'll find out the details. I'm sure Dr. Paton knows. And Carson, who I sent over when we first got the call. He's had a busy afternoon."

Maria nodded and walked out the door. Everyone else trailed behind her and went their own ways. Once she and Ten were back in the car, Ten started the engine and pulled onto the street. "You were tough on her."

"What ever happened to doing the right thing?" Maria said in a huff.

"She was frightened to death. I know it came out as anger, but she's still scared as hell. Cooke must have been some strong woman."

"She can be charged. She should be."

He put the wipers on low. "Try to calm down." Even as the rain came down, the sun peeked from behind a cloud and burned through his window and across his chest.

"I'm usually telling *you* that." She faced him. "My buttons were pushed. I'm sorry you had to see that. Why can't people do the right thing? I mean, the government is so fucked up, which is why we're on the inside trying to straighten things out. Then you get into a situation like this and it's just as fucked up."

"The human condition. That's what you'd say to me, *have* said to me, when I get tired of people."

"I just got off a case where young girls were abused in so many, many ways, and then I have to walk into something like this."

"Along those lines, do you think Superintendent Cooke was involved in the breakout?"

"Hell no. I think Dr. Paton was correct when it dawned on him what type of person Cooke really was, how much control she really had to have. I think he was heartbroken and relieved and didn't know which emotion to focus on."

"Those were my exact thoughts. I suppose he was scared too. Like Nancy. You don't have to see the video to know how violent it must have been. All you have to do is look into Nancy's eyes when she tells you."

"And Paton. He spent twenty years close to that woman and finds this out about her in a matter of hours. Yeah, I'd say he's going through a lot of emotions as well." She stopped talking and neither of them said anything until they were parked at the hotel again. Maria reached back for their gun case. "Tomorrow we work on the breakout. Maybe we let the police deal with the rest of this mixed-up shit."

Ten agreed with her.

When they got to their rooms, Maria said, "Give me some time to unwind. Maybe an early dinner?"

"Try not to think about this."

"It's hard not to."

CHAPTER 8

Ten sat across from Maria at Mulan with a plate of sweet and sour chicken in front of him and stir-fried rice in front of Maria, which she just stared at. "That's a lot of food," she said.

"Too much. And we don't have a microwave in the room."

"There's one downstairs where the hotel's continental breakfast is set up. I looked."

"Good." He put a forkful of chicken in his mouth, then a pineapple chunk. He pointed to the food on his plate. "This is good. Glad we can reheat it. There'll be plenty."

"So what do you think?"

He stared across the table at her. "I think you're going to ruin dinner."

"We'll just be postponing the conversation, not ending it. And not solving anything either."

"Fine." He stopped eating, holding the fork upright beside his plate. "That place is scary, and the people involved are all nuts."

She laughed briefly without commitment, then got serious. "I think Nancy may have caused the escape to get out of having to deal with Cooke."

Ten placed more food in his mouth but stopped chewing at her words and cocked his head. He swallowed hard. "I hadn't thought of that. She was pretty upset about the whole thing. And she was caught in the middle. She never asked for it. I can see where you'd think that. I hope not though. That would put her into a lot of trouble."

"She's in a lot of trouble now. When I think of what she was going through, a year is a long time to put up with what Cooke and Andrews were doing."

"She didn't actually say how long she was involved," Ten commented, "only that she had been there a year. Soon after, she said. Less than a year. Either way, you were pretty hard on her."

"Oh no you don't. You saw her, how she reacted. It's been long enough." Maria took a sip of her green tea. "And it's hardened her. That's why I think she could have been involved in the breakout."

"Let's look over the control system in the morning. I don't like the whole *there's an app for that* thing she mentioned either. Christ, there are so many holes in security for systems. I'm surprised we can keep any secrets from anyone or, in this case, keep any prisoners behind bars."

"I hope you don't mean that."

"Oh I do. But this isn't my expertise. We should talk to Jacob, or Roger Floramo."

"There's a name I haven't heard for a while. I thought he went back to work for Practical Robotics."

"After all the shit that went down with that killing machine we were all involved with, I'm surprised. The guy's a fucking genius though."

"You say that, but have you looked at your own resume?"

Ten ignored her comment. "We should talk with him. If he'll talk to us at all. If I were him, I'd be standing way away from all of us, anything to do with ISTI, in fact."

"And yet, here you are."

"Smartass." He smiled at her, and it felt good to do so. He sometimes felt like he carried a permanent scowl around with him, or a sadness that displayed as a scowl, perhaps the result of his disappointment in the world, in life.

They ate for a few minutes in silence. The restaurant bustled with activity, families coming and going. They seemed to have as much traffic for takeout as eat-in. People came in from the rain still coming down, although not so hard. Ten commented on the food a second time. At home, he didn't eat so well, and the Chinese food in front of him felt like a huge treat.

Maria seemed equally happy with her fried rice. Her head bent down as she ate. Her curly hair hid her cheeks and forehead. When she looked up at him, she gave her head a shake to clear the hair from her face. "What?"

He had been watching her and his stare had stuck into one of those can't-stop-staring glitches his mind sometimes got into. He didn't know why he'd fall into a staring loop like that except that it was when he had a lot on his mind. Maybe that's all it was. The moment reminded him of sitting across from Amy. The thought only flashed through for a moment, but it penetrated deeply.

Her word was lost in his memory, but her wide, piercing eyes shocked him back to where he was, sitting in a restaurant eating dinner with his partner. "Nothing," he replied. "Just mulling things over."

"I thought you didn't want to think about it."

"It could have been Dr. Paton. He could have been lying about what had happened. Maybe he found out about Elizabeth and Sarah earlier than he said, before instead of after the suicide. Maybe he couldn't stand the thought and hoped once Sarah Andrews was out of jail, she'd disappear and Superintendent Cooke would need a shoulder to cry on."

"Yuck. I can see why you didn't want to talk about this during dinner. The thought of him wanting her after what she did is creepier than what she did."

"Love," Ten said as an answer.

"I hope that's not what love looks like, or what love does to a person."

"So, to get off that subject, what do you think about Texas?"

"If it's the same system, like you suggested it might be, then they *might* be connected. Unless we can find a reason, though, I don't know if we should count on that. Not yet. Otherwise, it's a copycat case. I suspect that's why Jacob didn't send us out there right off the bat."

"We should focus on the escape here, then. Make sure it's not technical, that it only has to do with emotional upset and people trying to right some wrongs. If it is technical, then we have something greater on our hands. We'll have to find out how many other prisons are being upgraded or using the same system, or the same company, or the same electronics or software, even if it's not the same company." He shook his head and stared toward the ceiling in thought for a moment. "Yeah, this could get complicated, but a lot of it would be researching down to the component level, what exactly these systems look like." He looked up at Maria. "I have to admit, I like this better than getting shot at."

"Don't blame you there, but it's not over yet."

"Don't even say that out loud."

"I can't help you with the electronics or software stuff. If you can do that research on your own, maybe I work on the love triangle."

"That sounds even worse than what you first thought. Nancy being involved in a love triangle. You think maybe she wanted Cooke too? Or are we back to Paton?" He wiped his mouth with his napkin and placed it to the side of his plate. He nodded. "Good plan. I'll stick with the tech." He motioned toward a waitress and pointed toward his half-eaten plate. She seemed to understand and held up one, then two fingers. Ten answered with two fingers raised and the waitress turned toward the back. In a moment, she came out with two to-go boxes and set them on the table.

"Any dessert?"

"Not this time," Maria said. She widened her eyes toward Ten. "Unless you want something?"

"Watching my figure."

The waitress set the bill on the table beside Ten and walked away.

He reached for it and Maria snatched it away. "I have the company budget, you don't."

"Thank you."

"I don't know why they always assume the man will be paying. Drives me nuts. They used to do that with me and Ben too." Her eyes narrowed for a second and her mouth tightened, probably with a memory of her boyfriend.

Ten gave her a second in case she was in a mental loop of her own. He made a similar face, he was sure, when memories of Amy crept into his everyday life, and he wondered if Maria had noticed earlier and just not said anything.

Would they never forget the ones they loved?

Probably not.

He dumped his remaining meal into the box and then reached over and scooped Maria's fried rice into the other box. He closed them both. By the time he was finished, she was looking across the table at him.

"Thank you," she said. She pulled out her ISTI charge card and waved it at the waitress, who swung by and plucked it from Maria's raised hand.

"Long day," Maria said.

"It started earlier than most, for sure."

"It's hard to believe it's still the same day. I'd like to get a good night's sleep. Start fresh."

"I've got some PDFs to read over, some schematics to analyze. I think I will contact Roger. He can help with the software stuff."

"Talk with Jacob first, okay. Don't go all rogue on me."

"You make me laugh."

"And maybe you should get some rest first too. We have all morning tomorrow. Chief Carney won't be meeting us until ten o'clock."

"I'm too curious."

Maria signed the ticket with the waitress standing next to her and handed it back.

They got up to leave when Ten's phone interrupted. He pulled it from his pocket, looked at it, and held it up for Maria to see. "Jacob," he said before answering. He brought the phone to his ear as they left with their extra food.

Jacob was quick and blunt. "Same equipment," he said. "It's not new, but a lot of it was picked up by a series of prisons that either belong to a private group or are run by that same group. I'll get more information to you through Maria's secure system as it arrives here, but I'm suspecting something bigger than a single breakout is in store."

"A mass event," Ten said.

"Two down," Jacob said. "And close together. Someone might be testing their capabilities."

"What better way to test results than with two prisons so far apart," Ten said.

"We might be in a time crunch."

"I'm working on it."

There was a pause on the end of the phone. Then Jacob said, "I heard about the suicide too, of course. Horrible. At a women's prison. I know Maria won't let that go. I want you to back her up the best you can without taking efforts from the real issue. Stay on track. That's an order."

"She can handle herself. We've decided to split duties for a short while, but I hear you. I'll keep watch."

Jacob hung up as Ten and Maria reached the car.

"Seriously," she said. "We were just talking about that."

"What?"

"Jacob calls you when I'm the agent and you're the consultant. It's a boy's club."

"It was concerning the technology," Ten explained. "The systems are the same."

"I'm the agent," she said again.

They got into the car. "He's going to send information to you concerning the equipment and the prison owners. They're private. Through your secure link."

"I thought you said nothing was secure."

"Only if someone wants the information. There's no reason right now. It's just information. He also said it's okay for you to review the suicide, figure out what's going on there. I'm supposed to support you as much as possible."

"Did you tell him that I was going to work on that anyway, even though the locals can probably figure things out?"

"He knows you can't overlook something like that."

"Good."

"The locals, as you call them, might be biased in this case. They all appear to know one another. Small town," he said. "You'll get to the bottom of things much quicker and easier coming from the outside with no attachments."

"Thank you. You're right about that."

They drove to the hotel and Ten suggested they get an extra key card for each room. "So you don't have to knock every time."

"Yeah, and so you don't have to quit what you're doing and answer the door. It might be safer too. Once we get into the nitty gritty, there's no telling where this might go and who's involved," she said.

"I'm not expecting a lot of trouble."

"Famous last words."

CHAPTER 9

After discussing several of the eight primary computer game design engines being used, Mr. Hobart let his students work on their own projects using the computer room systems for an hour. He loved teaching high school Computer Club. The students' minds were open to whatever he thought to teach them, and their enthusiasm to learn on their own often took rewarding and interesting turns. Being in a club, for students, meant they were all in. A strong interest had already taken hold, unlike standard math, science, and English every student was forced to enroll in whether they liked it or not. A club meant self-motivation kept them engaged and moving forward.

He also taught a night class for adults at the local college, which was considered retraining by the state. There was the contrast. Unlike the kids from high school, the adults he taught were taking his course in order to get jobs. They did only what they thought they needed to do, which meant they did absolutely nothing extra. No playing around, no additional reading. It was all about getting the certificate, getting the job, and getting paid. Sometimes he wondered how self-motivation and enthusiasm had been torn out of the adults. Why didn't they go after something they were truly interested in? Or had they never had outside interests in the first place and that's why they were in the situations they were in?

That's why he admired Ken Hemming, even though the kid overstepped the rules—a lot. Mr. Hobart hoped Ken listened to his warning and chose to stay out of trouble. If he could rein in his illegal explorations, he'd make a great programmer someday.

Mr. Hobart walked over and stood behind Valeria. He worried about her too. She and Ken were partners on more than one project. She was as good as Ken and could easily have helped him if he had asked. Mr. Hobart hoped Ken hadn't asked, that it truly was just Ken's work. The truth was, though, any one of them could have helped. They were all good friends. But Valeria's uncle and her cousin, both from Mexico, were programmers. One at the bank and one at the police department. They were good role models even though she was in the thick of it now that Ken had hacked the FBI. "How's it going?" he asked from behind her.

Valeria swung around. "You snuck up on me." She looked nervous but then laughed and turned back to her screen.

"I didn't mean to scare you. It looks like you've chosen to check out Unity. That's a good game engine. You'll be able to work in 2D and 3D, but you knew that."

She smiled over her shoulder. "You can tell what I'm using that easily?"

"I'd better be able to," he said, "or you'd all let me know about it."

Bill and Craig laughed at his remark. Valeria put her head down and removed her hands from the keyboard as though waiting for him to stop peering over her shoulder.

"Any of you hear from Ken?" he asked the group as casually as possible.

Roger raised his hand, then the rest of them raised theirs one at a time.

"Oh, don't tell me you're mixed up—"

"Nooooooo," Roger said a bit too quickly. "But he is our friend. And you told us to keep him up to date on our lessons."

"I get it. I do. Just be careful. Don't get into trouble, and don't let him get into trouble either. I'm counting on you guys." He tapped the back of Valeria's chair. "You be careful too," he said.

"You don't have to worry, Mr. Hobart," she said without looking at him, her head still down. Then she reached up and began to shut down. The end of the evening.

Mr. Hobart stepped away. "Let him know I said hello." He wanted to say he was sorry again too, but didn't. He hoped they knew how he felt. They all seemed a little uneasy when he asked about Ken and a little too adamant about not helping their friend do anything illegal. They were good kids. He had to remind himself of that, not get too concerned, too over-the-top about the possibilities.

As the students left, Valeria hung back again.

He noticed her waiting. "You were off tonight. Everything going okay at home? Your mom and sister doing all right?"

"It's not easy," she admitted. "I might miss a class or two coming up. I wanted to tell you. Maybe more in the summer. Emma and I might have to work more hours."

"I'm sorry. It's been a long time." He waited for her to respond.

"My uncle is helping out." She glanced away but didn't move.

"Is there something else?"

"Ken's sorry. He said he made a mistake."

"I can't let him back in," Mr. Hobart said. "But I do appreciate that he knows what he did was wrong."

"He knows that. And he knows you can't let him come back yet." She still didn't look him in the eyes. "I'd better go."

"If you need anything... If I can help… Look, I know it's tough, but there are worse things to go through, trust me. You'll get through this. You all will." He meant it.

"I know." Valeria gave him a wave as she left the room.

He heard her walking down the hall.

Craig must have been waiting for her and asked if she'd told him. She said, "No."

"Do you think he knows?" Craig asked.

Mr. Hobart stepped closer to the door without going into the hall.

"It didn't look like he knew anything," she said.

The students were walking away. He had to strain to hear them.

"He'll find out soon enough," Craig said.

"It doesn't matter. We didn't do anything."

"He'll think we did."

The outside door opened with a loud clunk as they pushed through, and he lost the conversation. He walked back to his desk. What had they been talking about? What didn't he know? He packed up, locked the door, and headed out to go home.

As he approached his house, he saw a black sedan in his driveway. He parked on the street and got out. Two men stepped from the sedan as he walked up. He was reminded of Valeria and Craig's discussion while walking down the hall. She said they'd done nothing. Right now, he wished he knew what *nothing* they were talking about. Regardless, he believed them. They had no reason to lie to each other. Yet the FBI were back, so someone had done something.

"Friendly visit?" Mr. Hobart asked as he walked up to them.

Agent Munson had done most of the talking the last time he'd seen them only a week before, and that's who started the conversation this time as well. "Pretty much."

"Come on in." He wandered to the front door and unlocked it, but they didn't move to follow him. "I was just with the kids. Did something else happen?"

"Yesterday. I guess you didn't hear." Munson stood at the edge of the driveway.

"I taught yesterday, been teaching all day today too. Had a quick sandwich down the road and went back to school for Computer Club. I seldom listen to the news if that's what you're referring to."

"Prison breakout," Agent Smythe said.

Mr. Hobart cocked his head in question. "It wasn't my kids," he asserted.

"No. We're not sure what happened," Munson said.

"We're here as a courtesy," Smythe said.

"Courtesy?"

"It's a small town. We want to be sure you know so you can keep a closer watch."

"You think it could have been one of them?"

Munson shook his head. "Just a courtesy," he repeated. "And to tell you we're not working the case."

"Oh? Who is?"

"Some big government operation. ISTI."

"This is a big deal then," Hobart said with full understanding. "I don't know who that is, but you're telling me that they won't be so easy if it's one of the kids."

"We don't think they'll be lenient at all," Munson said. "We sat with two of them today. They can be pretty rough. Really hammered one of the employees at the prison."

"Relentless," Smythe said.

Mr. Hobart lowered his eyes then brought them back to meet Munson's. "This is really nice of you guys. Really nice. I'll be sure to keep an eye on the kids." He shook his head. "Jesus."

"My son's in Computer Club in Lewisburg," Munson said. "Kids can get enthusiastic, and think they're invincible." He smiled for the first time. "Especially when they want to protect their dads. My son would have done the same thing Hemming did. I just hope the warning from you helped. We thought that if he knew your job was on the line, he'd listen. I know how my son looks up to his teacher."

"But this other group won't care about all that," Mr. Hobart said.

"We're off this case."

"Thank you."

"People could go to prison."

"Me, as an accomplice, and any of my students." Mr. Hobart understood. "I am well aware."

"You'd just get into trouble. I'm more worried about these kids. They're young. They don't know how much damage something like this can do." The agents nodded to him and were off in a moment. They had provided their warning.

Mr. Hobart remained standing outside his door. He watched them back out of his drive and travel down the street. He had heard Craig and Valeria say they weren't involved, but they didn't say if they knew who was. He hoped it wasn't Ken trying his hand at something much more serious. But his dad wasn't in prison anymore. Was Ken just keeping his doors open?

Let's hope not.

CHAPTER 10

After a long night reading through the installation and repair documents for the P280 LockDown System, Ten still got up extra early to get some exercise in before breakfast. He knew Maria would be up early too and left a text that he'd be ready around nine. At the bathroom sink, he pulled his shoulder toward the mirror to look at the scars that bubbled from his skin. They reminded him of everything he'd been through. At the moment, he didn't feel lost, which is what he typically felt just before cutting himself. Maybe Maria had been right. Maybe he needed work to keep his mind occupied. Maybe he needed to keep moving. Maybe he needed to keep thinking. A lot of maybes and few guarantees that any of it might help him forget. The truth was, he didn't want to forget. He wanted to remember Amy forever. It was the least he could do.

He blew out a long breath, then turned on the faucet and cupped a few handfuls of cold water over his face. He leaned against the sink shirtless and in his boxers. He wiped his face dry with a hand towel.

He'd spent the previous day in his car for hours, then sitting across from Blake Paton and Elizabeth Cooke in the conference room, and then sitting across from Nancy Wilmoth and Blake Paton at the police station. Then sitting through dinner, sitting and reading until late. After a good night's sleep, although short, he needed to move his body.

The hotel had a small gym and a small indoor pool, but he decided to stick to his room for the morning.

He yanked the bedspread from the bed and folded it onto the floor, on top of which he went through a regimen of squats, sit-ups, leg lifts, and back and side stretches. Then he pushed into a handstand against the wall near the TV cabinet and began doing handstand pushups. He heard the door click and Maria walked in. "You're early," he forced as his body rose up and down.

She walked toward the bed to sit down. "You should wear underwear under your underwear."

"You're early," he said again as he lowered his legs and sat cross-legged on the bedspread.

"I shouldn't have barged in," she said. "I thought you'd be up and ready."

"I have fifteen minutes. Long enough to shave and shower. I said nine."

"You'd be late." She got up from the edge of his bed. "Three choices: I'll wait here until you're ready; go downstairs and grab a couple coffees and wait there; or, if you like, I can grab you something and bring it up. Give you time to get ready?"

"You don't have to," he said.

"Any one of those work for you?"

"It would be great if you brought something up. I'll hurry."

"I'll give you fifteen. Don't walk out of the shower and into the room naked."

"It's a little late for you to care, sounds like."

"You were flaunting."

"I was exercising."

"Fifteen," she said before leaving.

Ten walked into the bathroom and brushed his teeth before shaving and showering. The P280 drawings flashed through his mind while getting ready. He had marked up the PDFs and wanted to review them on the way to the prison that morning. Then he wondered who he'd meet there. Nancy sat in jail. He finished up and got dressed in a loose, short-sleeve button-down shirt, jeans, and tennis shoes. He remembered that Maria was wearing navy slacks and a more subdued, ocher blouse. Maybe he should dress more formally too, as though he were actually part of ISTI. But she'd introduced him as a consultant, which gave him plenty of leeway in how he dressed. Maybe jeans and a shirt made him look the part. He wouldn't want anyone to get the wrong idea.

He opened his laptop and pulled up his notes from the night before.

The door opened and Maria pushed in using her shoulder. Her hands were full, and she had Styrofoam plates and bowls running up her forearms. Ten jumped up and went to help her. "Let me get some of those."

"I got two bagels, two small bowls of fruit, two Danishes, and two large coffees, which are still sitting outside."

Ten took the two bowls of fruit from their wobbly positions, brushing his fingers across her forearms, and set the bowls on the cabinet in front of the TV then swung back for the plate holding the Danishes.

She placed the bagels, which looked toasted and had several pats of butter sitting beside them, next to the other plates. Maria went back out for the coffee. She smiled as she came in and handed him one. Then she reached into her pocket and pulled out a couple creamer cups. "Sorry, I blanked out and didn't remember whether you liked cream or not. I got several flavors. I did remember you don't take sugar."

"Anything works for me this early in the morning." He took one of the coffees and set it next to his laptop.

Maria delivered three other plates and set them beside him. "Eat."

"I will. I just wanted to skim through my notes from last night."

"You can do that in the car on the way over."

He turned in his seat. "You want to talk?"

"I want to apologize for being rude this morning when I arrived. I don't know what I was thinking."

"It's okay. I didn't expect you to walk in or I wouldn't have been... exposed."

"I shouldn't have barged in. I shouldn't have looked."

"We've been through a lot together. Let's not let that be an issue." He took a bite of his bagel.

She nodded and sipped at her coffee. She reached over and put a grape in her mouth. "It's not like me."

"We should talk about the case we're working on. Like I said, we've been through a lot together and some small indiscretion shouldn't come between us. Besides, nothing you haven't seen. Don't beat yourself up." He smiled. "It was actually a funny comment. Underwear under my underwear." He laughed.

Maria smiled. "You're a good guy, Ten. A good friend." She pointed at his laptop. "You can look over your notes, then I want to discuss Nancy and Paton."

He turned back around, dumped two creamer cups into his coffee and started reading as he ate and drank. When he was through, his bagel was gone, half the fruit cup eaten, and two bites had been taken from the Danish. Only a little coffee remained in the bottom of his cup.

Maria had finished all her food.

"Ready," he said as he turned toward her.

"I heard from Carney. They had a tussle out at Cooke's house, but sure enough, Sarah Andrews was there hiding in the basement. One of his guys got stabbed. Nothing too bad, but he did go to the hospital to get patched up."

"So Sarah is back in prison?"

"Big time. He said she didn't appear to be too distraught that Cooke was dead."

"I can only imagine."

"The woman had killed her husband for cheating on her. Sounds to me like she was heterosexual. Cooke's advances probably made her sick, maybe as sick as Nancy."

"Unless Nancy was jealous," Ten said, reminding her of their previous conversation.

"There is that. And Paton." She held up her cup. "I could use another. You?"

"On our way out." He closed his laptop and put it under his arm. He glanced at the pistol case. "We won't need those for this job."

"I doubt it. We'll have a police escort."

"You think they'll be hanging around all the time?"

"Carney doesn't appear to want to be too far from us. And I suspect he's talking with those FBI guys regularly, although he didn't act like they were his favorite people. But I'll have time, maybe later, to talk with Nancy on my own."

"How's that?"

"I also talked with Jacob this morning to make sure Carney and the others were out of the room."

"You've been busy."

"A few phone calls is all." She downplayed what she'd done, but Ten noticed how hard she worked when she was interested in a case. He needed to get on board with a bit more commitment.

Ten drove the car with the windows down. The morning air rushed in cool and moist. The rain had dampened the smell of manure, although the air still stunk more than they were used to. As they arrived at the prison, there were police all around, tape across the front doors, forensics, the whole team. Ten didn't see either of the FBI agents.

Carney saw them, though, and walked quickly toward the car even before they were out. He aimed straight toward Maria. "You went over my head." He sounded more impressed than angry.

"I'm sorry, Chief, but once we get into an investigation, there are some government factors that make it difficult to have anyone in the room. If this whole mess is what our boss thinks it is, it could be more widespread and dangerous than what we thought originally. The fewer people who have critical information, the better."

Carney looked around Maria at Ten. "You think this is going to affect a lot more prisons," he surmised.

"And we don't know when," Ten said.

"Secret stuff is involved," Carney said to Maria.

"A lot."

"I'd like to help. I had top secret clearance while in the Navy. It still holds."

"I'll let my boss know. You never know, he might be in agreement with that."

"Well, tell him that I know all the nitty gritty about this community. In fact, some things I'm sure you can't possibly know." He halted and raised his chin. "I wanted to tell you, this morning, the teacher for the local Computer Club called and wanted to be of service too."

"Computer Club?" Ten questioned as he took a stand next to Maria.

"The FBI. They were hanging out because one of the kids Mr. Hobart has in Computer Club hacked the FBI."

"Why would he do that?" Ten asked.

"Change the records they held on the kid's dad. He was held on some tax evasion problems, and it was affecting who would hire him. According to Munson and Smythe, the teacher, Mr. Hobart, was warned. They asked Hobart to talk with the kid. They gave him a break. Turns out Munson's son is in Computer Club at another school and Munson knew how kids were prone to break the rules."

"You think he's involved in this? The kid, I mean?"

"No, no. Not at all. Neither does Hobart. I think he just wants to be on record that he's watching, keeping his kids' noses clean. He talked with Munson too. Asked for your number." He put his attention back to Maria. "Surprised he didn't call yet."

"Not yet." She smiled at the chief. "We appreciate everything you're doing to help. Can we go in now?"

"Oh yeah, sure." Carney walked them through the line, under the tape, and into the building.

"She killed herself where?" Maria asked.

"Sorry to say, but in the computer room where Mr. Ten was yesterday, talking with Nancy. We think she was trying to erase some video but didn't know how. She was down here while Nancy was on break or something."

"She had a gun? In a prison?" Ten asked.

Carney walked them downstairs toward the computer room, other officers coming and going from the crime scene. He talked over his shoulder. "Appears so." He stopped outside the door. "Can't go in just yet. We're still cleaning up. I thought it would be okay by now." He addressed Ten. "Can you do your poking around in other areas until they're finished up here?"

Ten shrugged. "Who can I talk with about the location of all the interconnections? There must be terminals where the guards hang out."

"PJ is Nancy's assistant. He's part time. Been helping with the installation, I heard. He'll be here directly."

"Who's running things now that Cooke is dead?" Maria asked.

"Paton. I let him out this morning. We couldn't hold him with what we know."

She turned toward Ten. "This is a mess."

"A real clusterfuck," he said. "Look, I'm going to require a guard or something while I wander around and look at things. I want to see how the doors are opened, how the cameras are wired in, all that sort of thing. And PJ. Once he gets here, I'm going to want to know a lot about the installation. I suspect I'm actually going to need to talk with Nancy about it, so don't upset her."

"I'll have Paton take care of getting you an escort."

"You trust him?" Maria asked.

"I don't mistrust him, and I don't have reason to hold him. Close as it gets for now," he said. Two more people walked down the stairs and into the computer room. He turned and motioned for Maria and Ten to head back upstairs. "We can regroup in the conference room while we wait."

Maria said, "You two go. I'm going to see what's going on here if that's okay."

Chief Carney paused to look at her for a few seconds, his face unreactive. He turned around and yelled at one of the officers at the door. "Carson, I want you to let Ms. Tanner have full access. Anything she needs."

"Yes, sir," Carson said.

So that was Carson, Ten thought. A pudgy, balding officer with a quiet voice. If he was a prime example of the Muncy police, no wonder one of them got stabbed.

CHAPTER 11

Josh Hobart wasn't a big news watcher until now. After Agents Munson and Smythe had stopped by twice in the past week, he thought he'd better at least pay attention to the local news. When he saw a mention of what had happened at the Muncy Correctional Institution, it reminded him the FBI wasn't involved in that. Then when the news mentioned a Texas prison having the same problem as the local one, he didn't know how to react. He had heard Craig and Valeria talking about "what happened" but didn't want to approach them and have them think he was snooping around behind their backs. At the same time, he needed assurance that if they weren't involved, none of the others were either.

He could try hacking into the systems himself. Maybe. He'd have to research the systems and find key inroads, which would take some time. But why would he consider something that would surely put him and his job in jeopardy? And the fallout. Since he had already been contacted by the FBI about the Computer Club, a stunt like that would put every one of the students under surveillance as well. He couldn't do that—not to himself and not to them.

With the news still blasting in the background, he went into the kitchen and pulled a bag of coffee grounds from the cabinet and counted three scoops into the auto-drip coffeemaker that sat on the counter. His hands shook a little. This new knowledge about the prison breakouts affected him whether he liked it or not. He had to do something, but what?

His wife walked into the kitchen and stood in the doorway behind him. "What's bothering you?"

He turned and smiled at her. She was fair skinned and wore her light brown hair to her shoulders. She had dressed in her work clothes, black slacks and a white blouse. She managed a local restaurant, Family Dan's, and was on night shift for a few days.

"I didn't hear you come down. Just got home from school and thought I'd have a cup of coffee." He glanced at the clock on the microwave. "You heading to work soon?"

"You didn't answer me." She walked over and put her arms around him.

"The kids."

"Computer Club again. Is that still bothering you?"

"Not just Ken. At least it doesn't seem that way." He turned into her and kissed her on the forehead.

She placed her cheek against his shoulder. "Maybe you can break the club up for the summer."

"I've thought of that."

"You're not sure."

"I heard a few of them talking among themselves, saying they weren't involved. I didn't know what they were talking about at first. I have to believe what they said. They weren't talking to me. I just overheard it. Then I watched the news."

"You believe them. I can tell."

"I do. But it's still worrisome. After what Ken did, the FBI showed up again last night, and I don't know what to think or what to do."

"So what did the news tell you?"

"There was a prison break in Muncy. And one in Texas."

"You didn't tell me about the FBI." She backed away and looked into his eyes.

"You're tired by the time you get home. And to tell the truth, I didn't want to even think about it myself."

She reached over his shoulder and opened the cabinet and took down a to-go cup. "I'll have some of that."

The small auto-drip was almost finished with its cycle. Josh turned around and poured coffee into her to-go cup and his mug. She opened the refrigerator and took out a carton of half-and-half and poured a dollop in each container, then capped it and put it back. She pulled down a lid and pushed it over the top of her cup before leaning in to give Josh a peck on the lips. "You will figure it out. Muncy and Texas are pretty far apart. I doubt they're connected. Maybe you should discuss this with your students. They'll understand your concern. They look up to you." She headed for the door.

"Mel?"

"Yeah, honey?"

"Maybe tonight we'll talk about all this. You can help me think it through."

"Be happy to." She hesitated for a moment and glanced around at him. "You have a good sense about the kids. You knew Ken was susceptible weeks ago, remember? You were worried about him then. Pay attention to that. If you believe the others are playing it safe, trust your intuition."

"I called the police." He shrugged. "Just to be on record."

"As long as it doesn't ruin your relationship with your students. You don't want to disappoint them."

He stared after her and heard the door shut a few moments later. He took his coffee into the living room and sat down. The television was on but Mel must have muted the sound. He flicked the whole thing off and sat back to think. His cell phone rang, and he jumped and spilled some of his coffee onto his lap. "Shit." He ran to the kitchen where he'd left his phone on the counter but missed the call. He quickly went into missed calls on his phone and saw who it was. "Double shit." His concern spiked as he called back.

Craig answered the phone on the first ring. "Is everything all right?"

"Yeah, but I'm nervous about something, Mr. Hobart."

"Go on."

"I don't want to get into any trouble, and my dad says that, with all that's going on, being Black could make me vulnerable." Josh didn't comment. "After what Ken did. I mean, I was in the room when he did it. Me and Valeria. I left early. But I was there at the beginning. Anyway, this whole thing about the prison. You must have heard. I just want you to know that we have nothing to do with that. And... I... well, I don't want someone coming by asking questions. I'm too nervous, and I'm afraid they'll ask me questions and find out I was with Ken and maybe think that I might be involved in—"

"Hold on, Craig. I can hear how scared you are, and although I might not agree totally with your dad, you might want to be more careful right now. I hate to say that. You know I do. It pains me terribly."

"I know, Mr. Hobart. That's why I called. I wanted to talk with someone from the outside who I trusted."

Josh felt strange even having the conversation about race in such a small town and with a student as bright and capable as Craig. "Your dad knows you called me?"

"Yeah. He suggested you might want to be prepared, you know, to, like, stick up for me if it comes to that. I don't know. Maybe I should quit."

Josh agreed that Craig's skin color might make him more of a target, but he also knew that Munson and Smythe seemed like good guys. He could ask for their backing, even though a different agency was involved now. Then there was Valeria's involvement too. "Valeria was there too?"

"Yeah, but she's not as worried. I guess I'm just like that. I was stopped last year when a few of us were hanging around the Go-Mart, and the cops told us to disband, like we were planning some big heist or something. We were just meeting to agree on a bike ride. Anyway, that kind of scared me."

"It's okay to be cautious, Craig. Trust me. But I don't want you worrying yourself sick. Try to calm down. Nothing has happened yet."

"But we didn't have anything to do with any of the prison stuff. I mean, Texas? Why Texas, even if the two breakouts are connected?"

"No one on the news said that, did they?"

"Copycat."

"Oh. I can see why they might think that. But then, they're not connected, really."

"What should I do?" Craig sounded eager for an answer.

"I've been thinking about that. Maybe we should suspend Computer Club until September."

"If you think so."

"Not yet, though. I haven't fully thought about it. Let me think for a few days. Next Tuesday I'll have an idea what to do. Come to Club then. Keep up with your work. I'll know more then. I might talk with the people investigating this. That might help me understand things better, where they're looking and all that."

"My dad thinks I should quit for now, but I'm afraid that will make it look like I'm involved, and I'm not."

"Tell your dad that I'll take care of things. You may be right. It would look suspicious. If you can, wait until Tuesday."

"Sounds good, Mr. Hobart. Thank you."

Josh waited for Craig to hang up, then decided to call Valeria and come clean about what he overheard. He called her number and waited. Her mother answered. "Mrs. Marin, this is Josh Hobart from Computer Club."

"Is something wrong?"

He smiled into the phone. "No, Mrs. Marin, I just wanted to talk with Valeria if she's around."

"She's at work. She just got a job at the McDonald's where her sister works. I'm off to work soon too. Can I tell her to call you?"

"Yes. Please do that. Whenever she has a chance. I'll be up late, so maybe when she gets home." He lowered his eyes as he hung up. Their whole family had to work now that Mr. Marin wasn't in the picture. This was the first time he'd called her house. There was something about her mother's voice. He felt the heaviness of the house behind her, the heaviness of the past few years. He worried about Valeria and her sister, her family. He worried about each of his students more than he would like to admit.

He put the phone on the counter and walked back into the living room where his coffee sat on the side table. Their cat, Do-Little, lay in the spot where he'd been sitting, and he couldn't bring himself to move her, so he picked up his mug and sat at the other end of the couch where Mel usually sat. He sipped the coffee. Something inside him churned. Muncy was a small town with a number of Black and Latinx families who were seemingly always getting into trouble. He wondered how much of it was really them. He only got to work with the brighter students, teaching high-level math and then Computer Club. The children of color in his classes were bright and capable and didn't have a bad bone in their bodies. They had caring parents, like Craig's dad. He knew that there were ruffians—of all colors—in town but they weren't *his* kids. Except... His thoughts quickly morphed into Ken Hemming's illegal hacking, which burst the *all innocent* bubble he held to a moment earlier.

He reached over and pet Do-Little, who perked her head up, mewed, then lay her head back down again.

Mel would get home late. Valeria and her sister and mother would probably get home late too. In the meantime, he could worry about everything that was going on or think of a way to nip the situation in the bud. He walked into the kitchen and poured a second cup of coffee, then opened the junk drawer and found Agent Munson's card. Who did he say was taking over the case? It was time to find out and have a chat with them.

CHAPTER 12

Josh carried an umbrella when he met her at the park. It wasn't something he was totally comfortable with, but when Valeria refused to talk while at home, he felt he had no other choice. And since she wanted to talk with him in person, he wondered how serious their conversation might get. He lowered his umbrella when he saw Valeria walking toward him in a slicker with the hood up. She had fine features, smooth skin, a slight body. All that. A high school girl yet with confident, adult-like eyes. He wore a sweatshirt, but the rain had turned into a midday mist, and he felt he didn't want to be seen walking under an umbrella together. If anyone saw them walking that close, it could be misconstrued.

She peeked her eyes up from under her hood. "Dad and I used to come here. Just the two of us," she said. "It's the only place I thought of where we probably wouldn't be worried about someone hearing our conversation."

"Mel and I walk the trails through the woods sometimes on weekends when neither of us are working," he said. Mel was working this Saturday, so he had plenty of time to talk with Valeria about the breakouts, about his overhearing the conversation, about Craig's call, and about Computer Club in general.

She smiled at his mention of he and his wife walking together. "That's nice. Our whole family hasn't done that for a while." She lowered her eyes and turned down the path.

He took a few steps behind her. "I'm sorry," he said.

"Nothing you can do. It's just taking so long. My Uncle Philippe helps as much as he can. He and Mom have worked with different lawyers. Now they work together with just one. Uncle helps us out financially too, sometimes. Mom never said so, but I heard them talking. He has his own family. Two at home still, even though Ana is working at the police station." Valeria shrugged and looked around her hood. "You probably remember Ana. She was in Computer Club, then went to college."

"Your whole family seems to be into computers."

"Not Dad."

"What did he do before ICE picked him up?"

"Best mechanic in town," she said in a spirited, proud voice.

He heard her laugh at her own response and appreciated how strongly she felt about her father. "I don't think I ever heard what happened," he said.

"Something Dad did years ago. Mom told us it had to do with when they had nothing. Dad had lost his job and was trying really hard to find work. No one was hiring. It was their most difficult time. He stole some food from the grocery store and got caught. I was really little. The store didn't do anything. I think the manager knew our situation at the time. Dad actually made friends with the store owner, fixed his car for free a few times once he was working again."

"Why'd he lose his job in the first place?"

"The garage Dad worked for couldn't make it in the downturn. Mom said it wasn't their fault or Dad's. Everyone who worked there, including the owner, was out of work. ICE," she said with some contempt. "They do what they want. It was a long time ago. A small thing. He was desperate. He's been stuck in some immigration hole for too long. It's been almost two years. I miss him. Mom misses him. My sister misses him. We had a good family. We all work hard."

Mr. Hobart heard her voice crack. She was too young to worry about supporting a family while going to school. Her sister too. Even worse. He didn't want to diminish her need to get things off her chest, but he also wanted to warn her of the dangers if she or any of her friends from Computer Club were poking around where they shouldn't be. He had heard her and Craig talking about not being involved, yet she definitely had good reason. He had no idea where her dad was being held—definitely not at the women's prison in Muncy. Texas seemed too far, but it was possible. She seemed to be done with venting, with explaining her situation. They had come there to talk about potential problems—as though she needed more trouble.

He took advantage of the pause in conversation. "That's why I wanted to talk with you about Ken and Craig and the others."

"I know. You're worried. My mom worries a lot too. I didn't want her to know we were talking about the prison break. I never told her about Ken. She would freak out and make me quit Computer Club. It's all I have."

Her words cut to his heart.

Her dad had been retained as an immigrant for nearly two years, which Josh had not known until now. He knew of the event, just not the timing. He tried to stay out of his students' personal lives, as difficult as that was, especially hearing them talk at Computer Club. He often missed details on purpose. But now he knew. He could only imagine how difficult their lives were. And Ken's life. He was beginning to understand what Ken's family must be going through.

Valeria, along with her mom and sister, worked low-wage part-time jobs to keep the house going. She and her sister were still in high school, and now there was the disruption in Computer Club, the only place Valeria had for herself. He heard it all in the way she delivered her words, could see it in her shoulders, the way she slogged forward, slumped, head down. People talked with their whole bodies, especially children who hadn't learned to hide their feelings yet.

"I want to be sure that you understand the ramifications of hacking in general, let alone a federal organization. I hate to say this, but it might be best to stay away from Ken for a while. It's up to you, but your family is already, well..." He didn't know where to go from there. "I'm thinking of holding off Club for the summer. It might be best for everyone."

She slowed. "Don't you think it might be best to continue?"

Was she not wanting to let it go? Would that be more than she could handle right now? "Maybe. I wanted to talk with you, with each of you separately, before making a final decision. Mel actually suggested I check in to see what all of you prefer." Although the rain had stopped, every slight breeze brought drops falling from the leaves overhead. Water from his soaked head ran along his cheek.

In a moment, Valeria stepped off the path and he followed, wondering where she was taking him. He moved a low-hanging branch from his way and stepped high and cautiously through a bush that soaked his pants and the bottom of his sweatshirt. Why was she taking him this way? Where were they going? It wasn't that the woods path was busy. Since they'd seen no one anywhere on the path so far, and there was only one car in the parking lot when he arrived, besides Valeria's mom's car.

She threw her hood back as they entered a clearing where a tree had fallen some time ago and taken several other trees with it. Saplings pushed up from the rotting wood around them, and moss formed humps over dead branches and the long trunk of the tree. Valeria reached her arms outward and turned in a circle with a big smile on her face. "Dad and I used to come here before ICE picked him up. We'd sit and talk. No one around, just us, no matter how busy the trails were at the time. We could hear people talking as they passed by but would keep our voices low so they didn't know we were here. Isn't it great?"

Mr. Hobart's shoulders relaxed. He had no idea where she was taking him. He understood now. Valeria wanted to share this place with him as a father figure, nothing more. He loved her innocence and trust. Country kids. When he first became a teacher, he taught in Philadelphia for a year. Those high schoolers were world wise. A young woman might pull a teacher away like this just to get him into trouble with the school, blackmail him into giving her a better grade. Out here, at Milton High School, the kids were still kids. "This is a wonderful place," he said while looking around. "I can see why your dad would bring you here, why he'd want to share it with you."

She pointed at the largest lump of moss. "A nurse tree. Dad told me how it dies so other trees can live. It's not far from the path but, as you can see, it's private. No one else comes back here. I don't know how he found it. Mom doesn't even know it's here. It was just us, him and me. We can talk freely here."

"I thought we were doing that."

"We were. I'm sorry." She turned her head away. "I wanted to show somebody."

"It's okay. I'm glad you showed me. It's the perfect place to have a talk. Like you said, it's private."

"So," she said, and his earlier concern came back.

He worried what might be said next.

She lowered her voice. "The thing is, I helped Ken break into the FBI servers, not Craig. Like he told you, he left early. He called and told me he talked to you about him being there. I told him he didn't have to worry, but his dad is older. Craig has an older brother and sister who have grown up and moved out. His dad remembers race riots and tension way beyond what Craig has seen, and I think Craig's picked up the concern." She wandered around and kicked at the moss. "I don't blame him."

"I don't either. Things have changed a lot since his dad was young, but that doesn't change the fact that Craig might be more of a target than the white kids. I hate to say that so bluntly, but it's true. And since we're being honest."

"I know. That's why I wanted you to know it was me who helped Ken. Now that you know, it's easier to protect Craig if something happens."

"Again, since we're being honest, you are at greater risk too. I want to protect everyone in Computer Club, not just Craig." He walked closer to her. "You said *in case something happens*. What do you think might happen?"

"You know about the prisons. The news made us all nervous. After Craig, Roger called me, then Ken, then Bill. Everyone's worried."

His curiosity pushed into their conversation. "Why'd they all call *you*?"

"Because I helped Ken. Because Ken and I have worked together on other projects. They wondered if he was involved, but he's not. None of us are. I needed to tell you that in private."

"You're all pretty tight."

"We are. And we talked and we want you in on everything. I was elected to tell you. If anyone comes after any of us, like the FBI did with Ken, we figured they'd go to you first."

"I'm your buffer. Or maybe your insurance policy."

"That's why I think we should keep up with Computer Club."

"It keeps us in close contact," he said. He found it interesting, like always, how astute and creative his high school students were. Once again, they thought ahead, even further than he had. While he was thinking they should separate, they were thinking they should band together, and they were probably right. Strength in numbers.

"They wanted me to talk with you," she repeated. "They thought you might believe me more. Nobody knows how much I helped Ken though. You're the only person either one of us told. Even Roger, Ken's best friend since grade school, doesn't know."

"I'm glad you told me. Everything. Now it's time for me to come clean. I talked with Agent Munson about the group that took over the prison investigation, and it's a high-tech group out of Washington, DC. The International Security for Technological Innovations." He looked her square in the eyes. "I'm going to be proactive about this and contact them as well. Let them know I'm willing to help if they need me. I already talked with the police chief. Maybe I'll give them profiles on each of you so they know I'm aware."

Valeria blushed for a moment, then grappled back her composure. "I'm glad you're willing to stick with us."

"Absolutely. You can tell the others that too."

"And Ken?"

He swallowed. Was that what she really wanted to ask about? "I'll have to think more on that issue. He already did something illegal. Bringing him back might jeopardize the rest of you." *And me.*

"We trust your judgement," she said.

Which only made him feel more responsible.

CHAPTER 13

Cleanup at the correctional institute took longer than Ten or Chief Carney expected. Even after PJ showed up and Paton—who never showed his face—assigned a guard, the four of them waited in the conference room until late Saturday afternoon. The chief was interrupted a few times but stuck around as PJ and the guard arrived at different times, chatted with each about their day, and explained they would have to wait for cleanup to be completed.

All morning, a slight, sun-filled mist hung in the air outside the window. As people came and went to report to Chief Carney, Ten and his future cohorts exchanged very minor interactions, greetings mostly, with long periods of silence between. The four of them missed lunch.

PJ let loose several long exhales indicating his impatience. Ten was right there with him. The guard Paton had assigned to them looked happy to be off the floor, as they say, and sat, stuffed into her uniform, in a chair at the end of the table. She spent her most intimate time with her cell phone, either communicating through texting or watching videos from what Ten could tell. A white earbud cord draped over her shoulder and down to the device. She didn't even look up for small talk. Ten had forgotten her name and couldn't see her nametag, which twisted away from him and hung as though it had slipped from its pin attachment. The woman wore her hair short, which only made her face appear rounder than it was. Her middle-aged skin showed few wrinkles except around the eyes. She wore no makeup except thick eyeliner.

Seconds before Ten went completely out of his mind, Maria walked into the room and sat down next to him. "If you're still waiting, maybe we should head to the station and have another talk with Nancy." Chief Carney, who had been standing near the window, stepped closer to the table. "I can take you in my squad car."

"We'll follow you," she said. "Ten and I have to catch up on the way."

PJ stood up too. "If I'm not needed..."

"Tomorrow morning?" Carney said.

"It's Sunday."

"Both of you," he asserted.

The guard looked up with disinterest. "I'm working tomorrow anyway. Much rather wander around with you two."

"Then it's settled," Carney said while looking at PJ. "Sorry, Paul."

"It's okay. Just my only day off," PJ said sarcastically.

Ten and Maria left the room first and made their way through more policemen than Ten would have expected the whole town to have employed. When something happened in a small town, everyone seemed to come out to see what it was about. Everyone wanted to be a part of it. The air outside wrapped tightly around them, hot and muggy, less misty than earlier in the day. The sun showed through thin clouds. The hills behind the prison shimmered in the moist air. "Rain's over for a few days by the looks of it," Ten suggested.

Maria wrinkled her nose. "Let's hope that doesn't mean it gets smelly again."

"I suspect the manure is sinking in after all the rain." He looked over at her. "It really bothers you."

"Why I don't have a dog or cat. Why would anyone want to smell shit first thing in the morning, let alone pick it up?"

"That bad?"

"The smell makes me want to gag. The manure we smelled coming in burned my eyes. I could hardly stand it. You didn't notice?"

"I noticed but hadn't realized that it was that bad."

"It was worse when I was little."

"I'll be sure not to fart in the car."

"Gross."

They drove along the fields. Smelly, but not obtrusive, according to Maria.

"You wanted to talk," Ten said.

"Mostly I wanted to save you from sitting there all afternoon and save us from driving with Carney. These small-town police move slowly. By the time I came up to spring you, they were still searching and collecting what they thought was evidence, dusting everything imaginable, cleaning up, and doublechecking every step of the operation. Maybe triple checking. I was so bored watching them, I couldn't be sure. There were so many of them running in circles. Enough to make me dizzy."

"You found out nothing?"

"A little. They whispered a lot, probably not wanting me to hear."

"Even through all that, you picked up bits of information."

"I did. It seems she carried a small-caliber pistol in her purse, for God's sake. Enough to do the job. I didn't see the body, of course. They took that to the morgue already. But I heard them mention that the bullet went through the roof of her mouth and out the top of her head. Pretty instant."

"Small caliber. Like a .22?"

"I don't know, why?"

"It may not have been so instant depending on where in the brain it tore through. It could have been pretty, I don't know, painful, distressing, weird."

"I didn't think of that. Sounds terrible."

"Anything else?"

"That wimpy guy in the conference room with you."

"They call him PJ. What a fucked-up name. Probably fit when he was four, but once he grew up? No wonder he acts so shy."

"We should call him Paul," she said. "Treat him like an adult. I noticed Carney did that. He must have some sensitivity going on under that uniform. Anyway, Paul was down there for a little while. Nancy's assistant. He mentioned some tests they were doing. I thought you'd want to know. He didn't appear to know very much about the system at all though. Like he was just helping Nancy with wiring and that sort of thing. She's the brains behind the installation. I thought you'd want to know that too."

"It helps to know it's just the two of them for the most part. If that's the case, at least there aren't a half dozen people who could have fucked up. Narrows down our possibilities."

She waited for a moment and watched out the windshield.

"I sense there's something else," he said.

"Not about the case."

"What? You know you're going to tell me sometime. It had might as well be now."

"I was wondering how you're healing."

He let out a long, exhaustive sigh. "Are you wondering how my latest wound is healing, or are you wondering if I cut myself again? The answers are fine and no." He lowered his eyes for only a second, then brought them back to the road in front of him. "You might be right about staying busy. I haven't had time to get depressed. This isn't the most interesting job, not yet anyway, but it does keep my mind busy." He leaned across the console and pushed his shoulder against hers. "Don't gloat because you're right for a change."

Maria sniggered, then looked out the side window again. "I wouldn't say *for a change*," she said.

At the police station, they walked inside and instead of going down the hall past a WRONG WAY sign, they took a quick right where an arrow pointed. They talked briefly with the desk clerk, who was also the 911 dispatcher, telling her that they were there to talk with Nancy Wilmoth.

The woman hesitated as though trying to figure out what to say next when Chief Carney saved her by walking through the back door and up behind her. "Marge, I'm taking these two into the back to talk with Nance." He motioned back toward the rear of the building.

"Are they new?" she asked. "FBI?"

"No, Munson's still the local agent. These two are from ISTI. I'll tell you about that later. It's Maria and Ten, like the number ten."

"Nice to meet you both," she said as she let them through a half door which was part of the counter to her right.

"We could have gone around," Maria said as they snaked past a few unoccupied desks and back into the main hallway behind Carney.

"We're official now," Ten whispered.

The chief brought Nancy in without cuffs this time. He looked slightly annoyed as she sat down across from Maria and Ten. "You want me out of the room, I suppose?" he asked Maria.

"Would you mind?"

He shifted on his feet in a jerky motion that said he did mind, but he nodded anyway, resolved. "I'll be outside if you need me." He walked out and the door clicked behind him.

"How much longer you going to keep me in here?" Nancy asked right away, rather boldly. "I didn't do anything."

"You held back information about Cooke's wrongdoing. That makes you an accessory."

"I could have lost my job! She threatened me physically!"

Maria's face reddened and her eyes got fiery as she leaned slightly forward. Ten placed a hand on her forearm before she blasted the girl. "That's not why we're here," he said.

"Then what do you want?" Nancy asked, not knowing who to look at.

"The P280," Ten said, getting her full attention for the moment, probably gladly.

"What about it? The corporate offices sent all the equipment. We're just installing it. They didn't even send help. Assholes. We're not experts on this shit. If something went wrong, I didn't do it. I wouldn't even know how."

"According to PJ, you're the brains in your department."

"Sure, according to PJ. He's an idiot."

That answered one question, Ten thought. "PJ said something about testing. Did you perform some kind of testing procedure?"

Nancy sat back into her chair. She was thinking.

"You know anything about that? What kind of testing?" Ten pushed.

She sat still.

"Is something wrong?"

She suddenly looked relaxed. A little smile sneaked across her lips. "I'll help as much as I can," she said calmly.

"Great." He waited.

"But you have to drop any charges you have against me." She glared at Maria while keeping her face toward Ten. "I know you think I did something wrong, but I was scared." She let her eyes settle on Ten again as though looking for some kind of sympathy or understanding. "I'll help. Really. Anything you want. But I can't go to prison." She paused for only a second. "She threatened me."

Ten waited for Maria to answer, but she said nothing. He knew this wasn't like her. She must have been battling through her anger, her disappointment that the girl didn't just do the right thing. But he also knew, from experience, the right thing wasn't always what you thought it was. Other emotions got in the way and tangled things. "Can you call Jacob?"

This snapped Maria out of her trance. "I don't think he'll go along with this."

"I need to know what she knows. I'm dead in the water without it." Which wasn't exactly true, even though it would be easier with Nancy's help.

Maria turned her head toward him, confused. "You can figure this out. You're like ten times smarter than she is."

Nancy's head went back as though Maria's insult was physical.

"There's already been a second breakout," he reminded her.

"A second one," Nancy repeated, fear in her eyes. She shook her head. "That couldn't have been me. Proof—"

"We don't care about your proof," Maria interrupted.

"We've lost today and don't know how much time we have," Ten said. "Just call Jacob. I know it's not what you'd like."

Maria stood and walked toward the door. It didn't open when she first pushed on it. Carney was probably leaning against it, maybe with his ear.

"You finished," he said unconvincingly as the door cracked.

"I need to make a private call. On my cell," she said. "I'm going to step out back for a moment."

It wasn't long before paperwork sat in front of Nancy Wilmoth. She read it carefully before even picking up the pen that lay beside it. She looked up. "This is legal?"

"Don't question us," Maria said.

"It's legal," Ten said.

It looked like Nancy was going to pass, then she glanced up at Ten as though doublechecking to see if she trusted him, and picked up the pen and signed. "I can leave?"

Ten handed the paperwork to Chief Carney. "Could you make a copy for Nancy and one for yourself if you'd like to keep it in your file? We'll want the original."

Chief Carney took the paperwork and walked out.

Ten placed his attention back on Nancy. "You probably read the part that said you had to be available to participate whenever we needed you, and that you would be around and not leave the state," Ten said.

"Where would I go?"

"You can stop the tough-girl act now," Maria said rather rudely. Her hands had fisted. "And remember, *we* get to say whether you are participating or not. The fine print."

Nancy looked as though she were going to cry. "It only said I had to talk with him. About the technology." She hesitated as she waited for Ten to say something, but he didn't. "What do you need to know?"

"Everything," Ten said. "Details. It's hard to know what information matters until I hear it. We'll get to your testing procedures too, eventually. I want to know if the equipment looked used, if it had the right packing, if the black boxes have the proper labeling. Anything you noticed, then your installation process." He tapped the table in front of him. "I want to know about PJ and how he was involved."

"Then I can leave?"

"Only if I'm satisfied. And if I call in the middle of the night because something dawned on me, I want you to answer."

Nancy rubbed her face with her hands as though she were already exhausted. "I said I'd help, and I will."

"You hungry?" Ten asked.

"What?"

"Hungry. Do they feed you? I missed lunch and am starving. This is going to take some time. I'll need my computer and a sandwich." He stood.

Maria stood with him. "You stay. I'll get your computer, then run out and pick up something." She nodded her head sideways toward Nancy. "Find out what she wants to eat." Ten handed her his keys and Maria walked out the door just as Chief Carney returned with their signed paperwork and a copy. "Chief, I'm going to get Ten's laptop, then run out for lunch. Would you like to join me?"

He looked surprised. "Yeah. Sure."

"I'll catch you up as to what we're doing."

He smiled as though he'd just won the lottery.

"Try to be quick." Ten admired how well Maria handled the chief.

Once the two of them were gone, he turned back to Nancy. She was a cute, petite girl who had aged a year overnight. She looked tired. At the moment, he could see how stressful this had been for her and was satisfied that they'd kept her from prosecution for now. "Don't think too harshly toward Maria. She's been through more than she should have in this life and because of that has hardened to a few beliefs."

"She hates me."

"I wouldn't go that far." But he didn't say how far he would go. He sat back in his chair and crossed his legs. "You can let Maria know what you'd like to eat when she gets back. At least it won't be jail food." He laughed. He tapped the table, then saw how it affected Nancy and stopped. "Relax for a few minutes."

Maria came back in and handed him the laptop and took their orders before leaving with Carney. Once he had his laptop opened in front of him, he opened a new file and started taking notes about what Nancy noticed.

She leaned forward and talked more softly. She hadn't showered and her hair looked a bit greasy. Ten pivoted over his laptop and she had her elbows on the table across from him. Her breath smelled stale. She had slept, perhaps eaten at least once, and hadn't brushed her teeth. Ten tried to ignore the smell as Nancy started explaining about the multiple boxes the equipment arrived in, which, according to her, looked okay. "I didn't unpack any of it though. I had PJ do that one evening after work. He has another job and only works when I need the extra help. I figured since this was new equipment and the company wasn't sending anyone to install it that they'd might as well pay for another hand."

"That means that PJ was alone with the equipment for an evening?" Which also meant that he'd have to have this same long conversation with PJ.

"Several times. In order to get things done, we have to work separately. But I wasn't kidding when I called him an idiot. Don't get me wrong, he can follow wiring diagrams and cable identifications, but he's no engineer."

"And you are?"

"Top of my class," she said. Another thing that suggested she was more capable than she originally expressed.

"You were really pissed at Superintendent Cooke. For what she made you do."

Nancy's eyes narrowed. "It was horrible," she said quietly. "But it wasn't enough reason to let a known murderer loose into the community. I would never do anything like that. You have to believe me."

"Perhaps," he said.

Nancy didn't appear to like that response.

CHAPTER 14

Nancy explained that she'd need the installation guide if she was going to remember the specifics. A half-eaten sandwich sat next to Ten, and a scrunched-up wrapper from an already-eaten sandwich sat next to Nancy. Now she had tuna-sub breath on top of the stale-sleep breath. It wasn't her fault. Besides, he probably had cheesesteak-sub breath, so he tried to ignore all the odors in the room. Hopefully they balanced out.

Maria had come and gone more than once, openly bored with all the tech talk. Chief Carney appeared to be in a much better mood after his lunch with Maria. He didn't stick around for the tech talk though. Finally, Ten had enough too. He closed the lid to his computer. "That's it for now."

Nancy had been focused on their discussion and looked confused at first, then really happy, a big smile crossing her face. Relief blatantly showing in her every move as she sat back in her chair. Just to be sure, she asked, "Can I go home?"

"If I think of something, I'll call," Ten said.

"I know—any time, day or night. Once I get my cell phone back, we'll swap numbers. That way when you call, I'll know who it is and not ignore it." She glanced reluctantly toward the door. "Maybe I'll do that with your partner too. I don't want her hating me more than she does."

"Good plan," Ten said. He stepped to the door and opened it, then called for Chief Carney. "She's all yours. Do whatever you need before she goes free." He turned toward her before walking out. "I'll be in touch." Ten found Maria chatting with Marge in the front. "I'm toast," he announced.

Maria told Marge how pleasurable it had been to talk with her, then left with Ten. He asked her to drive.

"I still have your keys," she reminded him.

"Then it's settled. I've had enough for one day. Too much sitting, listening, and typing. They have a small pool at the hotel. I wonder if I can do laps there."

"I doubt it. But it shows in their brochure that they have a treadmill. How about that? At least you won't have to sweat as you would if you took a long walk in this humidity." She fidgeted with her phone for a moment, then set it on the center console and started driving.

He heard it vibrate. "Jacob?"

She glanced at the phone quickly. "I don't recognize the number. I'll let it go to voicemail."

"I doubt I'll use the treadmill. I need to clear my head and a treadmill doesn't provide enough variation in scenery. They usually stare at a wall, a TV, or other people. I feel like I'm not really walking but actively standing still. It's weird."

"It is actively standing still if you think about it. I like that. For me, it's less distraction." She thought for a moment. "There might be a real gym around somewhere. Maybe you can practice your martial arts thing."

"Taekwondo. Good idea."

She stared in the rearview mirror and reached toward him.

"What?"

"Brace yourself."

He turned in his seat just as a big silver Dodge Ram hit their bumper and their car jumped forward with a slight swerve. "Texting," Ten said.

"Oh no." Maria sped up.

Ten turned further around in his seat. "What's this about?" The truck had fallen back but now sped toward them again. "Get out of his way and slam on the brakes!" he yelled.

Maria gunned it, bounced over the side of the road, past a gulley, and pulled into a field, the back end of the car swerving to the side as she slammed the brakes like he said.

The truck whizzed by.

Ten noticed it didn't have a license plate. He swung around and Maria held a hand to her chest and shook her head. "This was supposed to be easy."

"He kept going. You okay?"

The car had stalled, so Maria started it again and spun the tires a little until they grabbed. She made her way onto the shoulder where she stopped and put it in park. "Your turn to drive." She got out of the car unsteadily, holding the roof for stability. As she walked around the back, she ran her hand along the vehicle to maintain contact.

Ten met her as he came around from the other side. He took her shoulders. "You sure you're all right?"

"I don't get it."

"Me either. You talked with Carney. Did he say anything that indicated someone might be mad at us? Come after us?"

"Not that I remember. Some crazy shit about what they found out by interviewing the guards who were on duty that night. Maybe one of them got pissed?"

"What'd they find?"

"One guard fell asleep at the terminals while the other two were 'taking a break.'" She used air quotes.

Ten glanced down the road and Maria followed his eyes. "We'd better get going." Once they were back in the car, Ten pulled onto the road but kept close watch for any other cars exhibiting strange behavior. There weren't many cars in general, and he never saw the Ram again. "What'd you mean by *taking a break*?"

"They were having sex in the back room. At least that's what the report appeared to indicate, according to Carney. The officer who filled out the form didn't actually use any words that explicitly said sex, just *intimate time*, things like that." Her hands shook as she talked.

Ten reached over and took one of her hands in his. "It's okay. We've been through worse."

"I just didn't expect it. I think it surprised me. I should know better."

"That was a warning for us to be careful where we're going with this case. Had they wanted to hurt us, they'd have used a gun, which means we might want to get ours out of storage."

She let go of his hand. "I'll be okay. I just have to relax, breathe." She purposefully took several breaths as though she were in yoga class. "Anyway, Jake said that some of the officers are pretty religious, his term, and probably wouldn't want to write down any specific words besides *intimate*."

"Sex isn't a bad word by any means."

"Yeah, well, I have no idea how religious you have to be to avoid writing it down if it were true. But he knows his own men."

"If that's true, this whole suicide thing must bother the hell out of them."

"If they know the reason why she did it, which I doubt," Maria said.

"A lot of sex going on in this prison," he said. "Is that how it is?"

"I've read about how much shit goes on inside our prison system, as I'm sure you have."

"Seen it in movies too, but I never thought it was that prevalent. I thought it was just drama."

"I don't know what to do about it," she said. "It's a side point, a distraction. We're here about the breakout—breakouts. We need to find out what they're about. Why it's happening. How. There's got to be something bigger going on. All this other sex-related stuff is just sidetracking us from the real issue we came here to solve."

"You think that? Or maybe it's all connected."

"From what I've read about prisons, a lot of crazy stuff goes on inside, all types of violence, but random prison equipment failure says something more than the usual behind-the-scenes crazy. And after that truck tried to run us over, I'm even more sure of it."

"I'd better figure this out sooner than later. But I worry that all the rest of it might be just as important. They might overlap."

"How about you keep your mind on the tech and leave the other distractions to me?"

"And if they do overlap?"

She put her window down. "We're working together," she said. "We'll know if it overlaps."

"Are you able to keep your head about these distractions? You were pretty pissed toward Nancy. And now we have people who won't even write down the word *sex*. If that person knew what was going on inside the prison, what then?"

"Then the two situations overlap. Here. At this prison," she said. "But what's that got to do with Texas?"

Ten pulled into the hotel parking lot and scanned the area for a silver Dodge Ram. Nothing looked out of the ordinary. He pointed toward her phone. "Did that caller leave a message?"

She looked. "Yeah. Let's sit for a second." She punched keys to get to the voicemail box and hit speakerphone.

Ah well. Voicemail. Okay, then. Ah, look, my name is Josh Hobart. I'm a teacher at Milton High and work with students in Computer Club. You probably know that we recently had a kid hack into the FBI. Ah yeah. Anyway, I've been monitoring them to be sure they're clean here. I mean about the Muncy breakout. But that's not it. Not really. I'm calling to let you know I might be able to help with whatever investigation you're doing. If it was a hack, that is. It looks like it. So... There. You have my number now, so give me a call. Either way, if you can. Well, thanks. Maybe I'll hear from you soon.

Maria laughed for a moment. "He was nervous."

"Voicemail tongue-ties some people. He sounded sincere, but why would he have to mention the kids in Computer Club unless he thought one of them might be involved?"

"He said one of them was caught hacking the FBI. I wonder if they believe the two incidents are connected. If so, no wonder those two FBI agents wanted to be included," she said.

"Yeah. But it didn't seem like any love lost between them and Chief Carney."

"Stereotypical police-versus-FBI story."

"Maybe," Ten said. "So what do we do with this Josh Hobart guy?"

"We get back to him like he asked and maybe use him instead of bothering Floramo. He's local and willing. And if one of his kids hacked the FBI, he must be teaching them something."

"Let me think about it. Local might mean he has his own agenda."

They got out of the car and walked through the lobby up to their rooms. Maria followed Ten into his.

"Are we still talking?" he asked.

"Promise me you won't go out for a long walk without me, or without telling me at least. That thing that happened out there spooked me."

"I don't think they meant to hurt us."

"Maybe not. Like you said, it was a warning, but a warning for what? For us to stop? And which part?"

"I see what you mean." He thought about their two cases. Everyone knew about the breakout. It was on the news. But the sex tapes Nancy was involved with were still not public knowledge. "Do me a favor and call your buddy Carney. We want all this sex stuff, the guards, the super and inmate, Nancy's involvement—all of that needs to stay under wraps. That way it limits the number of people who could be involved and also lets us know if our recent road attack was an inside job."

"If we work both ends, how will we know?"

"I don't know yet. But like you said, we're working together. We'll figure it out." She lingered for a moment. Ten held her gaze. "Tell you what, I'll try the treadmill. If I hate it, I'll give you a call."

"I'll be down in a few and spend some time in the pool."

"You don't need to keep an eye on me," he said.

"Who said I was? Maybe I just want to cool off."

He cocked his head and shot her a disbelieving look. "Either way, give Carney a call first and see if we can keep this all tight to the vest. I'll call Nancy before I change and let her know that her mouth has to be shut too. I'll check to see who else she might have told already and start a list of people to interview if necessary."

"I'll do the same. Including the cop who took the statement and couldn't use the word. He might complain to someone." She paused at the door. "The list is growing."

"You mean about the person who ran us off the road?"

"Yeah."

"Have faith."

"This job isn't making that easy," she said before leaving his room.

CHAPTER 15

Josh Hobart explained to Mel that he'd had a private talk with Valeria and each of the young men from Computer Club. She had worked eight to five that Saturday and had just returned home. They were in the kitchen together. Josh stared into the backyard from the window over the sink. Mel stood in the doorway.

"You sure she wasn't trying to trap you into a compromising position so she could blackmail you if they *are* involved?"

"You're not serious," he said. "You suggested I talk with each of them."

"Maybe I watch too many movies. It sounds like you trust her, then."

"I trust all of them." He turned around and leaned back against the counter. Mel looked tired and her white blouse bore several food stains. It was always like that after a shift, and Josh often wondered how messy the place really was. How was food always splattered? At the moment, though, his head reeled from all the conversations he'd had that day—on the phone and in person—and the decision about Ken that was tormenting him, not fully ready to be resolved. "At the same time, they're a tight group and might protect one another," he explained.

"There you go. So you don't completely trust them." She pulled out a chair and sat at the table and leaned heavily on her elbow.

He shifted his weight against the counter but stayed in position. "I want to trust them completely."

"I know you do, honey. You want to see the best in everyone." She smiled at him. "My advice, if you're asking, is to follow your gut, not your heart. Your love for those kids shouldn't cloud your judgement."

"Yeah, well, for backup I called the woman from that ISTI group. They're involved with security and technology or something. I forget what Munson told me it stood for, but I suspect they'll bypass any poor judgement I might have."

"Is that what she indicated when you talked with her?"

"She hasn't gotten back to me yet. I left a message."

"Do you think she'll get back to you?"

"Who knows? I have to assume that if they're professional, they'll at least let me know to buzz off."

About that time, his phone vibrated on the counter where he often plugged it in to charge.

"Speak of the devil," she said.

He swiped at the phone and nodded toward Mel before picking up. "This is Josh."

"Josh, this is Maria Tanner, from ISTI. I'm sorry it's kind of late but we've been busy pretty much all day, as you can imagine."

"I understand."

"About your offer—"

"Yes?"

"My associate is handling the technical stuff so I'm going to pass you off to him, I'm afraid. His name is Tempest Nesbit. I suspect he'll want to talk with you sometime soon, so I gave him your number. I hope that was okay."

"Yes. Absolutely. I'm surprised. I wasn't sure..."

"Hey, like most government operations, we struggle for funding. We aren't a high-visibility group like the FBI, CIA, Homeland Security, or even the NSA for that matter. So a little local support is welcome."

Josh hesitated to ask at first, then went for it. "Is the FBI involved?" He heard her laugh on the other end of the phone.

"I heard that you dealt with Agent Munson for your other little ordeal. The one you mentioned in your message. I doubt we'll be using their services, but you never know. They do have additional information since they've already been involved, even if minimally. But for now, no."

"He's not a bad guy," Josh said. "He gave my student a break, and I appreciated that. These are good kids."

"You mentioned that before," Maria said.

"I did. Well, it's true. Anyway, thank you. I appreciate the call and will wait for your assistant to touch base. What's his name again?"

"Tempest Nesbit. He's my associate, not my assistant. Although that sounds better to me."

Josh imagined her smiling after saying those words and thought that perhaps her associate was in the room where she was calling from. "Tempest. I'll be glad to help. Tell him that."

"I will."

The phone went dead, and Josh turned toward Mel. He gave her a one-shoulder shrug to the question she never asked. He walked toward her with a slight, tight-lipped smile. "Looks like they're okay working with me. I almost didn't expect it. She said her associate would be calling. A Tempest Nesbit. The tech guy."

"You think he'll call? Or do you think that was her way of passing without you holding her to it?"

"Yeah, I think he'll call. She wouldn't have informed me if they didn't mean to call. She sounded very official and said they'd been busy all day. Pretty cool." He sat across from Mel and reached out to take her hand. "I'm actually excited about the opportunity. Working with a government agency. Never thought that would be part of my career path."

"You're a smart man. You can do anything. I'm sure they'll find how much of an asset you can be."

"Maybe we should go out. Celebrate this milestone."

Mel rose from her chair. "I'm all for not cooking or cleaning up. Let me spruce up and change and I'll be right down. At dinner, you can tell me more about your discussions with your Computer Club kids."

Josh kissed her on the cheek. After she left, he sat back down and thought about what he'd just agreed to. It was exciting, but it was also scary. What would he do if one of his students were involved? That was a big question, one that led directly into the question about what he needed to decide about Ken.

CHAPTER 16

Ten placed both feet on the carpet and rubbed his face, forehead, and back of his neck with his fingers. The clock said 3:32. It was still dark. He went to take a pee and then sat down in front of his laptop. He sent Nancy a quick text for when she got up, letting her know that he needed her to be at the prison as soon as she could that morning. It was Sunday morning, and he had no idea when she would be up. If he got there early enough, he could beat both her and PJ, and start running through the installation parameters they'd completed. He then switched his focus to the operational guide and searched for testing procedures. Even though he'd heard from Maria that PJ had mentioned a test procedure and he'd asked Nancy about it, he had forgotten to check it out on his own. Long day. What better time to catch up to things he'd forgotten than three-thirty in the morning?

He skimmed through the PDF from the beginning again, looking for specifics. When he found what he looked for, he copied and pasted the information into a Word document and kept reading. Each time he found something that left him wondering, he copied and pasted that element into the Word doc. He labeled each page he pulled information from so he could reference back quickly if he needed context.

After an hour, he needed a break, and slipped on a pair of jeans and a Yes t-shirt. Even with the band split up, somewhat, Steve Howe still made the rounds. The last time he'd seen Steve and the newly formed group play, he bought a tee. He liked tees that provided a history and never bought one where he hadn't been. Like, he wouldn't buy an Adele t-shirt if he hadn't gone to see her. He wouldn't buy a Tower Bridge t-shirt if he hadn't been to the Tower Bridge either. He had a few threadbare classics he didn't wear very often and considered picking up another version, like The Rolling Stones. He'd seen them in concert a couple times years ago, so he could justify that.

On his way to the lobby for a fresh cup of coffee, promised by the hotel to be available 24/7 in their brochure, he thought about the breakout and how it might connect to the Texas event. Or were they separate events? If they were connected, it meant the culprit could be anywhere in the world, which was most likely anyway. But history would suggest the crimes were local. At least that was his first thought. There was a lot to consider any way he looked at it. He didn't like where his mind was taking him and pushed *whole world* thoughts out of his head as he poured a cup of coffee into a Styrofoam cup. He passed the person at the front desk and said good morning.

"Early morning," she said.

Couldn't disagree there.

She was young, early twenties, and had her head down reading a book, shoulder-length brown hair hiding much of her face. She held a highlighter in her hand, so he figured she was a college student studying for a final. It was mid-June after all. Colleges and schools would be ending soon.

He sat off the lobby in one of their comfortable, stuffed leather chairs. He stared out a large window in the front of the lighted entryway. He let his mind wander as he held the coffee cup and sipped every once in a while; he'd forgotten cream but didn't get up to remedy the fact.

He wasn't sure how he was going to work with Nancy or PJ, and after Maria called the teacher from Milton who ran Computer Club there, he'd have to add him to the mix. Ten was not a delegator. He wasn't looking forward to having to separate what he was up to and try to manage it without being intimately involved. Plus, there was the fact two-thirds of the people weren't trustworthy, maybe one hundred percent if the teacher was actually trying to protect his students rather than help solve the crime as he suggested. Ten took note to have Carney talk with Agent Munson and ferret out as much information as possible about the FBI hack and maybe have someone check the background of this Josh Hobart guy, as well as his students. Ten shook his head and closed his eyes. There were already too many people involved. He liked it better when he and Maria worked on their own, just the two of them. Of course, that never really happened, but it was a satisfying thought to have so early in the morning. Fewer problems. He could trust her.

While he rested with the coffee cup between his hands, he heard the elevator ding behind him. For a brief second, he wondered who else would be up this early in the morning. What was it now, close to four-thirty or five?

A rustle of movement came from behind and toward him. Before he could turn to see who approached, Maria came into view and sat with a thump and gush of air from the cushion in the chair next to him. "I was worried."

He shot her a questioning look. "You're early."

"Your phone kept vibrating." She handed it to him.

"You could hear that in your room?"

"I don't sleep quite as soundly as I used to."

"And you worry about me? More than you need to, by the way."

"I went to your room and you weren't there. Just your phone. I didn't know what happened."

"I'll leave a note next time." Ten realized that Maria wasn't doing as well as she seemed to want him to believe. Maybe what Carol, her psychologist, helped her with wasn't working as well as she'd said. He didn't address that. He understood. "Let me see who needed to talk with me so early." He opened his phone and text messaging. "Nancy.

Three times. First to say she'll be there at five. Two more times to see if I got the message." He sat up quickly. "Five?"

"What is she thinking?" Maria asked.

"Fuck. I texted her when I got up this morning around three-thirty and asked her to meet me as early as she could. I didn't expect her to even get the message until late morning, if that."

"People keep their phones on their bed stands. Even you. Of course she got the message. Probably woke her up."

"I can't make it by five. It's 4:53 already."

Maria laughed.

"It's not funny."

"You got everyone up early. Nancy. Me. And now *you're* flustered? That's karma."

Ten drank down half his coffee. A little bitter. He stood. "I'd better get going."

"Text her back. Tell her you fell back asleep and will meet her at seven or eight."

He sat back down and started texting. "Good idea. Jesus." After sending the text, he apologized to Maria. "I have to start thinking before I do things."

"Agreed. Maybe call Josh Hobart too. He could meet you. If you really want his help."

"I've decided to call him tomorrow. Let the man have his Sunday."

"He'll be teaching tomorrow."

"I'll figure something out," Ten said, not knowing if he really would.

Maria got up from the stuffed chair and the air sucked back into the cushion. She didn't appear mad or put out in any way. Tired, but not mad. "I'm going to get ready. Meet you down here in forty minutes?" She brushed stray strands of curly hair from her face. "Or I can deliver again."

"No need. I have to do a quick morning workout to get my blood flowing. You don't want to walk in on me again."

"How do you know?"

He stood up to follow her to the elevator, but she walked toward the coffee pot instead, so he went up without her. He knew he was pressed for time all of a sudden and shortened his morning routine, which included not shaving. In all, it didn't take as long as he had thought for him to get ready. Maybe the caffeine did the trick. He checked his phone once he was dressed, and Nancy had agreed with his change of plan. She was probably relieved. He couldn't tell. Her texts were short, not chatty at all. He was sorry he'd gotten her up so early, but at least he knew she was serious about working with him. She wasn't going to disappear. He liked that.

CHAPTER 17

Nancy sat near the control rack with one of the circuit boards pulled partially out and held fast using a jumper cable. She sat on a desk chair, held a meter on her knees, and had the leads touching a few points on the board, checking for some kind of signal when Ten was escorted into the room by the guard he had met the day before. The same guard who had spent all her time in the conference room plugged into her cell phone. Her name was Lisa Bennet and she looked as though she'd slept in her uniform. A slight musty smell drifted from her clothes whenever she created a breeze. As soon as they arrived in the room, Bennet walked right over and sat in a chair in the corner.

"Hey, Lisa."

"Hey, Nance."

Ten noticed a familiarity he felt went beyond work. "How well do you two know each other?"

Lisa pointed toward Nancy, then herself. "Went to the same schools. Known each other since, what? Kindergarten? Small town stuff. You'll get used to it."

Ten nodded, then bent near Nancy to see what she might be doing. Nancy smelled a lot better than she had the day before. She showered recently, washed and dried her hair, and pulled her hair back into a short ponytail. She wore makeup and a light-colored lipstick that brought out the fullness of her lips in a subtle way. "Can I ask what you're doing?"

"A few checks," she said. "We're in the second phase of installation. Since you weren't here and I didn't know where you wanted my attention, I figured I'd continue where I left off. I still have a deadline that I'd like to stick to."

Ten liked her work ethic. "And PJ?"

"He's here too. I sent him to wire more of the remote units into the facilities. Building E." She glanced over her shoulder at Ten. "Keeps him out of my hair."

"You don't like him."

"He's okay, but he's also a bother when I'm trying to get things done. Asks too many questions. I can trust him to wire things in, fix the cables, remove the older equipment. He has his place." She was much more lenient on PJ than the day before when she called him an idiot more than once.

"I like Paul," Lisa said from her corner.

Nancy snarled but Lisa didn't notice, her head bent down, chin to chest, face plastered near her cell phone like the day before.

A guard who never looks up. No wonder people escape from these places.

He brought his attention back to Nancy and started asking questions in a rapid-fire dialogue. For a moment, he thought she might think he was like PJ. She kept up with answering him easily and politely—again, impressive—while continuing her checks. She must have memorized each test location. She knew exactly what she was looking for. Finally, she got up and walked over to a computer connected through a patch cable to the bank of printed circuit boards. "Let me show you where I am," she said.

Ten followed and leaned next to her to see what she was doing.

A list of test points appeared on screen when she refreshed. Judging from the last measurement he saw her make, it looked as though she had memorized about half of the list. He waited as she read through the second half.

Ten straightened. Already his back felt the pain of being cantilevered over her desk. He'd have to eventually find a seat or do warmups and stretches so his muscles didn't lock up on him. *Keep moving.* He kneeled next to her. She never offered for him to sit, nor did she suggest that Lisa find another chair. She switched to a new screen and pointed at it. A system diagram popped up. She pushed a few keys and hit ENTER to switch to a screen that showed colored wires.

"The green lines are installed, red need to be installed, yellow in the process." She flipped to another screen. "This shows the whole facility. See this building?" She pointed to a section on screen. "This is where it happened. The escape. The first portion we'd installed. The test you asked about was completed three days prior to the escape. It couldn't have had anything to do with that." She clicked on a link in the corner. "The result of the test. You can see that everything went smoothly. We were good to go. We put that portion online, which is what the installation guide said to do, and started to install the second system in the next building. Building E, where PJ is."

She turned to look at Ten. "I can't find anything wrong. I was checking all the interconnecting circuits when you came in. I'll finish when we're done here. But I have to tell you that I don't expect to find anything weird. Unless there is some strange intermittent problem, I can't see what went wrong. Maybe the guard made a mistake from her end, hit a button she wasn't supposed to. That could happen. It is a new system. Plus, guards can override or go to a manual setting from their own observation room. For emergencies. That would be my bet."

Ten stood and paced in a circle while Nancy ran through more screens, then sat in her chair near the printed circuit board and continued her hardware checks. He stopped pacing in front of Lisa.

She looked up slowly. "Yeeeees?"

"Can you take me to Building E? I want to look things over."

"Sure." She got up and said, "I'll walk him around the campus and talk with you later, maybe."

"Sounds good. Maybe we'll break together," Nancy said as Lisa walked out.

Ten wondered what Lisa and Nancy would even talk about. They said nothing while in the same room together, both preoccupied with their own devices, as it were. He followed Lisa up the stairs and outside. He texted Maria to let her know he was taking the tour, starting with Building E to check on PJ. She texted back right away with a message that she was waiting to talk with Dr. Paton, who appeared to be overworked with all of Superintendent Cooke's duties as well as his own. *We can regroup around lunch*, she texted.

The outside air blistered with sunlight, yet there was a lingering undercurrent of coolness left over from the morning. The humidity threatened to burn that off quickly though. The day was hot for a June morning and by the time they entered Building E, both he and Lisa were sweating. Ten less than Lisa, who looked as though she'd run several miles to get there.

She hadn't said a word the whole time.

Lisa had a pass card she used to get into the building, and led Ten down a hallway and into a small equipment room.

PJ sat on the floor, his body half stuffed behind a rack of circuit boards similar to but slightly smaller than the rack Nancy had been working on when Ten had walked in on her. PJ peeked out from around the rack as Ten and Lisa shuffled in. "Hi, Lisa."

"Hi, Paul." Her voice sounded much more cordial this time than when she'd greeted Nancy. Ten could tell there was an attraction. He doubted PJ could tell though.

Lisa put her phone in her pocket.

PJ said, "One second." He did something behind the rack, then scooted out. "Ten, if I remember correctly."

"You remember correctly. Nice to see you again, PJ. Is PJ okay? Sorry you have to be here on your only day off."

"Yeah, well, once I got here, it wasn't so bad. I'd rather you call me Paul. Anyway, about this, I'm getting extra hours in, which is why I'm doing it at all. Going to buy a new car, get rid of my junk heap."

"What are looking to get?" Lisa chimed in with more words than Ten had heard from her in two days.

"Don't know yet."

"If you want help looking, I could go with you."

Paul looked confused. He glanced at Ten and then back to Lisa. "Sure. I guess so. Won't be much to do."

"It would give us a chance to catch up."

Paul shrugged and pulled himself up to his feet. He turned toward where he had just been and said, "Just shifting some wires around."

"Shifting wires?" Ten asked.

"We're using the old wiring and I'm having to change out most of the connectors for the new equipment. Different pin-outs. It's not terribly difficult; just pop the pin out of one slot and into another. Data pins are different for the new equipment. Power pins are the same. It's just not easy to get to all the time."

"Doesn't the old equipment work properly?"

"Sure, it does, but you know how these companies are. They all want the latest technology. Not that this system handles a whole lot more than the old one." He smiled. "Look, I just help out. Whatever they want me to do, I do."

"And the recent test? Since something went wrong, no one's concerned it might be a defect? That it might happen again?"

"If you ask me, it was the guard. Bertie. That woman isn't all there. Always looks out of it. Maybe she was futzing around and pushed the wrong buttons." He laughed at his own assumption. "Sorry, that wasn't quite right. She'd actually have to go through a sequence to open the doors, something she'd have to do on purpose. Honestly, I doubt she'd do anything like that, no matter how bonzo she is. She'd have to know they'd fire her."

"And that's exactly what they did," Lisa said. "The same with Buddy and Gwen. Idiots."

"They were the ones taking a break," Ten said, noticing that the word for the week was *idiot*.

Lisa laughed. "They weren't on break; they were fucking in the back room." She looked over. "Sorry, Paul."

"It's okay. Everyone knew about them."

"Everyone knows they're a thing and yet they were allowed to work together?" Ten asked.

Paul and Lisa gave each other a knowing glance. "Superintendent Cooke didn't know," Lisa said.

"And their spouses," Paul added with a shake of his head. "Well, Buddy's spouse and Gwen's boyfriend."

"Really?" What was it about small towns that the people lived soap opera lives? "Anyway," Ten said to break the conversation, "I'd like you to show me what you're up to and talk me through how the installation's been going and generally how you understand this thing works." He had read through all the documents and chose Paul to explain the operation because he was less likely to skirt around any issues they may have found during implementation. Nancy was smart enough to know when to avoid an operation and clever enough to do so without being caught.

As Paul walked Ten through the system operation—Ten followed along in his head—Lisa appeared to listen to every word as well. She had it bad. And Paul didn't have a clue. Maybe he didn't want a clue.

Every few steps along the way, they performed their own testing, even though it wasn't required according to the installation guide. "Nancy likes to doublecheck everything. She's probably right though, since we're swapping the wiring like I told you. A small mistake could make a big problem if we don't catch it right away."

"And the first actual test?"

"Pretty innocuous. Line-Tech handles that remotely. We just download the test algorithm from their site and run it through the system. The quick brown fox sort of thing."

"Quick brown fox?"

"You know, like in computer class when you're learning all the typing keys. The system runs through every step whether it's something you'll use every day or something that's only there for redundancy or emergency."

"The algorithm comes from the Line-Tech site."

"Yeah. Don't worry, we're present for the whole run-through and watch every step. Nancy knows her shit."

"So she's told me," Ten said.

"She can be a bit arrogant about it. She treats me like I'm stupid sometimes, but she's a smart girl and probably assumes everyone else needs their hands held. I don't let it bother me."

"She should let you do more," Lisa said. "You're just as smart as she is."

Paul laughed. "I appreciate your saying so, but I don't have her training."

Ten asked if he could run through the test sequence and Paul opened the terminal connected to the system. "I can do one better. I can download what we did, the checks and the results, step by step, onto a thumb drive and let you look it over later if you like." He finished the download and handed Ten the thumb drive.

"This will help." Ten put the drive in his pocket.

"You can go online to the Line-Tech site and download the first test too, but you'll have to get security codes from Nancy."

"So it is secure?"

"Yeah. Well, as secure as it can be."

Ten stuck around for a while longer and they talked about the upgrade to the new system and what other changes they were making. Nothing Paul said set off any alarms inside Ten's head except maybe the security issue that Paul threw out offhandedly. After that, he asked Lisa to walk him around the rest of the campus and introduce him to a few of the other guards. She seemed happy to oblige, even though they talked very little as they walked in the heat from building to building. The air was thick with moisture and the insects were out in force. Ten noticed Lisa sweated through her uniform in several places. At one point, on their way back to the administration building, they passed a small side building.

"What's that?" Ten asked.

"Psychology," Lisa said.

"Dr. Paton has his own building? I thought his office was in the main building."

"He meets patients in there. We have some crazy people, and the state requires we have a psychologist on staff."

"But his own building?"

"They don't want inmates going in and out of the admin building. You can imagine why. Too many civilians who don't want to interact with the prisoners, I suspect. Maybe there are laws against getting prisoners that close to the office staff. I don't know. I just know that's how it works."

"Can we go inside? I'd like to look around."

"Locked up. I have to get permission. Dr. Paton doesn't like people popping in."

"He's not there anyway, what would it matter? He's in the admin building. Maria's talking with him."

"Still have to check. I don't have a key either." She tapped at her phone. "I doubt he's going to allow you in there when he's not around."

Ten thought about why that might be. He smiled briefly. "I bet you're right."

CHAPTER 18

They didn't get permission to visit Dr. Paton's separate office space. Lisa laughed as she held up her phone. "Official text."

Ten read the message: *With all that's going on, I don't have the time. Besides, I'm with his partner right now in the administration building. No one goes into my offices without me present.* "Pretty direct."

"He's not a nice man," Lisa said.

"What makes you say that?"

"I don't know. It's just that every time I see him or say hello, he looks grumpy, mad at something or somebody, maybe everybody. He makes me feel like I'm below him, like I don't matter. And I mean *every* time I see him. You see how he answered my request. Doesn't that sound mean?"

"I want to see inside that office," Ten said.

"You'll have to do more than ask," she said.

Ten smiled broadly at her. "Oh, I'll not only do more than that; I'll make sure he feels it."

"I like you," she said.

"Glad I'm growing on you."

Back in the main building, before walking up to Superintendent Cooke's old office, Ten texted Maria about lunch while he stood at the bottom of the stairs.

She instantly texted back for him not to come up; she'd meet him downstairs.

"I'll meet you back here in about an hour and a half," he told Lisa. "Let Nancy know too. If I change my mind, tell her I'll text her."

"I usually get a half hour for lunch."

Ten smiled. "I'm sure you'll find something to do."

In a few minutes, Maria bounced down the stairs and took Ten's arm as she walked by. "We have a lot to discuss," she said.

"Uh oh."

"So how did you make out?"

"A lot of nothing." He pulled the thumb drive from his pocket. "Although I do have this."

"And what's that?"

"Results from their test run. I'm going to go through it later. I want to get Nancy's security code for Line-Tech too, so I can download their algorithm." He shoved the drive back into his pocket. "That's for later."

They got into the car and drove toward downtown Muncy hoping to find a place for a quick lunch. Maria started in about Paton as soon as they were in the privacy of the car. "He is a piece of work."

"Lisa, the guard who takes me around, said he's mean to everyone."

"He's a literal ass. Says very little. Answers questions with as few words as possible. Looks down his nose at you like... I don't know, like..."

"Like you're beneath him. You aren't important," Ten said.

"Exactly."

"Lisa said that too. Did you know he has a separate building for his offices? According to Lisa, he won't let anyone inside without him there. Well, and according to his response to my request. I think he's hiding something."

"You two sound as though you were chatty next to my conversation with Paton."

Ten laughed. "Yeah. I wouldn't exactly say that either. So did you get anything out of him?" Once Ten had pulled to the curb, they got out and walked back a half block to the Muncy Diner. It had that old, metal trailer look to the front but was much larger than a trailer on the inside. "Nice façade," he said once they were inside.

A waitress of about forty walked them to a table while casually carrying a coffee pot at her side. "Coffee?"

"Not for lunch, thank you," Maria said.

"Know what you want?"

Ten let Maria answer, since she'd started, and watched as she stared at the woman longer than necessary.

The waitress said, "I'll give you some time, then," before walking away.

Maria turned back to look at Ten. "We don't even look like locals."

"It's a diner, how varied a menu do you think they have?"

"Don't you side with her," Maria said with a smirk. "I had to deal with one asshole already today."

"So? Nothing?"

"All morning I waited, and he couldn't even be polite once I got in the office. There was paperwork everywhere. He'd answer his cell phone, text, look out the window. In between, he answered my questions with single-word answers. Nonetheless, he did seem upset about Cooke. At one point, he stared out the window and I thought I saw his eyes well up. He said that she left a big mess for everyone and I got the sense that he meant him. There was something going on there."

"He was in love with her. Strong woman, wimpy guy."

"Deeper than that."

"What's deeper than that?"

"I haven't figured that out yet." She pulled the menu from a rack near the window and opened it. "You should look at the menu too."

"I'm getting a grilled cheese and half a cup of their soup of the day, whatever it is."

"I'll get a ham on rye and Diet Coke."

"Water," Ten said. When he glanced out the window again, he shifted in his seat.

"What is it?" Maria looked where Ten was staring. "That's the truck."

"Wait here." Ten slid from the booth and walked out the front door. The silver Dodge Ram finished parking and a big man stepped out. He wore baggy jeans and an old, threadbare blue t-shirt with one breast pocket. "Hey," Ten said.

"Hey," the man said with a questioning look.

"You tried to run my car off the road yesterday."

The man stared down at Ten. He was maybe an inch taller. "Don't know what you're talking about."

Ten walked to the front of the truck and pointed. "I think you do."

"It's a truck. It gets banged up." The man started to walk away.

"What the fuck did I do that you'd pull such a stunt?"

The man kept walking toward the diner. He was on task.

Ten grabbed his arm and turned him around.

"You don't want to start nothing."

"I asked a question."

"I think you should get out of town and let the locals deal with whatever is going on. You've messed enough things up."

"So you know who I am."

"You're an outsider who's stirred things up. Like I said, I ain't gonna let that happen and neither is Carney or the rest of 'em. Get out."

"Is that a threat?"

The man shrugged Ten from his arm. "It's a suggestion." He wandered off and into the diner.

Ten wasn't sure what to do. Blatant. He walked in just as the man yelled at one of the other waitresses, "You ain't leavin'!"

The waitress stared wide-eyed at him. "Buddy? You can't be here." She turned and yelled into the back, "Hank, I might need some help here!"

"You ain't leavin'," Buddy said again.

The waitress—a short, dark-haired woman with more than her share of wrinkles around her mouth—began to cry.

Hank came from the back, a dirty apron hanging over a big belly. "You can't come in here and make trouble, Buddy. You made your bed."

"I'm takin' her home."

Ten slid in across from Maria.

"Is that him?" Maria asked.

"I'm getting the picture," Ten said.

"Explain it to me, then."

There was a little tussle as Buddy walked toward the waitress and Hank stepped between them. Ten tapped the table. "Tell you in a minute."

"I called the police," Hank said, but even Ten knew he didn't have time.

"I'm takin' my wife home now." Buddy shoved Hank into the counter.

The waitress was in full distress, arms up, backing away. Her hair moved back and Ten saw a bruise on the side of her cheek. *So that's how it was.* He rushed between Buddy and his wife and held up his hands to stop Buddy from getting any closer. "You're not going to hit her again."

Buddy pulled back as though he had time to swing at Ten, but Ten blocked the slow man's punch with both of his fists raised, then took two steps toward the man's wife and kicked Buddy's knee, bending it in the opposite direction it should normally bend. Not hard enough to break it, but enough to hurt like hell.

The big man screamed and dropped to his other knee. On his way down, Ten punched him once to the lower jaw and Buddy jerked backward, then lay flat on the diner floor. Ten turned toward Hank. "Now you can call the police." He looked toward the older waitress and placed their order as though he'd just gotten back from the restroom.

She nodded, blank faced, and walked into the back.

He hoped she heard him.

Buddy's wife rushed around Ten and bent toward her husband. "Oh, Buddy. Oh, oh." Her hands shook, and she looked like she didn't know whether to touch him or not. One hand brushed through his hair.

Ten reached down and helped her stand. He held Buddy's wife's frail shoulders and looked into her eyes. "He's been hitting you."

She was full-on crying now and staring toward Buddy lying on the floor. Through her tears she said, "Only last night. I wanted out. I told him. After what he did. He got mad. I can't blame him."

Hank reached toward the two of them but never touched either one. His fingers waved. "I'll call Carney to pick him up." He then turned toward Buddy, who was out cold on the floor. "Can I move him?"

"Yeah, but you'll need some help."

Hank motioned toward two young bucks mesmerized by the confrontation and watching from a booth against the wall while waiting for their lunch.

"You going to be okay?" Ten asked Buddy's wife. Two other waitresses had come from behind her. He motioned for them to come forward. "Take care of her. Make sure she has someone with her at all times until this is over. I want you to call the police if he tries to stop you again. If he tries anything."

Buddy's wife nodded. Both the other waitresses agreed too.

Ten searched for their waitress. "I'll be back at our table." As he swung around to walk back to his table, he heard one of the young men say, "that was badass," as they helped Hank with Buddy.

He slipped in across from Maria.

"Carney is going to want to talk with you."

"I know."

"You had to interfere." She leaned forward. "So what was that about and why did he try to run us off the road?"

"He was the guard who was banging his coworker in the back room. Somehow his wife found out why he was fired and couldn't live with him. That pissed him off and he took it out on us, thinking we exposed him. He was just mad and had to take it out on someone."

"But we didn't expose him. Whoever caused that breakout did."

"Maybe that's what happened. Someone trying to get back at him or her, who knows," Ten said. "Maybe the other woman's husband had something to do about it."

"Both were married?" Maria looked shocked.

"Not married, but according to Paul, PJ, it was a serious relationship. Same thing."

"You got a lot more out of your morning than I did."

"I guess so, when you add it up."

"She looks like she's been torn apart," Maria observed.

Ten lowered his eyes at the table in front of them. "One day you're happy and everything is fine..." he said.

"We both know what that's like. My heart goes out to her."

"She should move out of town, out of state. Start fresh."

"She won't," Maria said. "Some people just can't. She might even take him back."

"Why does that happen to people who don't deserve it?" What Ten didn't say was that it wasn't fair—what happened to him and Amy, Maria and Ben.

Buddy was taken into a back office and his wife whisked away. In no time, their waitress brought out their lunches as though nothing had happened. Ten wondered how often they had a brawl in the diner that it would go back to normal so quickly. Their waitress set down their food and stood there for a moment. Either she was slow, or her pauses meant something. Ten didn't know which. "I'll get your drinks." She still didn't move. "That was impressive."

"Thank you," Ten said.

"Your boyfriend's quite the man," she said to Maria

"We just work together," Maria said.

"Whatever." The waitress walked away and came back with her Diet Coke and his water, dropping them off on her way to clear another table before going into the back again. More people trailed through the front door and were walked to an empty table. The lunch crowd was filling the space. The new patrons knew nothing of the altercation.

They were halfway finished eating when Chief Carney walked from the back. He sat next to Maria. "What was that about?"

"Ask Buddy."

"I will when he's fully awake. He's sitting up a little dazed right now. Not very talkative. Should be able to focus by the time I get back there. Thought I'd check your story first."

"He's been hitting his wife. Looked like he was about to do it again. Couldn't let that happen." Ten set his spoon down. His soup was getting cold. He didn't look at Carney. He moved slowly, picked up the uneaten half of his grilled cheese, and took a bite.

"He always like this?" Carney asked.

"You're seeing his good side," Maria said before the chief stood back up and walked away.

"You trying to make me sound mysterious for a reason?"

Maria smiled. "A little drama for a small town. Carney can tell the story to his grandchildren. At least we know no one will try to shove us off the road tonight."

"They won't hold him for long."

"I think he'll leave us alone and focus on getting his wife back."

"I hope you're right."

CHAPTER 19

With Sunday behind them, Ten spent the whole next morning with Nancy going over the P280 electronics and couldn't find anything out of the ordinary. They spent part of the time in Building E with Paul rechecking his wiring. They would then do the ground checks between systems on Tuesday and probably download the algorithm and do Line-Tech's test on Wednesday. She really did know her stuff and proved it every step of the way. And she was thorough.

At lunchtime, Ten and Maria ate at the same diner as the day before. Ten felt their lunch had been interrupted and wanted a chance to taste his food without a fight. He also asked Maria to check with the other waitresses about Buddy's wife. He still didn't know her name. Before they were settled, Maria got a call from Jacob about yet another breakout. This time in Kentucky. "Same system too."

"Before you hang up, tell Jacob to find a way for me to get into Paton's offices without Paton having to be there." He didn't mention that none of the equipment they were checking was located there. If anyone could get him access, it would be Jacob.

Monday afternoon, after running more tests and watching Lisa tap away on her phone (when she wasn't staring at Paul), Ten decided they could continue their installation without him. Nancy looked relieved not to have him glaring over her shoulder all the time. Paul didn't seem to care one way or the other. Ten wasn't sure his decision had actually gotten through to Lisa.

Nancy stood and reached to shake his hand before he left. "Thank you for letting us move forward without interfering."

"I'm just here to figure something out. It has nothing to do with you."

She looked down. "Some of it does. What Maria's looking into. I know she wants to grill me about it eventually. You can tell her I'll answer any questions she wants. I know how much a favor it was for you to do what you did. You have no idea how grateful I am." She finally let go of his hand.

"I'm glad," he said before leaving everyone to continue their work. When Maria joined him outside the admin building, he told her, "I'm starting to trust Nancy. She's been very helpful. She's grateful as hell for what we did. She's thanked me more than once. And she said she'll talk with you whenever you wish and won't hold back."

"She's grateful for what *you* did. I would have liked to have seen her in jail a lot longer."

"She was scared. We've seen that before."

"When have you been too scared to do the right thing?" Maria asked bluntly.

"I've killed people. When is that the right thing?"

"Different circumstances."

"She's a good kid. Smart. I'd hate to see that wasted for a single mistake."

Maria squared her shoulders. "We don't have to agree on everything."

On the way across the Susquehanna Bridge into Muncy, they decided on an early dinner. They found a nice place called the Twin Archer Brewpub. They ordered a couple of burgers with fries and discussed the day's accounts.

"Jacob's wondering how it's going. I keep asking for favors and he doesn't feel like he's getting enough return, I can tell. He's anticipating more breakouts at other prisons. Says it's only a matter of time and we don't have it." Maria went on. "Said there are about twenty prisons going through upgrades, including another one right here in Allenwood."

"Tell him I know he's worried. If he wants to put someone else on the project, I'll go home."

"Don't, Ten. I'm sure he trusts you. He just wants this to go away. He's got a lot of other things going on."

Ten looked up from his meal. "I want it to go away."

Maria matched his glare. "I'll let him know that but doubt it will relieve the tension."

"It's good for him. How about you? Is he still okay that you're looking into this suicide thing?"

"I told him they might be connected."

"They might. I don't think either one of us believes that though. Maybe if Cooke let Sarah out, which we both doubt, or if someone else did it to expose them."

"Paton?" she asked.

"Why'd you say that?"

"Something about that man bugs me."

"Well, if he did," Ten said, "why Texas? Why Kentucky?"

"Hide his tracks?"

"I don't think he'd know how unless he got one of the guards to do it. Locally, I mean. That could have happened. Except that they all got fired. If it was one of them, they'd have no reason not to come clean. If he's as big an ass as everyone keeps saying."

"Unless whoever it was happened to be involved with Paton," she said.

"Two things," Ten said. "There is way too much behind-the-scenes sex stuff going on here. And second, who the hell would be involved with a man like Paton?"

She didn't answer either question.

Finally, Ten said, "Let's widen our search. How about we get Carney to get reports on everyone we know who could be involved?" He poked a fry into his mouth. "All the guards who had access that day, Paton, maybe interview the prisoners who escaped. Get those FBI guys involved. It might be nice to know what their take is on the kid who hacked them. Which brings us to Hobart and his Computer Club. He touched base with us, not the other way around. Maybe he's trying to hide something he did or something one of his geniuses did." He took a breath. "I'll give Hobart a call and if I sense something odd going on, I'm calling Roger Floramo."

"You usually don't want that much help."

He gave her a wide, fake smile. "If it makes Jacob more comfortable, let's do it." He went back to his food, picking up his burger in both hands. Before taking his next bite, he said, "Can't hurt. You can pick and choose who you sit in with, or you can interview some, and Carney or the FBI can interview others. Just a suggestion."

"Thanks for the go-ahead. Since I'm the lead here."

He laughed. "I thought you were asking for my opinion."

"Maybe." She smiled at him. "It's always welcome. You know that."

He looked at his burger, having not taken that next bite yet. "Make sure you include Paul and Lisa in your interrogations. She's really interested in him and he doesn't seem to give a shit or notice. Maybe that's something she might do to get his attention." He took his bite finally, changing his focus for a few minutes.

Maria finished her burger and chased it with water. "During the process, I'll get backgrounds on everyone I can."

"Good idea."

They paid for dinner and, once again, Maria drove them back toward the hotel. While she drove, Ten called Josh Hobart, who picked up on the second ring. "Josh Hobart here."

"Mr. Hobart, this is Ten. I'm working with ISTI concerning all the breakouts that are happening."

"All?"

"You may not have heard. There was another one in Kentucky. Look, this puts us on a tighter timeline. We have to figure this out pronto. You said you might be able to help. We're about to give you that opportunity."

"Uh, yeah, sure. I'm pretty sure I can help." His voice wavered as he spoke, almost like he didn't know what he was about to say even as the words left his lips.

"Look, Mr. Hobart, I don't need *pretty sure*."

"Call me Josh." His voice strengthened. "I can help. What do you need me to do?"

"I know you were teaching all day, but could you meet us at our hotel? We're at the Holiday Inn Express."

"Absolutely. Do I need to bring anything?"

"Nope." Ten hung up.

"You think he can help?" Maria asked. "You didn't sound so sure."

"I hope so, but we have backup if not." Ten watched out the window the rest of the drive. He noticed Maria watching her rearview mirror even though Buddy was spending a night in jail. It wasn't the first time during this trip he'd seen her acting on edge. Maybe this work wasn't for her.

Maria told Ten she'd clean up and then head to his room. "I want to be in on what you're finding out. Jacob wants me to report in and I don't think he trusts you'll tell him everything."

"I thought you said he trusts me."

"Yeah, to do the job, not to report in."

"He may be right," Ten said with a grin.

"You are so contrary."

"I don't have to kiss his ass."

"I don't kiss his ass."

"No, I can agree with that. You don't kiss anyone's ass."

"I'll be back," she said.

A few minutes after she left his room, someone knocked on his door. He opened it to a thin, dark-haired man with a nervous smile.

"You must be Tem," he said.

"It's Ten, no M at the end."

"Tempest, though. Right?"

Ten was used to explaining his name to people, even though it got a little old. "An acronym. My name's Tempest Eugene Nesbit."

"Oh." Josh laughed nervously. "Clever. I get it."

"I'm sure you do." Ten stepped from the door and let it close as Josh Hobart followed him to his laptop. "That thumb drive has the test sequence for the P280 LockDown System on it. The sequence and the results. I didn't download the algorithm that was used because I wanted you to get familiar with what's going on first. When we need to, I have the security codes to get us in. Five layers."

Josh interrupted as he sat down. "Yeah, first two to verify your computer and location, next three to get into their system where the download is hanging out. I got that."

Ten smiled. "Glad to hear it."

Josh opened the file and in a matter of seconds had already dug deeper into workings than Ten could have gone.

Ten was slightly familiar with what Josh explored, but his expertise wasn't software so he hoped Josh could fill that gap. He struggled with having to rely on someone local instead of someone from ISTI, or Roger, his preference, but Jacob had okayed it through Maria. Ten couldn't help wondering if that was yet another way Jacob distanced ISTI from the project, or something he did regularly, whether Ten was involved or not.

I can't be concerned about that right now.

Josh mumbled explanations of what he was doing while he did it. "I'm examining the code used to create the sequence as well as the operations the sequencing engaged and disengaged." He kept hitting keys, sometimes with one hand, other times with both hands as he stared at the screen. "Now, the results that are expected, and the ones it got." He looked back at Ten. "That's just to create the GO/NO-GO response. After that, things return back to the results and analysis process. I have a little ways to go still."

Maria let herself into the room while he worked. Ten stood and waved her in. "How's it going?" she asked.

"Great," Josh said. "Fairly straight forward so far. Nothing too weird. I want to doublecheck my progress though."

"Nothing *too* weird?" Ten asked.

"Nothing weird at all. Sorry." Josh turned around and put his hands on his lap. "You people are pretty literal. No room for nuance."

"Finding anything?" Maria asked.

"So far, I'm looking at a lot of activity, but I don't have a whole lot of reference as to what that activity is. Are we opening and closing doors, locking them, bringing up video? A lot of switching, redundant checks, that sort of thing, but..."

Ten walked over and brought up another window and opened the manuals. "If you just read the first few pages, the intro, you'll get a feel for how the P280 works. It's not overly complicated, but there are some hoops to run through. I can see where you need a reference."

"Thanks." Josh started reading. After a few minutes of reading and some more time looking deeper into the thumb drive material, Josh said, "Nothing so far. This helped a lot. Some of the switching could have been screwy and I wouldn't have known it if I didn't know what the system was trying to do. You want me to look at that algorithm? *Line-Tech* I believe is what it said on this drive. Let me see." He pulled up Line-Tech's internet page. "The P280?"

Ten poked his hands in each of his pockets. He checked around the room. "I know it's not the best practice, but I jotted down Nancy's logins and security codes. If I can't find them, I'll have to give her a call."

Josh continued to type and wait, then type and wait. "Give me a minute before you call." Ten and Maria shot each other a look, then shifted focus to Josh. "Okay," he said. "But," he swung around in the chair, "do I have to get special permission? I mean, breaking in like this probably isn't legal."

"You're in?" Ten said. "Through their roadblocks?"

Josh held a finger over the RETURN key. "Not in yet, but I could be. I don't want to get into any trouble."

Maria stepped toward him. "I'm the lead on this job and I give you permission to hack into their system. If you need something in writing, that might take a while." She shifted to look at Ten. "Although it's a bit alarming that you could do it that fast."

Josh Hobart made a big show of lowering his finger onto the RETURN key. He smiled broadly. "I'm in."

Ten didn't need to watch the fancy display. Maybe it was a hacker thing. "Once you download the algorithm, what are you looking for? Can you tell if someone fucked with it?"

He looked over at Ten. "We don't swear in my house. To answer your question, only if it's still in there. If for some reason it was stripped out, then no."

Ten was about to tell Josh that he was in Ten's house now and that swearing was allowed. Maria must have noticed because she reached out and stopped him. She nodded toward Josh, indicating they should let him do what he does best. So Ten shifted his response. "Do you teach how to do that in Computer Club?"

Josh's jaw tightened. "Never. In fact, Rule One in Computer Club is *never do anything illegal.* And if you don't know if it is, then don't do it until you find out. That's why I asked you for permission."

"But one of your kids did hack the FBI."

Josh turned around slowly and cocked his head toward Ten's laptop. "When companies aren't as smart as teenagers, who's at fault?"

"The person who illegally hacked in," Ten said. "A lot of old people make mistakes out of ignorance of the system; should their identities get hacked?"

Maria took a step to interrupt their conversation. "These kids can learn this stuff in more places than Computer Club, right?"

"All over the place. That's why I started Computer Club. It's like martial arts training; the first rule is to avoid the fight."

"You train?" Ten's interest perked.

Maria said, "Ten's a black belt."

"When I was younger," Josh said. "I was only using it as an analogy for how I work with the students. I haven't done that for years. My point was that all I can do is drive home what's morally right."

"Morals are fluid," Ten said.

CHAPTER 20

Ken made his entrance slowly, pausing at the doorway. The others looked up toward the movement. Mr. Hobart smiled first at Ken and then the others.

"You let him back in!" Valeria squealed.

Hobart walked over to greet Ken as he walked into the room. "Several of you suggested I keep the group together; I agreed. This way we can talk about this whole hacking business as a team. We get to help each other stay out of trouble." He heard his voice quiver and hoped they didn't notice. He felt strongly about keeping them safe.

"You're the coolest, Mr. H," Bill Newbury said.

"How come you didn't tell us?" Roger asked his best friend.

Ken glanced toward his teacher. "Mr. Hobart asked me to hold off. Sorry."

"I wanted it to be a surprise," Hobart said.

"It is." Roger walked over and slapped Ken on the back. "Good to have you with us again. I wondered why you seemed happy all day in school."

"That could be because it's ending for the summer soon," Ken quipped.

Mr. Hobart interrupted their banter. "We need to talk about this though. Seriously. Everything has to be in the open. Especially now. We all have to be on the same page. I talked with the people from ISTI and they trust me to keep you guys safe, keep you out of trouble, so we all have to be honest with each other and with them." He looked around the room and everyone seemed to avoid eye contact, maybe from embarrassment. Yet they all nodded their heads. It was an uncomfortable subject and he knew it was his job to get them onboard. Like Mel had said, they looked to him for guidance. This ordeal might be the best learning experience any of them would have for a long time.

Ken broke the brief silence. "Were you helping them?"

Mr. Hobart smiled and narrowed his eyes. "You can't tell anyone." He figured he had to reveal something important before they would fully trust him and allow themselves to be open as well. "I offered my help and they accepted," he said. "I went over last night. To where they were staying. They asked me to hack into a company's system." It wasn't exactly true—they hadn't *asked* him to, but he needed his students to believe he was trusting them with a secret, offering them inside information.

"That is so wired," Craig said.

"Cool," Bill and Roger said at the same time.

All the students had closed in, looking at him and asking questions. He didn't know who asked what after a while. Among their interests were how he did it and if it was his first time. He had done some things in his past, but nothing harmful or totally illegal in his assumptions, and more importantly, nothing that was ever found out. For sure nothing as illegal and threatening as hacking the FBI. In and out of minimally secure systems? Yes. He wouldn't expose them to everything he had done in the past; he didn't have to. For now, there was Line-Tech. And of course...

"Which company was it?" Valeria asked.

"Line-Tech, the company that makes the equipment that's going into the prisons. They're upgrading or swapping things out. Something. Those ISTI people don't exactly give you a lot to go on. There's something pretty top secret about the project they're involved with and I was just excited to be helping even in a small way."

"When was that again? Yesterday?" Bill asked.

"Yesterday after school. I told them I had Computer Club on Tuesdays, but I think they want me to work with them again tomorrow."

"I knew the Muncy prison was putting a new system in," Bill said, causing everyone to stop talking and Mr. Hobart to stare at him with his eyes wide.

"You didn't say anything. How'd you know about that?" Hobart asked.

"Don't look at me like that, Mr. H. It was just something my dad mentioned. He's friends with a bunch of the guards over there. That's all I know, really." He swung around. "I told you guys, didn't I? I'm pretty sure. But I didn't check into it. I didn't know what company was involved. It was just a comment Dad made one night when complaining about how they're spending our tax dollars on new equipment when the old equipment still works fine."

"Thank you." Mr. Hobart looked around at the others. "That's what I want from each of you. Total openness and honesty. No matter how unimportant it may seem. Without it, I can't keep you safe." He straightened. "I'm not trying to scare you, just letting you know that this is serious business. So I'm going to let them know what you told me. They may want to talk with you or your dad to find out who those guards are so they can check in with them. Understand one thing," he said loudly, "no one is in trouble. All they're going to do is find out what you know. If all you know is what you said, you're fine. Do you see how this works? We keep each other in check, we're totally open about what's going on, and we let ISTI know so they learn to trust us. Their trust is important."

Hobart wasn't sure why he was so adamant about this, but the thought did cross his mind that he didn't know enough about any of his students to be sure they weren't involved. Especially after what happened with Ken—he was totally blindsided about that. As soon as the thought came into his head, he shoved it aside. He couldn't let that happen again. Their trust was all he had to work with.

"I don't know if I want to be talked to?" Bill said.

"Hey, look at it this way; you'll be able to tell your kids and grandkids how you were involved in a super-secret undercover investigation."

Bill smiled and looked around. "Yeah."

Valeria raised her hand. "Are they going to interview all of us?"

Mr. Hobart nodded. "I suspect they will. Or someone will. Each one of you will have to tell them about this meeting. Feel free to repeat anything I've said or what Bill just told you. If we're all open and aboveboard, they'll get the same story from each of us. They'll see that we're all together and we're all trustworthy." He waited for any other questions, then clapped his hands together. "Okay, let's get going. We have a lot to cover tonight."

"Can you give us more details about what you did, first?" Ken asked.

Mr. Hobart laughed jokingly. "Yeah, I suspected *you'd* want to know." The others laughed too, although not-so-comfortably and with a slight edge of concern.

"No, it's not like that, really. I backed out of the hacking business. I told my old man what happened, and he was worse on me than being kicked out of CC. I'm just curious. You don't have to tell us how you hacked in. Maybe just what they're like. How the conversation went."

"A half hour," Hobart said. "Then we get to work." He nodded, then gave them the rundown of what happened, how literal Ten seemed to be, how friendly Maria was. He didn't tell them how he hacked into Line-Tech, only that he had and hadn't found anything out of the ordinary. "That's why I know they'll want me back. Supposedly, they're going to download the algorithm again and this time, want me to analyze it pre- and post-operation."

"Do you think you'll find anything?"

"I don't know. It would be pretty cool if I did. I mean, it would mean I helped them solve whatever case they're working on. But at the same time, I suspect they have other people working on the case too. I doubt I'm the only one."

"You can do it, Mr. H," Bill said with Ken's quick agreement.

The others remained quiet and once the conversation petered out a bit, he turned to his class notes and began where he'd left off the week before. He noticed some reluctance, some nervousness, in the group but that was to be expected.

Wasn't it?

CHAPTER 21

Ten asked Nancy to wait until that afternoon to download the algorithm from Line-Tech. It was Wednesday and he wanted to wait for Josh Hobart to arrive after school. Ten introduced him to Nancy.

"I've heard of you," Josh said.

"How so?" Nancy asked.

"You were in one of the first Computer Clubs the school offered. My predecessor—"

"Mr. Carlson," she said.

Josh nodded enthusiastically. "Yeah. He raved about you. Said you were the smartest student he'd ever taught. Didn't you win several academic awards? Like math, science, chemistry?"

Nancy smiled broadly. She was almost in tears. "Thank you. Sometimes I forget that I was ever good at anything." She looked around. "You end up with a job like this, you start wondering a lot of things."

He glanced at Ten and then back at Nancy. "A woman with your talents could go anywhere. Trust me. Carlson believed in you."

"She was top of her class in college too," Ten said, repeating what she'd told him. For some reason, all the praise made him feel full of pride toward her. The way Nancy reacted made him think of how his own daughter, never born, never given the chance, might have grown up. He turned away slowly while taking in a long breath.

Nancy must have caught sight of his reaction. "Are you all right?" Her attention quickly shifted from herself to him, which made things worse. Ten had to excuse himself. He walked out of the equipment room and into the next room over. The one that Nancy used as an office. He heard them whisper behind him, "What's that about?"

He leaned forward, placing his hands on her desk for a moment of support. His knees went weak. He closed his eyes and lowered his chin. *What am I doing here?* He waited but no answer came. None ever did. After a few moments, he composed himself and walked back into the other room. "Sorry."

"No worries," Josh said. "So, how do you want us to proceed?"

Ten regrouped. "Nancy, I want you to get him to the page where the download occurs. Then I want Josh here to follow it every step of the way, looking for anomalies. You saw what it looked like the first time; this should be similar, I suspect."

"Should be the same, except with the subsystem information. It's not the main control so there will be differences," Nancy said.

Ten acknowledged her. "Perfect." He narrowed his eyes. "If I understand what I read, that shouldn't change the sequence or activity, only the location."

"Not a whole lot. Remember, these are just system checks. The high points, not every little detail," she pointed out.

"Okay. So I guess that's it."

Nancy reached for the keyboard.

Josh said, "I could hack in again."

Ten shook his head. "No. I was thinking about this and thought that maybe the algorithm knows Nancy's passcodes. Maybe it switches to a different download if it's her."

"Brilliant," Nancy said before Josh could comment. "That is a definite possibility." She went back to the keyboard, smiled up at both of them, and said, "Here we go."

Ten observed as Josh and Nancy worked together, talking about what they were doing and what they were noticing. Whenever Josh asked about the hardware, Nancy had the answer to that as well. They made a good team. They kept up with each other very well. Ten learned a lot just listening to them. The only problem was when it was all over.

Nancy and Josh both looked up at the same time. He said, "Everything went smoothly. No glitches."

Nancy sat back in her chair and said, "Intermittent. That must be it. There is no other answer."

"Not a chance," Ten said. "This happened at three prisons so far. There's something going on."

"What else would you like us to try?" Josh asked.

Ten paced the floor with his hand on his head, then reached down to rub his neck. "Something. There must be something." He considered calling Roger Floramo, whom he'd worked with before. Considered calling was as far as it got. At this point, he wondered if Jacob had a reason not to use Floramo. He'd wait. Let them give it another try. "You saved the tests?"

"Yes," Nancy said.

"Can you put that on a thumb drive again? Make two copies. Josh, I'd like you to take another look at it if you don't mind. I just want a copy for our records."

Nancy nodded as she prepared to download what they'd done. "Do you think the download might have opened a channel that stayed open? Through the internet?"

Josh thought for a moment. "Definitely feasible and doable. Verification of updates is a hot topic in InfoSec, since a safe update requires a chain of trust all the way up to the writer of the code. Honestly, that's feasible in practice. Yet, so far, I don't think so. I checked for ways in and didn't find anything at first blush." He looked over his shoulder at Ten. "I'll take a closer look tonight."

"Could it be hardware?" Ten asked. He'd been away from design work for a few years now. Was it possible he'd forgotten that much? He looked at Nancy for the answer.

Her mouth twisted and she looked into the corner of the room, deep in thought. "Perhaps. I suppose there could be a particular control circuit with a particular code that activates after a particular test has been completed."

"That's a lot of particulars," Ten said.

"Plus, it might not do it again after the second test. Or it might."

"There are *minor* differences in the test sequences," Josh said.

"I can't get inside the chips," she added.

"I know," Ten said. But he also knew it was possible. The question was, did it make sense?

"Maybe check the timing of the other breakouts," Josh said with Nancy's agreement. "Can you do that?"

"I can do pretty much anything," Ten said.

The other two smiled, and Josh nodded approvingly. "Now that's cool."

Nancy handed each of the men a thumb drive. "Have a nice evening, you two. I'm going to go home and rest."

Ten dismissed himself. He had given his car to Maria for the day and wondered if she was back yet. Luckily, as he left the building, she was walking toward him.

"Just coming to get you," she said.

"Have a productive day?"

"Absolutely. You?"

"Not so much."

"Guess what?"

"Shit. Don't tell me—another prison break?"

"And Jacob is pissed. He asked me what the hell you were doing—those exact words—and if I thought you were up for the job."

"I don't need to do this. He can assign someone else if that's what he thinks."

Maria stood back. "Jesus Christ, Ten. You've said that a half dozen times since we've started. What the hell's gotten into you?"

"It's true. He only asks me to get involved so he can keep ISTI at a distance. Why? I don't have to do this either." She had her hands on her hips as though she were about to scold him. "Don't," he said. "It's bad enough that I can't figure this out. That I need all these other people to help me."

"So that's what's bothering you."

"Please," he said.

She scoffed. "You're feeling sorry for yourself because you need help?"

"Well, what do you want from me?"

"A commitment. That's all anything is about, isn't it? You are either committed or you're not." She waited.

Ten felt attacked. He felt vulnerable. But who better to feel vulnerable in front of than someone who understood? And she did. He hated that fact and was also lucky to have it. He didn't know how to answer her. So he simply said, "I'm committed."

"Are you?"

"I am now."

Then she hugged him. "I'm sorry."

"You're right. I need to get out of my own way. Stop worrying about what I can't do and start doing what I can. We need to figure this out before someone gets hurt."

"Or whoever is doing this lets everyone out," she said.

"That's what Jacob thinks, I'm sure."

"That's what he fears."

"Let's go." Ten took the keys from her and they headed to the car.

"I have good news too," she said.

"I could use it."

"At midnight tonight, while the admin staff is home in bed, a team from New York is coming in. They're going to lock down Dr. Paton's office. You'll be able to lead an investigation of that space like you wanted."

"Shit. I just committed to solving the breakout problem and I'm getting the okay for a second job."

"You can handle it," she said. "I'm here to help."

While driving back to the hotel, Maria filled him in on discussions with several guards as well as the escaped prisoners. "Sarah Andrews was damaged by what Cooke was making her do. Ashamed. Felt tainted, almost." Maria's face puckered as she mentioned the fact. She looked as disgusted as Sarah must have felt.

"Yet she was found at Cooke's house. I'm not sure I believe her," Ten said.

"Why do you think she was there?"

Ten had both hands on the steering wheel and gripped it tighter. "Don't tell me."

"She was going to kill Cooke."

"Holy shit."

"She didn't care if she went back to prison. The whole time I talked with her, she wouldn't even look at me. She was completely ashamed. Even after all I read about prison inmates, rape, all that. This one thing disgusted her beyond any of that."

"Why?" Ten asked.

"Sarah is a tough cookie. She had to bow down to Cooke in such a demeaning way that it broke her. But only when they were together. Like two different Sarahs. She's a real mess right now. Hates herself, hates Cooke, hates everything. I asked them to put her on suicide watch."

"A fucking mess," he said.

"A royal fucking mess," she said.

"Did she know anything about who broke her out?" he wondered.

"Not a thing. She almost didn't escape. She heard the door unlatch but hesitated. She thought she'd just heard something at first. Then she got up to check. She thought it was some kind of miracle."

"And I have a sense that Dr. Paton is somehow mixed up in all of this."

"I know. I have no idea how, but you have a good sense about people. You can read them."

"I'm not sure I agree," Ten said.

"You don't have to. So, what is it about him?"

"He might be a wimp in a lot of ways, but if he was in love with Cooke, which is what I believe, he might have wanted Sarah out of the way. He couldn't have known that Sarah hated Cooke. How could he even fathom that if he was in love with Cooke. That would make it even worse. He'd be in complete denial."

"Until after Sarah was picked up. He probably saw the situation before I did. In fact, I'm sure he did. He had a session with her right after the police brought her back."

"He should have put her on suicide watch," Ten said.

"Unless he doesn't care. Or actually wants her dead."

"Even if he wanted her out of the way and thought she'd run off, I can't see him as smart enough to hack the system. Not his inclination. But maybe he knows someone. The sleeping guard. Could he have convinced her to let Sarah out?"

"That wouldn't explain all the other breakouts," she said.

"True."

"I suppose someone else might have helped him," Maria said. "But that still doesn't explain the other prisons."

"We'll figure it out," he said. "Maybe there's something in his office." He stopped. "He's going to raise holy hell about this. Maybe we search his home too." Ten smiled.

"You have a mean streak I don't think I've seen before."

"Just for Paton. There's something about the man."

"Like I felt about Nancy."

"We all have our buttons."

CHAPTER 22

It would be another few days before the next system test. Progress, despite Nancy's overnight stay in jail, hadn't slowed by much. The P280 LockDown System now controlled the first two buildings in the Muncy complex. The other prisons hacked did not have the same timing as the Muncy prison. Plus, as Ten looked into the breakouts, there were different cell blocks that opened; some of them unlocked and then locked within seconds, some within hours, causing the tech people to have to shut the system off and batten down whole areas manually. As he collected information, he began to see it as one person, even though everyone else on the team thought they were copycat crimes. "One person playing with all the pieces to see what works and what doesn't," Ten asserted.

"It sounds like everything this person—if it is only one person—has tried has also worked perfectly so far," Maria said as she drove.

Ten had just gotten off the phone with the Kentucky prison. "We don't know that. How could we? If one hack didn't work, only the person doing the hacking would know for sure."

"Yeah, I guess you're right. What's Josh and Nancy think?"

"Copycat. They don't think whoever is breaking in would know the specifics of each system, only a general software layout."

"Are they right?"

"Maybe. It takes a lot for me to get information like that from each prison. It would be even more difficult for someone to get the details for each breakout unless they were on the inside."

"So someone from the inside is doing this?"

"I didn't say that," Ten said. He stared out the window at the fields. "Maybe that's why each hack looks random. They don't have inside information."

"Takes you back to one person," she said.

A haze hung low over the fields as it lifted from the morning dew. The hot sunlight blistered across the fields. Ten opened his window and warm air with an undercurrent of overnight cool entered the car. Refreshing. "It's supposed to rain again tonight, but it doesn't look that way so far."

"That means wind later today, probably around sunset," Maria suggested. "So why didn't you want to go rummage through Paton's offices this morning? I thought you'd be eager to do that."

"He can boil for a day. I want to see how desperate he is. I asked Carney to have someone tail him, watch his house. If he throws any big garbage bags out or throws a full suitcase into the trunk of his car, I want to know, and I want it confiscated."

"If you think he has something in his house, why not get a warrant?"

"For what? He's not a suspect. No technical knowledge, no reason except what I think. Besides, this way he'll do the search for us. He knows exactly what he doesn't want us to see."

"And his office?"

"We have both places covered. At this point, his office is the easiest to search. We have control of that. It's all on the premises. Taking it like we have is enough to alert him that we are checking on him, that he isn't exempt. Force his hand. Get him to remove any evidence from his home."

"But if he's not part of the breakouts, why do this?"

Ten turned in his seat to look at her. "Aren't we also trying to figure out why Cooke committed suicide? We have at least two crimes going on here. Don't you want to know how he's involved?"

"You're the one who thinks he's involved in all this somehow. But I'll go along with that." She turned down a dirt road that had recently been oiled to keep the dust down. "Second house on the left. The creek side."

About a quarter mile up the dirt road, they came to the second house. The grass needed cutting and an old Honda with a patched rear fender sat in the drive. "Craig Hiller. His dad's name is Henry. He owns a local grocery store. He goes in late. Craig is the only Black kid in Computer Club. Gets straight As in school. According to Josh, both the kid and his dad are a bit worried that Craig will be singled out during all this."

"Because he's Black," Ten said. "I get that."

"Exactly."

He opened the door. "Let's go."

Maria stood slightly in front of Ten when a big Black man with a bald head opened the door. His eyes were dark, and he had laugh lines around his eyes.

"Please, come in," he said as he stepped aside. "You must be Maria," he said, holding out a nervous hand. His voice sounded dry, like he hadn't had his morning coffee yet.

"This is our technical consultant on the investigation," she said.

"Ten, like the number," Ten said as he shook the man's hand.

"Ten it is." He walked them into a living room where a tattered couch sat next to an equally used and threadbare chair. Two other wooden chairs had been brought from the kitchen. Craig sat in one of them and stood up as soon as Maria and Ten walked into the living room. "My son, Craig," Henry said.

Ten and Maria shook Craig's hand. He was a bit lankier than his dad, but Ten could see that he'd fill out as he grew older. His arms looked strong. He had the same dark eyes as his father and slightly lighter skin.

Maria sat on the couch while Henry took the other wooden chair. Ten knew he was about to sit in Henry's chair—the man of the house—and something about that kicked a nerve in him he wasn't aware he had. In a symbolic sense, it felt like Henry was relinquishing his power to Ten and Ten didn't want that to happen. These people were already worried. "We'll swap chairs," he said to Henry as he walked over.

Henry began to raise his hand in rebuttal, but Ten insisted. He smiled. "I don't think I can fit in your chair. Besides, it's your house. We're the intruders."

"Yes, sir." Henry looked quizzically at Ten, then walked to his chair and sat down, one big hand on each of its arms.

"It's not *sir* either." Ten was afraid every word he said would be misunderstood and already found he was coming across as bossy. *White privilege.* But he didn't know how to change that. What *should* he say? How *should* he say it? Finally, he looked right at Craig and said, "The only reason we came to see you first is because your dad was home this morning and we wanted you both to be here. Your mom too, if you'd like."

"She's working," Craig said quietly.

Ten looked at Maria, who said, "At the bank. It was difficult to get them all here. I forgot to tell you. I just thought, from what Mr. Hobart said, that these two were the most important."

"Why's that?" Henry asked. Ten ran a hand through his hair. "Is something wrong? Do you think my son did something wrong?"

Ten noticed how the man asked if they *thought* Craig did something wrong, not *if* his son did something wrong. The man trusted his son, which said a lot about the family. "Look," Ten said, perhaps a bit too forcefully, "we don't think he did anything. It's all part of a standard investigation as we try to piece things together." He turned in his chair to acknowledge Craig. "Hobart told us that you were concerned because you're one of the few Black kids in the school. And the only one in Computer Club." There. He came out with it.

He turned back toward Henry. "I can never fully understand how it must be for you and your family, in constant fear that you'll be singled out for any crime that happens near you. I can only imagine. My only experience was when the government hunted me down because I was involved in a top-secret technology that I literally didn't even know I was a part of. Once I realized people were after me, I was frightened all the time. The fact that you live that way, that this situation puts you on edge, is horrible in my eyes." He looked over at Maria and her mouth was open. No sound came out. Perhaps she thought he said all the wrong things? He didn't know.

He lowered his voice, as though that might help. "Henry, I assure you, we do not think your son did anything wrong. In fact, under the circumstances, I can only imagine that he's kept himself especially clean. Although your concerns about being Black are justified, I can't stress enough that those concerns are not warranted here. Craig's statements are only meant to help us see where things might differ when we talk with the rest of the kids." He turned to Craig. "You have a very impressive academic record. Mr. Hobart speaks very highly of your intelligence and integrity." He glanced between the man and his son. "I'm sorry if that was the clumsiest way to say this, but I'm just a white guy. I don't know what I don't know."

Henry smiled at him. "You're forgiven." He turned his eyes toward Craig. "My son was there the night Ken Hemming hacked the FBI. Scared the shit out of both of us. I told him to let Hobart know, but the FBI knew who did it too. I thought it was a lucky break and asked him to stay away from Ken for a while. Go ahead and let the man know any details you might have."

Maria and Ten grilled Craig like they would anyone else and the young man took it all with strength and integrity. As they left, everyone shook hands again. As Ten and Henry shook hands, Henry said, "I appreciate you trying to understand. You're not just another white guy. None of us are just another anything."

"I appreciate that," Ten said. "I know a lot of Black men and women, but none are close friends. Maybe I'm missing out on something."

"We're all missing out on something." With a slight nod, he repeated, "We all are."

As Maria drove back down the dirt road, she gave Ten a broad smile. "That was brave. Clumsy, but brave."

"It was desperate. He was very gracious about it."

"They both were," she said. "And so were you."

"It was easier for me."

CHAPTER 23

The conversation with Ken and his father went totally in the opposite direction. Even before they made it to the living room where they were to talk, Ken's dad, who introduced himself as Matt, said, "You're barking up the wrong tree. You have no right suspecting my son because of one mistake. I'll bet you aren't talking with the rest of the Computer Club crew."

"We already talked with Craig, and the others are on our list for today," Maria said.

He motioned for them to sit down, then walked over to a fireplace off to the side in the living room. He turned around, looking as though she'd interrupted his speech. His eyes settled on her for only a moment. "I'm talking here. You need to spend more time with those people at the prison. Nobody does that anymore and these prisons are getting away with torture. Torture, I tell you. The guards are all hoodlums, management is oblivious, and the inmates are running everything. People are getting hurt." He stared at Ten, who hadn't taken his eyes off the man yet. "You haven't said a word, son."

"I'm the technical consultant on the job. I came to talk with Ken about how he got into the FBI and what he might know about hacking in general. Where'd he learn how to do it?"

"Hobart. I don't trust anyone who's supposed to know what they're doing and then chooses to be a teacher. At a high school, no less. If he's so fucking smart, why isn't he working at a college?"

"Choice?" Maria said.

"Who the fuck is in charge here?" Matt wanted to know.

"I am," Maria said.

Matt smirked at Ten. "You said you're the consultant. So she controls the shots. Typical."

All this time, Ken sat in a side chair as though trying to disappear into the cushion. Maria turned toward the boy, her knees pointing in his direction.

"He doesn't have any information for you," Matt said. "Tell them, son."

Ken looked up and swallowed. "Every site has a back door. Usually more than one. I just found one by accident."

"Fine," Matt said as though he'd lost a bet. "Tell them who helped."

Maria kept her eyes on Ken. "Craig and Valeria were there."

"If you knew already, what the hell'd you come here for?" Matt yelled. He pushed away from the fireplace and walked toward her aggressively.

Ten stood and the man stopped. He looked at Ten and said, "He had nothing to do with the prison. He promised me. I trust my son. He wouldn't lie to me." That was something Ten believed, even though Matt didn't deserve that trust. "The FBI hack wasn't intentional. The kids were playing around. All three of them. Why are you picking on him? Just because it was his computer they used?" He threw his hands up and walked away, then turned and came back more slowly. "Hobart shouldn't even be teaching them things like this."

Ten could tell that Ken didn't agree with anything his father said but could hardly get a word in edgewise. He shied away with his head down. When his dad got really loud, Ken closed his eyes against the onslaught. Before Matt opened his mouth again, Ten decided to stop punishing the kid by letting his dad yell. He cut the man off bluntly, holding both hands up in front of him as though pushing Matt back and away from their space.

Matt, in fact, did back away as Ten took one step toward him.

"Well?" Ten said.

Ken's father went silent. He looked toward his son.

"Thank you for your time." Ten motioned for Maria to follow him toward the front door.

Matt was right behind them as though chasing them out. Before closing the door behind them, he yelled, "Talk to Hobart! He's the problem."

Maria walked ahead of Ten. The second he stepped out the door, he closed it firmly behind him, cutting off any other comment Matt might want to make. "Asshole," Ten said as they walked toward the car. He asked Maria to throw him the keys. He caught them while strutting around the back of the car, slapping the trunk lid as he went. "I have to drive off some of my frustrations after that."

Back on the road, Maria said, "He didn't let his son talk."

"I have a feeling that's the exact reason his son did what he did."

"To please his dad."

"Bingo. That's a pretty screwed-up relationship. He's either going to force his son to get into even more trouble or Ken's not going to come home one day and that man will never see him again."

"It makes Ken a key suspect," Maria interjected. "The opposite of what his dad tried to hammer out of us."

"We need to get him alone so we can talk with just him."

"Having a parent in the room usually helps get the truth out of the kid."

"Not this time."

"Maybe we need to check in with Josh again," she said.

"I have a feeling that he loves the kids as long as they're in love with the same thing he is. He doesn't appear to know anything about their actual lives." He held up his hand before Maria could react to his statement. "Not that I'm criticizing the man. He has his own life to deal with, I'm sure. It's just that if he doesn't know those kids and their motivations, how can he be absolutely sure that they're not involved in all this?"

"He can't."

"Exactly." He put his window up and turned on the air conditioning. Maria followed suit with her window. They didn't have to talk as loudly once the car was closed up. The sun blasted through the windshield and Ten began to sweat so he turned the blower on higher. "Who's next?"

"William Newbury," she said. "You'll want to turn left up ahead. He and Roger Bennet—that's the kid who Hobart said was best friends with Ken Hemming—live close to each other, so we'll hit him next."

"Bennet? He any relation to Lisa Bennet, the guard?"

"Cousins. The whole town's related."

"He may have known about the new system."

"Probably. Does that make him a suspect too?"

"Let's talk with him before we jump to that conclusion. So, then, who's after that?"

"Valeria Marin and her mother, Alejandra, I hope. They were not easy to schedule together. Everyone in the family works because her dad is being held pending immigration." She nodded. "I wonder about her."

"Her dad's being held? How long?"

"Ricardo Marin. It's hard to tell. Paperwork is funky because he was apprehended, thrown in jail, then moved, then moved again. All told, it looks like about two years."

"Two years!"

"ICE."

"Jesus. More assholes. Looks like that kind of day," he said.

"Makes her a suspect."

"Or not," he said. "I doubt the family would want another member in prison. They know how devastating it is by the sounds of it. Where's he at?"

Maria tapped her phone where she had taken notes. "Allenwood Federal Correctional Complex. About fifteen minutes from here."

"Wow. This thing is tightening down like a vise."

"Are you considering her involvement now?"

"That might mean that the other breakouts are copycat cases. I'm not totally convinced of that yet. But this Marin family looks suspicious."

"There's more. Her cousin Ana works in IT at the police station. Remember?"

"The whole family."

"Annnnnd," Maria dragged out, "her uncle is a programmer at the bank."

"The uncle sounds suspicious. Is that her dad's brother or mom's?"

"Dad." Maria raised her eyebrows. "We have the other two boys first." She pointed. "447, up here on the right. Again, the student's name is William Newbury. His dad isn't home, but his mom, Diane, will be."

"I sure hope she's calmer than Ken's dad."

They were asked into the house politely. It was a nice place on a clean street. A lot of the houses looked the same. Older but well-kept. Mrs. Newbury wore a light red and yellow shift in the heat. She was slender, well groomed, and pleasant in demeanor. She introduced them to William as she walked them into the kitchen. A fan was in the window over the sink. Her son was a bit meatier than his mother. Same eyes and nose. Must have been his father's body. He stood near the sink and walked over to shake hands with each of them. "Call me Bill, please. That's what my friends do."

"You know why we're here," Maria said.

"Yeah. I talked with Craig a little while ago. He said you asked a lot of questions but were nice. Made my nerves calm a little, I have to admit."

"Glad to hear that," Maria said. "With your cooperation, this won't take long." She looked at his mother. "Diane, we'd like for you to join us, in case there is anything the two of you may have discussed and you want to fill in any gaps."

"Would you like coffee? Lemonade?"

"Water would be great," Ten said.

Maria shook her head. She sat down across from Bill and introduced herself and Ten, then went right into questioning. Diane brought water for Ten and sat perpendicular to her son. After a half hour, Bill had told them little more than Craig. Maria said, "I do understand you knew that Muncy Correctional was installing new equipment."

Bill looked at his mom. "Mr. Hobart said he was going to tell them."

Diane said, "His father plays cards once a month with a few of the guards over there. They've been friends for years." She smiled. "He hears all the gossip and can get a bit grumpy about the government spending money on prisons instead of schools."

"I have to agree with him there," Ten said. He nodded toward Bill. "How about you?"

Bill shrugged. "Sure. I guess. How would I know. I guess if that's what Dad thinks... We sure could use better computers at school."

"But you're not angry about it. You wouldn't want the installation to fail for any reason," Ten said.

Diane shifted nervously in her chair but said nothing. She waited for Bill to answer.

"Never really thought of it that way. To tell the truth, it'd be worse to have prisoners escape than prove their equipment didn't work. Who would do that?"

"Who indeed," Ten said.

"What about Mr. Hobart?" Maria asked.

"What about him? He's a great teacher. Treats us like adults. Wants us all to do well." Bill looked at his mom again. "He'd never be involved. In fact, I can't imagine anyone from Computer Club being involved."

"Ken?" Ten said.

"That's different. He was trying to help his dad. The man couldn't get a job because of his record," Bill said as though it made sense.

Diane said, "I don't know about Ken and his father, but as far as Mr. Hobart is concerned, I've only met him during parent-teacher sessions. He seems like a capable teacher and the kids seem to like him. He can be a bit of a taskmaster, but that's a good thing." She smiled broadly. "It is a real good thing." She looked at Maria. "Bill's getting a scholarship to college because of his skills and a great letter Mr. Hobart wrote for him." She was obviously very proud.

After a few more questions, Maria was satisfied and they thanked Bill and Diane, who walked them to the door.

"Four-minute drive," Maria said once they were back in the car.

"Almost exactly the same story," Ten said as he found a parking spot and parallel parked the car.

"Do you think Josh Hobart prepped them?"

"I think, in the least, they talked. And Craig talked with Bill for sure. He said that. I suspect Craig and maybe Bill now too will be talking with Roger and probably Valeria. A tight-knit group. The good and bad of it."

"We're going to get the same story from each of them," she said.

"At least the interviews will take less and less time."

As expected, they got the same story from Roger. As Ken Hemming's best friend, Ten asked about Ken's dad and Roger's jaw tightened. "He's rough on Ken. I don't know why. Ken's a good guy."

"Ken never complains about it?"

Roger shook his head. "He's proud of his dad. Loves him. I've learned not to get into it with him. Keep my opinions to myself. Found out years ago it wouldn't matter anyway."

Once outside, Ten decided to drive again. "That kid is a good friend. He might help Ken, but he wouldn't do anything wrong on his own," Ten said.

"I think he's more apt to try to keep his friend out of trouble," she said.

"You're probably right about that, but he might not push too hard against Ken. Like he said about Ken's dad, he's learned where not to take the conversation."

"Are you saying what I think you're saying?"

"Any one of them so far." He looked distraught when he faced her. "But a kid? I mean, there is motive, but I expected someone more sophisticated, older. With more experience."

"Kids know computers," Maria suggested. "I know it's a cliché but it's also true. And they're too naïve to believe they'll get caught."

On the way to Valeria Marin's house, Maria got a call from Chief Carney. After she hung up, she said, "You might want to turn around."

"I didn't catch the whole conversation," Ten said, "but they found something?"

"You were right. Paton went home and cleared out his place, came out, and put a trash bag into the trunk of his car. He doesn't know he's been watched and is headed back to work as we speak."

Ten laughed. "Finally, something is coming together."

"Hey, I've learned a lot about Cooke and Sarah Andrews."

"This might tie in with that too."

"I'll have to let Valeria and her mom know we can't make it today and hope that we can find another time." She pulled out her phone.

Ten stopped her. "I have another idea. Why don't I drop you off? You won't have to reschedule. You can do the interview and I'll have one of Carney's deputies pick you up in a half hour and take you back to the prison. I'll have time to see what Paton's been up to. I'm sure it's going to take some time to get the paperwork needed to search his car."

"You're glad this happened."

"I knew Paton would do something stupid like this."

"I meant that you get to avoid talking with the only girl in Computer Club," Maria said accusingly.

Ten narrowed his eyes. "Drop it. Maybe I'm just bored with the same story."

"If you say so."

He ignored her comment. "Make sure to inquire about her uncle and cousin. Get details about them. Set up appointments. Have a nice chat."

"Sounds like this time won't be so boring," she said.

"For either one of us."

CHAPTER 24

The sun was hot, and cumulous clouds darkened in the western sky as they were heading toward Muncy. Ten drove into the prison parking lot and half jogged toward the front doors of the admin building. Chief Carney's hand jutted out as Ten approached. "Glad you could make it. Where's your partner?"

"Maria is running down some leads on the hacking side of things."

"You two switch interests?"

"We think they may be tied together. Besides, she's a better interviewer, so we split differently this time. That's all. I think she may have thought I'd intimidate the girl we were going to talk with and wanted it to be woman to woman." Ten hoped the excuse made sense to Carney. Ten shook the man's hand. "By the way, you did a great job with this. We're lucky to have you on our team." He hoped he didn't sound too patronizing.

Chief Carney puffed up a little. "We are happy to help. Told you from the beginning we were here for you."

Ten wondered what made ISTI an easier pill to swallow than the FBI, who Carney seemed to dislike. Proximity perhaps. Or the fact that ISTI was deeply secretive and shadowy to most people, which may have made them more intriguing. He followed the chief straight to Dr. Paton, who had gone back to Superintendent Cooke's office. When they walked in, Paton was collecting papers and piling them on the center of the desk.

He looked up. "They're sending someone from Lewisburg to sit in while they interview for a new super. I'll be glad to be out of here." He pushed his chin out as though he were in charge. "You'll have to let me into my building now. I have a job to do. Sessions. All of which are mandated by the federal government. You can't just block my session room off like that. I checked. You don't have a warrant or anything."

"Check again," Carney said with a sly smile.

Dr. Paton got flustered and looked upset, like he was about to break down. The uneven stack of papers in front of him slid sideways. He looked down. "This won't do. I'm calling a lawyer."

Chief Carney gave Ten a glance, then said, "I recommend it." Carney still hadn't told Paton that they were going to search his car. Somehow Ten sensed the police chief enjoyed the cat-and-mouse game a bit too much. Perhaps small-town policework bored the hell out of a man like Carney and this was his one chance to truly enjoy his job. Or maybe he had a vendetta against Paton.

Ten, on the other hand, had originally wanted a calmer life. Raise a family, work a regular job, do his martial arts for exercise. Ever since the government he'd thought he could trust sent someone to murder him and his family, things had changed. Here he was doing projects for that same government. But that's not how he rationalized it. No, he worked with Jacob—and Maria.

"You okay?" Carney said.

"Just thinking about the case." Ten motioned toward Dr. Paton. "Collect your things in a box." He pointed to a cardboard box sitting in the corner of the office behind the desk, probably the one Paton brought his work over in. Ten swung around. "I'll meet you downstairs."

At the moment, he and Maria had far too many suspects and not enough evidence concerning the breakout. There were motives all over the place. All they could do at this point was throw everything against the wall and hope something stuck. His head spun into a momentary despair he knew could take him down quickly if he didn't come out of it. His thoughts of Amy and their unborn child had started it. Maria had been right; it was the girl. All he could do was focus elsewhere. In that case, he hoped Dr. Paton was hiding more than just his feelings for Superintendent Cooke inside his car.

By the time they stood outside together, Chief Carney had the paperwork Ten needed to search everything Paton owned, including his house, car, office, and anything else he wanted. He let Ten know, then said, "Got a call and sent someone to pick up your partner."

"Shit, I forgot about that."

"That's what she said."

"Thanks for helping out." He nodded at the chief. "And for saving my ass."

"So what do we do about him?"

Paton stood near them, shifting back and forth on his feet. He wrung his hands. More sweat beaded on his forehead than the humid day might have indicated. His eyes darted away and back one too many times.

Chief Carney asked Ten, "Where to first?"

Ten kept his peripheral vision on Paton. "Let's check that garbage bag in his trunk."

Paton's expression widened and his lips pursed briefly. "What bag? What makes you think there's something in my trunk?"

Carney seemed to take pleasure in the fact that he and his men had participated with Ten and Maria. "We've been tracking your movements."

"You can't do that!" Paton yelled. Then he did something really stupid. His shoulders shivered, his body tensed and crouched slightly. His posture added up to one thing.

Ten was used to paying attention to body language. He saw it coming before anyone else.

Paton took off running exactly where his eyes had darted a moment before.

The doctor didn't get more than ten feet when Ten tackled him at the waist, reached around to one wrist at a time, and dragged both arms behind his back. Carney came up fast with his handcuffs ready. In a matter of moments, Paton was standing, and sputtering dirt from his mouth.

Carney held onto Paton from behind. He looked at Ten. "You are faster than I thought by looking at you."

"Must be reflexes," Ten said.

Carney had one of his men pat Dr. Paton down and retrieve his car keys, wallet, and some change from his pockets. "I'll keep his keys. In the meantime, take him to the station and lock him up. We'll talk with him later."

"I want to call a lawyer!" Paton screamed over his shoulder.

Carney nodded. "Have at it." Then he held up the keys and said, "Let's see what the sniveling psychologist is hiding, shall we?"

Inside the garbage bag were dozens of DVDs, each labeled with date and number; photos of Cooke and some of the prisoners rubber banded together; and sheets of handwritten poems, which read as though they were written to Cooke, paperclipped in batches. Some of the poems were dedicated to Cooke or mentioned features she had. Others were hard to tell who they were written about. Ten skimmed them. He noticed Nancy's name in passing but didn't pull that poem out or mention it to Carney. He flipped through each set of items and placed them on the trunk floor.

Chief Carney watched as Ten pulled items from the bag, flipped through them, and set them aside. Near the bottom of the bag, he removed a tube of hand cream and a variety of oils and lubricants. Even before Ten finished emptying the whole bag, Carney wrinkled his nose in disgust. "I don't like where this is going," he said.

"Let me put it all back," Ten said. "I've seen enough. More than enough. Have someone take it back to your offices and tag everything. I want access to it later though. Me and Maria." He twirled the top of the bag and looked for someone to hand it to.

Carney motioned for a young woman police officer to handle the job. She lifted the bag as though it carried a disease and walked away with it.

"I hate to do this to you, Chief, but let's go open up the office." Ten looked around at the other officers, who had followed them to the car. "Let's just make it the two of us. I don't want all this getting out."

Carney called Carson over. "Go with Susan and take care of having everything tagged, will you? Do it in batches for now. No need for anyone to look through each piece at this point. And make sure everyone keeps their mouths shut until I say so."

"Yes, sir, Chief." Officer Carson jogged toward where Susan had walked, and they started talking in private.

Chief Carney twisted his head to the side and his neck popped.

Ten could feel the pop in his own neck and understood the tension that must have settled there. "After you," he said.

Two officers, both very young, a man and a woman, guarded Dr. Paton's little office building. A cloud crossed the sun, throwing a shadow over the front of the building. The officers nodded and stood by as Carney and Ten ducked under the barricade tape strung across the front walkway leading to the building. Carney unlocked the door using the keys he'd taken from Dr. Paton. "Here we go."

The building had a few rooms, most for storage. They took a quick tour, then walked back toward the foyer and down the short hallway to the largest office with a placard on the door of Dr. Paton's name. They walked in slowly. The hardwood floors from the hallway turned into carpet in the office. At first blush, the office looked like any other psychologist's office. The walls were painted an off-white, a few scenic paintings hung on the walls, corner lamps spread an even light into the room, aided by two side windows. A large oak desk stood a few feet from the front wall across from the door, while oak bookshelves stood along the other two walls. A plush office chair sat at an angle behind the desk as though waiting for someone to sit down. A couch and two stuffed chairs were situated so a psychologist had several ways to communicate with subjects.

"Try not to disturb too much," Ten suggested as he took in the room section by section.

Carney had walked over to the desk, only a name plaque sitting near the front and an empty wooden in-basket to the side. He turned to face Ten. Carney pointed toward the top shelf of one of the bookshelves. "How about that?"

Ten walked over, reached up, and took down a small box with a hole in the side. He opened it to reveal a small camera. "Expensive camera." He looked around the room. "I'll bet there's more than one."

"And how about this?" Carney had walked across the room and opened a cabinet that looked like it might hold files, but there was a video terminal and DVD player sitting on a shelf.

"I'm afraid to say this but turn it on. Let's see what's in there."

Chief Carney picked up a remote that sat on top of the DVD player and turned the units on. He pushed play. The screen filled with Elizabeth Cooke and Sarah Andrews. There were sex toys involved, two nearly naked bodies, and before the action went too far, Carney turned it off.

"Thank you for that," Ten said. He shook his head. "I wonder why he didn't use thumb drives or cloud storage. There must be a lot of video if it's been going on so long."

"Selective shots," Carney said.

"Excuse me?"

"My brother videos his kids on a digital camera, then goes to his computer so he can pick and choose what he likes. He keeps it all on the thumb drive but burns the best parts to a DVD."

"Makes sense."

"Did you see her face?" Carney asked.

"Not what caught my eye. What did you see?"

"Sarah Andrews. Her face. She looked like she knew she was being taped. Her lips moved."

Ten walked over beside Chief Carney in front of the screen. "I hate to say this but play it back."

As the screen came back on, Carney reversed it for only a few seconds. Sarah Andrews lay on the floor, naked, with her legs bent at the knees. Elizabeth Cooke covered part of Sarah's body and held something in her hand and was moving her arm. Cooke's breasts hung over one of Sarah's knees. All that aside, Ten watched as Sarah Andrews turned her face directly toward the camera. He read her lips. It was easy.

"I'll kill you," Ten said out loud.

"That's what I got," Carney said before turning the DVD off.

"We can explore more of this later," Ten said. "Right now, have the place searched and tagged. I want to know how many cameras and where. Make a sketch of the room. You can do that, right?"

"We have a man we use. He's good. I'll have him come in." Chief Carney waited. "Anything else?" His face belied a certain shock that Ten couldn't place.

"Not at the moment."

Carney stood still, staring at Ten. "What's this mean? To you, I mean. You've done this work before. What's going on here?" He waited for some kind of answer that Ten couldn't deliver. The man looked upset, as though something he'd seen bothered him deeply.

"I don't know. To tell the truth, I'm the technical guy most of the time. This is way more crazy than I'm used to. I'm not sure Maria is going to be any more help. This is not our usual type of work."

"What is usual?" Carney asked as though trying to move the conversation as far away from the images they'd just seen as possible.

Ten understood that need. He was glad to move on. "Usually, it's some tech that's being misused and we have to go in and shut it down. That simple most of the time. It can get dangerous depending on who's involved." Ten's face tightened like he'd smelled something really bad. "It often does get dangerous. And pretty weird." He was thinking of the Humanzee experiments they were involved with. As he thought about that, this job was hardly any more horrifying than some he'd worked on. He couldn't say that to Carney though. "But it has never gotten this creepy and disgusting."

Carney heard him. "I've seen a lot of bad." He didn't go further with the statement and Ten knew this was beyond what he'd seen. The man just didn't know what else to say, so he let it drop.

"And to think that Nancy was forced into this," Ten said. "I can't imagine how she coped or how freeing it must feel for her to be out of this mess."

"She's too young to go through something like this. To have to be involved in any way."

"Maybe it's time we talk with her about the details. There's more to this than meets the eye," Ten said, remembering her name being mentioned in one of the poems.

"Do you think all this dovetails into the hacking of the system? Was it even hacked? Do you think Elizabeth or Paton, or both of them, may have let Sarah Andrews out?"

"All good questions. And I have no clear answers. It's downright depressing, I can tell you that."

CHAPTER 25

The rain slammed against the hotel window at an angle. Ten sat on the edge of his bed, leaning over his phone, looking at photographs taken a long time ago. He sometimes delved into his past like that, especially after witnessing yet another human failing. Dr. Paton, Elizabeth Cooke, Nancy Wilmoth, Sarah Andrews. Who else was involved? He didn't want to know. Right now, he had uncovered some demented individuals.

Nothing that helped with their original case. *That case is going nowhere.* Before heading to his room, Maria told him about another prison that had a very specific breakout—one whole cell block, then only one cell from a different block, and two cells from a third block. None of it made sense anymore. They were being played with and he had to get his mind off the job, forget about it so his subconscious could sort things out. It was all too messed up. He missed normal. But there wasn't any normal anymore. There hadn't been for a while. So he stared at pictures that had represented normal at one time.

He stared at his wife's face, her arms and hands. He had few photos of her whole body, which sometimes bothered him. Standing in the kitchen, she was cut off at the waist. He had one of her sitting lakeside on a blanket and one where she waited for him next to the car. Her body, head to toe, whole. Somehow, those photos meant the most to him. Then, perhaps a few close-ups of just her face. But mostly, at this moment, he wanted to see her whole—as whole as possible in a photograph.

Thunder cracked outside the window and he jumped. He stared at the window for a few long seconds, watching the rain hit the glass and run down in rivulets. In the distance, over the parking lot, trees bent way over, then snapped back, flexible but definitely strained. Ten went back to his phone and flipped through a few more photos. She wasn't very far along, but in one shot, she had lifted her shirt and held her stomach as though her pregnancy was evident. She had the broadest smile across her face.

From behind him, Maria said, "She was beautiful."

Ten dropped his phone and swung around angrily. "What the fuck! Why are you spying on me all the time?"

Maria stepped backward, shocked by his attack. "I'm not spying. I came in, like you said, when I was ready for a late dinner. It's late. That's all. It's just late..." Her voice broke and trailed off. Another crack of thunder let loose beyond the window as she finished. "Don't look at me like that. I didn't mean anything. You're allowed to look at her pictures. You don't have much." Maria's eyes welled up as she spoke. "I do it too. I miss that life. I miss Ben. I hate this job." She turned away and wiped at her eyes. "Not *the* job, *this* job. I don't know where it's going, what we're involved with, and why it's so fucking and horribly perverse."

"Maybe we should talk with Jacob," Ten said. His anger subsided as he observed how Maria was reacting to the unorthodox situation they were in.

"No. We're going to figure this out. We're going to put every one of the people responsible for the breakouts away, every person responsible for abusing these inmates away, every person who didn't come forward, didn't stick to some goddamned moral code. Every one of them," her voice screeched. "This is physically and psychologically abusive. And I have a feeling that Paton and Cooke and probably a half dozen others are to blame." She let out a huge sigh, swung her head away from Ten, and huffed toward the bathroom.

He heard the sink running.

A moment later, she came out wiping her face with a towel. "I'm sorry."

"This has got everyone on edge."

"It's unnatural. All of it. Something dark and evil."

Ten picked his phone up from the floor where he'd dropped it and looked at Amy's face. "I just wanted to see her. Sometimes I'm afraid I'm forgetting everything I had before all this started." He blinked. "I know I can't go back. I know it. And it's not like that's what I'm wishing for. I know better. I just want to remember her, us."

Maria walked over and threw her arms around him and lowered her head to his shoulder. He felt her body shiver briefly. "I know," she said, "I know." Another wave of rain battered the window. Maria pulled away and looked at him for a moment. "We'd better eat something."

"I want to hear about your meeting with the Computer Club girl."

"Valeria and her mother, Alejandra. Sweet people caught in a politically activated mess."

Ten followed Maria into the hallway and to the elevators. "Did you get the same story from her as the others?" They were both trying not to think about their pasts, their present. They were trying to focus on the job at hand. He knew that. They had been through a lot together and he knew why they were discussing the breakout again. Focus on one thing to forget another. He knew it.

"We had a lot of time to talk," Maria said as they approached the front of the hotel.

They looked out as buckets of rain poured over the parking lot in waves. Ten ducked down as though that would stop the rain from hitting him. They ran out together and leaped into the car, laughing once they were inside, both of them nearly soaked through. Ten ran a hand over his head and water dripped from his palm.

"That's some rain." He looked over and Maria was pulling rainwater from her hair and letting it drip onto her slacks. "That's the straightest I've ever seen your hair."

She laughed. "It won't last."

"Where to?"

"It's late. I'm okay with fast food. There must be a McDonald's or Burger King around here somewhere."

Ten pulled out his phone and requested Burger King. The phone brought up several to choose from. He poked his finger on the Lycoming Mall Road location, then closed the GPS app. "I think I remember seeing it when we first got here."

The rain came down so hard that at one point, he thought to pull over, but didn't. He slowed and leaned forward as his wipers slashed at the windshield. They made it to Burger King, ordered a couple burgers, fries, and two drinks, then paid at one window and waited at the next window for their food while rain came into the car. Once they had their food, Ten drove along the Susquehanna River and found a turnoff where they could park and eat. At first, they sat quietly, listening to the rain on the car roof, watching the drops hit the river in abstract patterns. The only sound inside the car was the rain and the rustling of food containers, wrappers, and bags.

Once Maria was nearly finished, she said. "Valeria loves her father very much. And misses him. It's heartbreaking. You're lucky you weren't there. When I walked in on you and saw you looking at pictures of Amy, it reminded me of how I feel." She shifted to lean against the door and look at him. "How Valeria must feel too. At least her dad is alive. He's missed his daughter growing up. I thought about you. How you've missed the same thing. It must be horrible for him."

Ten listened but didn't respond. Maria's mind seemed fuzzy as she mumbled and spoke in circles. "They go see him regularly."

Ten wanted to stay away from delving into their emotional states. He needed information, simple and straight. "How about the hacking?"

"She admits to helping Ken Hemming. Her family, her uncle and cousin, like I told you, are all good at this. I don't think she had anything to do with it though. She's smart, but the Allenwood prison hasn't been touched. They go and visit when they can."

"Maybe Ken's involved, but none of the others. That's what you think? Your best guess?"

"Near the end of our conversation, we just talked about her and her dad. Alejandra held her daughter's hand the whole time we talked. She just let Valeria go on and on about how great a mechanic her dad is, how they used to play when he wasn't working. She remembered when he'd let her ride around piggyback as a young child, when they'd play badminton in the front yard. Her stories were heartwarming. She included everyone in the family, her sister, her mom. She had that same face you did when I walked in on you tonight. She remembered her dad with that same yearning for the past."

"I'm glad you had time to relax and just talk. It was probably good for her to talk about it. But the hacking. Your thoughts?"

"Ken. Like you said," Maria answered and then started in again. "At one point, her mom asked her to get some pictures to show me. While Valeria was gone, her mom begged to know if we could do something to help. Her husband had been beaten up and was in the hospital for a few days, but she never told her daughters about it. She didn't want them to worry. I could see that she was eaten up over the news, that she felt helpless, and through all that helplessness, she had to go on for her daughters' sakes."

"What'd you tell her?"

"The truth. There's nothing we can do." Maria popped a french fry into her mouth. "Sometimes I think our government treats people outside the prisons practically as bad as they do inside the prisons."

"Maybe that's why I won't join ISTI. Maybe I don't trust our government. I trust me." He looked over at her serious gaze. "And you. I trust you, Maria. I'm sorry about earlier. You caught me off guard."

She looked into her lap where her hands held the last of her food. "She understood that I couldn't help. When Valeria came back into the kitchen, I looked through the photos with them. They were a happy family. Now they're struggling even more than they ever did. We talked about how he'd stolen some food years ago, after the garage he worked at had closed down, which is why ICE picked him up. The minor robbery happened such a long time ago! A desperate time for a young family. Ever since then, they'd been fine. They pay their taxes, their mortgage, all their bills. With Ricardo gone, things have changed drastically. Three women in one house, two still in high school, and every one of them works. It pains their mother. Yet Alejandra won't let the girls quit school. She finds a way to give Valeria time for Computer Club, for Juana to have time for gymnastics."

"There is too much wrong in the world, isn't there?" Ten said.

"That's why we're here. I often think that even if I can help a little..."

Ten scrunched up his wrapper and burger box, and stuffed them into the bag they came in. He drank the last of his lemonade and stuffed the cup in the bag too. "Anything that would make you think she's involved?"

"She helped Ken. No one has said this yet, but I got the feeling that without her help, Ken would never have gotten into the FBI servers. And one other thing her mother said."

"What's that?"

"That Valeria would do anything to help her sister not have to go through this anymore."

"She actually said that? Didn't she know that would be motive enough?"

"She said it as though Valeria was loving and kind, that she thought of others. I think her mom thought that sensibility would prove that she *wasn't* involved, that she cared too much about others."

"That care can go both ways," Ten said.

"I don't think so in this case," Maria said. "I think she wants to stick around to do as much as she can for her sister, for her family."

Ten started the car. The rain had slowed but still came down steadily. "Let's go look at some photos and poems. Maybe some videos, although I'm not sure I'm ready for that this late in the evening." As they drove toward the police station, he said, "I'm starting to lean into your camp in thinking this was just Cooke or Paton arranging for the breakout. Cooke may have wanted Sarah free if she thought they were truly a couple, and Paton might have wanted her gone if he wanted Cooke to himself."

"And the rest are copycat cases," she said.

"We'll see."

CHAPTER 26

It was late at the police station and only a few people were there. The night dispatcher, one officer doing paperwork at a desk, and an officer having a late, swing-shift lunch. A few others were out on patrol, the dispatcher told them after Maria showed her credentials and explained Ten was a consultant on the case. The officer doing paperwork, a portly man of about thirty named Gus, led them into the evidence room, where they sat at a long table to go through the tagged items they'd uncovered from Dr. Paton's trunk.

Maria flipped through photographs, making faces and noises of disgust. She didn't spend much time on any one photo. There was no need to study them.

Ten skimmed through the poorly written poems. Most rhymed terribly with no cadence at all, making them sound sing-songy while at the same time elaborating on abusive acts. Gross couplets mentioned body parts—*fits* and *tits*— as well as off-rhymes like *fussy* and *pussy*. Ten actually laughed out loud at the ridiculousness of some of the poems, as much as they were also grossly kinky and perverted. He searched for the poem he'd seen while flipping through earlier. The one that mentioned Nancy. When he found it, he sat up in his chair.

"You find something?"

"Probably not," he said. "I had noticed Nancy's name in one of the poems earlier and just found that poem again."

"And?"

"I won't read it to you. It's too funny and gross at the same time. I'll paraphrase." He looked up at her. "The poetry is really bad, but basically what he's saying is that he thinks of Nancy while watching Elizabeth and Sarah cavorting. It's the only place I've found any variance in sentiment. The rest are sex-ridden love poems seemingly aimed toward Cooke with some general disgust thrown in about Sarah. As though Paton didn't know what the attraction was." Ten made a face. "I don't know what the attraction is anywhere along here. They're all rather nasty in one way or another. Or maybe that's because I know what they've been up to."

"The photos are from inside the prison. To rooms I don't recognize, closets some of them, to a stuffed couch I suspect is what you found in Paton's office."

"Let me see," Ten said. Maria held up a photo. "Jesus. Yeah, that's his couch." Ten leaned in slightly. "Andrews is handcuffed to the leg of the couch." Both bodies were naked. Ten glanced at Maria and waved for her to lower the photo. "Do you think Paton was in the room at the time?"

"I don't know. But to answer your earlier question, I can tell you what the attraction was for Elizabeth Cooke. Control," Maria said. Then she cocked her head. "Speaking of Paton's office, you never said much about what they found there after you left. We were so focused on Valeria during dinner that I forgot to ask."

"After I found the first camera and Carney located a DVD player, we watched a short piece of what Nancy must have been asked to record. I'll spare you the details for now. After that, I let them handle it. That material is labeled as well. What I did do is skim through the report. I have to laugh at how Carson explained what they'd found."

"What?"

"Do you really want to know?" He shook his head. "You may not want to. You see how insane all this is getting."

"I'm a big girl. And after looking through these photos," Maria threw the stack in front of Ten, the top one showing a completely naked Elizabeth Cooke pulling Sarah's top off, "nothing will shock me ever again."

Ten laughed briefly. "Okay. Carson called it a *masturbation station.*"

Her eyebrows raised. "That is pretty funny. Nasty as all hell, especially about Paton, but funny."

"If this all wasn't so horrific, it would be a comedy. But we're talking about abusive relationships, suicide, and prison breakouts." Ten reached out and slid the photos across the table in front of him. They could have been stills from the videos. But why print them out? He imagined Paton's home office with a wall covered with the photos, a constant reminder. "I have to wonder if he loved Cooke like the poems seem to indicate, or if he was just kinky and loved to watch the two women together."

"Both," Maria said. "And then when that didn't excite him enough, he started to include Nancy. Do you think he would have pressured her like Cooke had, if he'd have tried to include her more?"

"I was just wondering that myself. Wondering a lot of things. Like, did he mention it to her? Did he pressure her already?"

"If so, she didn't tell us. But no wonder she seems so relieved." Maria gritted her teeth and hissed through them. "That girl still should have come clean long ago. This is why prisons are such awful places. People let this kind of shit happen because their job is more important than people's lives. Grrr. It makes me mad. Maybe they think prisoners deserve what they get, but they're not judge and jury. They shouldn't let it happen. It should be stopped!" She slapped the table.

Ten stared at her. This touched her deeply. "I've never heard you hiss and growl," he said in all seriousness.

"That's because I won't scream while here."

"That bad?"

"Yes, it's that bad," she said. "Isn't it for you?"

"I don't know. For some reason, I can see both sides."

"Well, I can't. And it's a little shocking that you can."

The tension in the room had tightened. "Let's call it a night."

They packed everything back the way they'd found it and left the building. The rain had practically stopped. A few drops here and there meant that Ten ran the wipers intermittently. It was late. Dark. He needed sleep. On the way to the hotel, he wondered about why he might see both sides of the story, each story, including Paton's and Cooke's. The more sides he saw, the less emotion he attached to any particular one. The less he felt at all. Could he feel anything about any of it? Even before he and Maria separated to go to their rooms, he thought about cutting into his own skin. Just to feel something. The thought flashed quickly by, but he noticed. He always noticed.

She turned toward him before he walked into his room. "Are you going to be okay tonight?"

"You mean after what we just learned?"

"You seem different. Yeah, after going through all that stuff, and after going through pictures of Amy. More that, I just want to know you're okay."

"I'm just tired," he said. "You don't have to worry."

She gave him a slight smile and leaned in to deliver a quick peck on the cheek. "See you in the morning. I'll bring breakfast up to you."

"You don't have to do that. I can get my own."

"But you often don't. I know you."

"I'll be up early." Ten went in and sat on the edge of the bed. He hadn't told Maria what he had seen Sarah say with her lips while he and Carney watched the video left in Paton's DVD player. "I'll kill you," he said out loud. Who did she mean? Cooke? Paton? Did she know about Nancy?

Exhaustion overcame Ten and he flopped backward onto the bed, his knees bent, his feet on the floor. Still dressed. He slept for about an hour like that. When he awoke, his knees hurt. He undressed and walked unsteadily into the bathroom. Standing before the mirror over the sink, he turned to look at his latest scar. It had scabbed over and was nearly only a streak of puckered skin. Although deeper than he initially expected to push the knife, he hadn't damaged anything and hardly felt he'd even cut himself. That thought pushed another his way: he wished he had a knife with him. Maybe he'd buy a pocketknife. He noticed how the thought rattled around in his head, how his heart fluttered for a second or two. He took a breath and stared at his image in the mirror. Tired eyes stared back at him. He wasn't the same person he'd been only a few years ago. Everything had happened so quickly. Who was he now? A person who could see all sides of an abusive event—events. He'd moved through all sides of such an issue before. He'd loved and murdered. He knew all those sides. He turned away from the mirror.

His thoughts shifted to Ricardo Marin. How might he have changed after a few years away from his family, after getting beaten up? Was it too late to help him, even if they could? As Maria had said, at least he still has his family. They are still alive. But if he can't be with them, can that lie even be said?

Ten pounded his fist onto the sink and felt the pain shoot up into his wrist. The loudness of the act woke him from his downward spiral. He rubbed the side of his hand. He hoped he hadn't woken anyone, particularly Maria, who obviously could hear almost everything through the wall that separated their two rooms. He turned out the bathroom light and walked into his room, pulled back the covers, and buried his face into his pillow. He was out in less than a minute.

CHAPTER 27

A knock came to the door and Ten yelled for Maria to come in. He sat at his laptop going through the installation instructions again, for like the tenth time.

It took a moment, but Maria eventually pushed against the door holding two coffees, one in each hand, while two bowls of fruit with a muffin atop each perched across her forearms.

Ten jumped up and grabbed the bowls resting on her arms. "I have no idea how you collect all this, make it to the elevator, push the button, and then open my door."

"You don't want to know," she said. "Although I have seen waitresses who could do so much more."

"With a hell of a lot of practice, I'm sure." He set one bowl on the dresser near the TV and one next to his laptop before sitting back down.

"You've been up a while. Did you get any sleep at all?"

"About as much as you."

"Even after your tantrum?" She raised both coffee cups and tapped them together. "Cheers." Then she handed one of the cups to him, picked up her bowl, and sat on the stuffed chair next to the window.

He looked over at her questioningly.

"Last night when you slammed your fist against the wall."

"It wasn't the wall."

"The noise woke me," she said. "How's your hand? Or was it your head?"

Ten lifted his hand and turned to see the bruise that covered the bone near his wrist. "I'll be fine."

"Why didn't you tell me what Sarah Andrews said into the camera?"

Ten closed his laptop lid and swung around to look at Maria. She wore a lovely flower-print blouse with tan slacks, along with her usual flats, only these were brown to go with her outfit. "We'd had a late night and were both on edge. I saw no reason to tell you right before going to sleep. Why put that in your head. Who told you?"

"Chief Carney called this morning. Early. He'd heard we spent time with the evidence and wondered what we were thinking."

"I'm thinking he likes you."

"I'm the lead on this and the only number he has," she said, "so push that idea out of your head."

"He asked about you right away when I showed up yesterday."

"Polite," she said.

"Interested. But we can argue that later. Who do you think Sarah Andrews was threatening?"

"Where did this episode take place? Or were there too many naked bodies to remember the details?"

"Paton's office. On the couch."

"Oh yuck. My guess: she was threatening both of them. An all-inclusive '*I'll kill you for this.*'"

"Do you think she knew Nancy was involved? I mean, she must have known someone was."

"I don't see any way she could have known the details. Cameras are cameras. They operate on their own. But it is something we have to consider, now that you mention it."

"Have you heard from Jacob?"

"Pissed. In a hurry. But no news of another prison problem."

"I'll take what good news I can get," he said.

While eating, they talked about the case, veering away from the abuses and back to the breakout. "The two problems are seeming closer together than I may have thought initially," Ten said. "There are all kinds of motives between the two people who seem to be involved from the inside. Paton and Cooke, I mean. If Cooke was bold enough to threaten Nancy, why wouldn't she threaten a few guards too? The guards are just as susceptible to coercion."

"It makes me wonder if our adulterous couple was actually doing what we think or did they walk away on purpose."

Ten shook his head. "Buddy's guilty. I could see it all over his face. His wife knew it too." Ten pulled the lid from his coffee and took a long sip, letting the hot liquid slide down his throat. He held the cup toward Maria. "Perfect. Thank you."

"I'm learning." Maria popped a grape into her mouth. "If that's true, then who else could have helped except Nancy?"

"We're back to the threats Cooke made. And I agree. Once Cooke pushed and got what she wanted, there was no reason to stop there. I'll pull Nancy aside and have another talk with her. She's been fully cooperative every step of the way, offers additional information when she thinks of it. She and Paul both."

"I'd like to talk with all three guards, but don't want to go alone."

"Take Carney."

Maria laughed. "Are you trying to get us together?"

"No. Of course not."

"You don't sound convincing."

"He'll protect you. That's what you're worried about."

She crossed her legs and set her bowl on the nightstand where she could reach it. She removed the top from her coffee cup and set it aside, then held her coffee toward Ten in salute. "For what it's worth, you have a sixth sense about people. You know when they're lying. You know when their heart is in the right place even when their actions aren't. Buddy and Nancy are only two examples. Oh, and Paton. You saw that coming a mile away."

"So, Nancy," he said. "I don't think she helped with the breakout. I think she wants to know what happened as much as we do."

"See?" Maria sipped her coffee after her salute.

"Maybe," he said. "Okay, I'll go with you. But let's make it quick. We have to figure who's responsible for these breakouts—this breakout, if the others are copycats."

"You're still not sure," she said.

"Something is bugging me about it."

"I've said it before. Follow your gut."

After their quick continental breakfast, they stopped at the breakfast room off the lobby for a second cup of coffee to take with them. The rain had ended, and the sun was out again, burning off the dew and rain from the night before, creating a lot of humidity in the air. Ten got into the driver's seat.

Maria put her cup in the front opening of the center console. She pulled out her phone. "I'll contact Carney and get the addresses of the three guards. They've all been fired, so they should be available. I'm not sure where Buddy will be, but I'm sure Carney will know."

"While you're making calls, touch base with Josh Hobart. He sent an email late yesterday that he hasn't found anything unusual, but I want to talk with him personally. I can't feel things out through email and—just in case—I want to know he isn't protecting any of his students."

"You mean Ken Hemming."

"Any," Ten said. He winked at her. "But mostly Ken Hemming."

While he drove toward Muncy, Maria started writing down addresses and motioned for Ten to turn around by circling her finger in the air.

"Scenic route," he said while making a U-turn in the road they were on. There were few cars and he had plenty of room to maneuver. They passed a house here and there, sometimes several in a row, a grove of trees, and recently manured fields. The drive was pleasant, the morning still cool.

After she hung up, Maria put her window down. "Nice morning."

"It's going to get hot."

"We'll deal with that when it gets here," she said. "We have a few miles to go and then we'll make a right. Buddy and Cassy, that's his wife's name, live back in the woods."

"They're still in the same house?"

"According to Carney."

"No alternatives," Ten said. "It's like they're both stuck."

"You may be right. It's sad, yet it might work. Who knows? It might even make them closer."

As Ten pulled up to the ramshackle house via a weedy quarter-mile drive, he saw Buddy in the front yard chopping wood with an axe. He stopped the car and turned off the engine. The two of them watched the man split a large log in two with one swing. He was shirtless and, even in the cool morning air, already had a sheen of sweat glistening over his back and arms.

"Jesus," Maria said. "Maybe we should come back another time."

"We're here," Ten said as he got out of the car.

As they approached, Buddy smiled at them. He took one look at where Maria's eyes were staring and dropped his axe to the ground. "Don't worry," he said defensively. Then he took in Ten from top to bottom as though sizing him up. "You saved my marriage."

"Excuse me?" Ten said.

"Cassy was real mad, but she threw it off like a horse throws off a fly. Said she felt responsible for me not being happy at home. We're seein' a counselor. Right off, the man said he could see we're still in love."

That was more information than Ten needed, but he was glad it was working out for the two of them. And just then, Cassy stepped out onto the small porch, wiping her hands on an apron. It all looked so country to Ten; he almost laughed. "Can we talk about the escape?"

"Not much to tell."

Cassy came down the few stairs. "You here for Buddy?" She tenderly placed a hand on his meaty arm in a protective motion.

"Just a few questions," Maria said. "You doing okay?"

Cassy nodded quickly a few times and turned her eyes away. "We'll get through this." Then she looked at Buddy. "If they're going to ask questions about the Sarah Andrews thing, I'll wait inside."

He bent toward her and kissed her on the forehead. "I'll be in afterward." Cassy walked back into the house. Buddy turned back around. "You're pretty scrappy," he said to Ten.

"Never been called that before. Makes me sound like a forest animal."

Buddy laughed. "Funny too. What do you need to know? I don't have any information. You know where I was and what I was doing." He looked wide-eyed at the two of them. He had nothing to hide.

"What about the other guard?" Maria asked.

"Bertie?" Buddy laughed out loud. "She falls asleep all the time. She got several jobs. I think the only sleep she gets is on guard duty at night." Maria turned to Ten and shook her head. "You don't believe me," Buddy said.

Maria swung back around and said, "That's not what that was about. I was simply indicating that this isn't getting us anywhere."

"One other thing." Ten asked, "Did you initiate the sex that night or did she?"

"She always did," he said. "Why? You think she was in on it?"

"Just asking," Ten said. "Thank you. And I'm glad things are working out for you and Cassy."

Buddy's earlier smile flattened and Ten noticed some doubt, but he turned and walked back to the car with Maria behind him. They backed out of the drive the whole quarter mile, never looking back.

"Bertie, as he called her, is next. If she's home. From what he said, she's probably at one of her other jobs." She pulled out her phone. "I'll try to call." Ten heard the call go to voicemail. Maria shook her head, shut down the call, and said, "Let's try anyway. I never answer calls that I don't have in my contact list. It's not far. Closer to town and closer to Gwen Hawthorne's place anyway."

"I'm willing."

She held her phone near Ten. "Here you go. It's an easy find."

He glanced at the phone's GPS map. "Got it."

"I'll leave a message for Josh to meet you at the hotel. What time?"

"Right after dinner. Say six-thirty or seven. We can eat at the Asian place again."

"Mulan?"

"Yeah."

As Maria made the call and left a message, Ten found Bertie's house and pulled up out front. It was a two-story home, probably three bedrooms, with light blue siding, white trimmed windows, and a well-cared for front yard. "Nice place. All those jobs must be working for her." They walked onto the porch and knocked. They heard footsteps and the door opened.

A Black man with short, cropped hair dressed in jeans and a t-shirt opened the door. "Can I help you?"

Ten glanced at Maria. "We're looking for Bertie?"

"You're lucky she's here. The storm knocked out the electricity last night and we got up late." He opened the door. "You the investigators? We was wondering when you would come by." After they were inside, he yelled, "Bertie! Those government people are here to talk to you." He motioned them into the kitchen. "She'll be right down. But you might want to make it quick. She don't like to be late."

Bertie was a stout woman, well-groomed and dressed in a white blouse with black slacks. She wore gold hoop earrings and light makeup on her dark skin. "You go on to work, sweetie. I'll take care of this and see you tonight." Her husband waved at Ten and Maria, who waved back. They heard the door shut a moment later. Bertie sat down at the head of the table and leaned in. "Am I in trouble?"

"You got fired for sleeping on the job. What other trouble is there?" Ten said. She sat back and he knew there was something else. A lot more of something else. "There's a lot more, isn't there?"

"I worked extra nights sometimes or double shifts. I was always really tired from my day job."

"Cooke knew you slept, didn't she?" Ten said.

"Encouraged it. Paid me extra when things were going on."

"Things going on?" Maria asked. Ten saw Maria's anger building. Heard it in her voice. The whole moral obligation thing.

"She said she was 'making rounds' and had me shut down my video terminals. I did what I was told. I don't know what she was up to. I truly don't. I was so tired most nights, it was easy to fall asleep." She looked from one to the other. "I can imagine."

"What about other guards?" Ten asked, while Maria just stared.

Bertie let out a huff. "Half the time people call in sick. Sometimes they call in another guard or two and sometimes they don't. Half the time I'm there alone." She looked between the two of them again as though she didn't know who to talk to. "Well, I'll just say it. If it's Buddy and Gwen, those two, they're off somewhere on their own anyway." She relaxed a bit in her chair. "Look. This is a prison. There are bars and locks and I been doing this for a long time and nothing, I mean nothing, happens much at night besides some yelling. I figured Superintendent Cooke was up to something, but I was so damned tired I didn't make it my business to find out what. Of course, knowing about the suicide and who escaped and all, I could probably guess." She stopped and looked at Ten in the eye. "But I'm not going to guess. I don't wanna know."

"You just took the extra pay," Maria said.

"Standard double-time if called in and running a double," Bertie said. "I did nothin' wrong."

"No. You didn't," Ten said. He stood. "I'd like to ask you to make a full statement. Could you do that for us?"

Bertie nodded. "I'd just as soon Harley doesn't have to be involved. He knows nothin' of what was going on and is already nervous about me workin' there."

"You can go down to the station whenever you like and make the statement. We'd prefer you do it today. They'll take care of it. We'll let them know."

"After work today," she said.

"That will be fine," Ten said. "Maria?"

She stood. "Thank you, Bertie."

"I'm sorry," she said.

"I know," Maria said.

CHAPTER 28

The apartment complex where Gwen Hawthorne lived looked more rundown than most in the area and gave off the appearance of a housing project rather than apartment building. Junk-littered balconies with bent metal sides overlooked weedy yards and untrimmed hedges. The paint on every door blistered and peeled in the hot sun. Soiled curtains partially covered about half the windows. Ten and Maria walked inside a small foyer. A small office sat to their right. The carpet at the entrance was worn almost to the plywood underneath. They walked up two flights of stairs and down a dimly lit hall to apartment 1318. The air felt moist and dirty and smelled of mold. Maria knocked. They heard bare feet running and the door suddenly opened. They looked down. A little boy in Pull-Ups and a t-shirt stained with, well, a lot of things, gripped the knob as though it held him up.

He looked at them with some surprise. "Mommy!"

A big-breasted woman in a housecoat walked through the living room from a back room, stepping around toys like an expert. She held a two- or three-year-old on her hip. The loosely tied robe showed a lot of leg. She wore lace underwear and no bra. A line of cleavage ran down the front of the robe. "Who are you?" the woman asked.

Maria stepped forward and held out her hand. "We're from ISTI and would like to ask a few questions." When she saw that Gwen didn't know who or what that was, she explained, "The government group that's investigating the breakout at Muncy, where you used to work."

"I didn't see anything. You probably know that."

"We'd just like to ask a few questions," Maria repeated.

"I can do that, but like I said, I don't know nothin'." She opened the door wider. "Punk, why don't you go in the kitchen and finish your Cap'n Crunch."

The kid let go of the doorknob and ran for the kitchen, flat-footed and awkward.

"You call him Punk?" Ten asked.

"His dad was some punk and the name stuck to Liam."

"His name's Liam, though?"

"Yeah," she said, "after his daddy." Bouncing the baby, she said, "And this here's Arnold, named after *his* daddy." As she set Arnold onto the floor, one breast slipped from the robe. She swung it back under the robe as she stood, wrapped the cloth a bit tighter, and tied the front. Arnold ran for the kitchen. "Sit down. Ask away."

The place smelled like wet diapers and mildew. It was already getting hot. Inside the apartment, the air felt only slightly less sticky than in the hallway, but that could have been from an open window somewhere. Ten and Maria both sat on the threadbare paisley-patterned couch and sank deeper than expected. Maria leaned forward. "You and Buddy?"

She smiled broadly, then frowned. "Well, until we got caught and fired, he was about to divorce that skank of a wife of his and marry me. I guess that's out the window now." She looked toward the kitchen. "Punk could have used the male influence. He's gettin' a little wild."

"You do call him Punk," Ten said as though that wasn't helping.

"Cute, ain't it?"

Ten glanced at Maria and asked, "What do you know about the breakout?"

"Nothin'." She shrugged. "Told you this would be useless. Nothin' ever goes on over there. I mean, a lot of fights and screaming sometimes. And we've had a few of the men guards trying to touch the inmates or watch 'em shower. Ask them to lift up their tops. That sort of thing. Happens sometimes. They get caught and fired. Then another crew comes in."

"Anyone get hurt?"

"Sometimes, but that happens in the day more than at night. When everybody's out and about. I don't see much of that. Don't work days. That's somethin' you have to talk with the superintendent about. I heard that she's rough on the girls sometimes too. Beaten a few of them from what I heard. It's hard to tell the truth though. A lot of mental cases in there, you know. I think that's most of 'em. Makes you wonder. But then, it's a prison and bad things happen. You don't go to prison unless there's somethin' wrong upstairs. Know what I mean? Anyways, it's a job. I got to pay my bills and raise my boys. That's all I'm thinkin' about while I'm there. Now I gotta find somethin' else."

"And Buddy," Maria said.

"Don't say nothing bad about Buddy. He's a gentle soul. I only wish he were mine." She looked disappointed again. Then she looked at Maria. "There'll be another." She smiled. "You know what I mean."

"I don't," Maria said as though she didn't want to have anything in common with Gwen.

"Had you heard anything about Superintendent Cooke abusing the women, other than beating them?"

Gwen looked confused. "How do you mean? What other way is there?"

"Verbally?" Maria asked. When she got no reaction, she said, "Sexually?"

"You mean woman on woman? I didn't think Cooke went that way. Shit," she turned her head away, "I can't say that I can even imagine that, so no. I don't think so."

"What about Nancy Wilmoth? You know her?"

"Computer girl. That's all I know. She's come to fix the observation equipment a few times when we had problems. But I only seen her once or twice. Seems like a nice enough girl. Why? Is she involved? She don't go that way, does she?"

"We're just trying to look at all angles," Maria said.

Gwen turned her gaze toward Ten. "What angle you lookin' at?" she asked with a grin and a wink.

"I'm just the technical guy," Ten said. "She's the boss."

Gwen asked, "You two together?"

"Not like that," Maria said.

Gwen turned her face toward Maria slowly. "You have more questions?"

"One more. What do you know about Dr. Paton?"

Gwen smiled. "He's a wimp. Scared of his own shadow. Creepy. Somethin' about him doesn't ever fit, like he's uncomfortable in his own skin. But then he's a psychologist. They ain't right most of the time."

Maria stood up and thanked Gwen.

Ten was surprised by the sudden ending but stood up as well.

"I'll walk you to the door." Gwen tugged on the strap around her housecoat to loosen it. She leaned slightly to the side while getting up, allowing more of her breasts to show again. She gave Ten a smile while Maria headed for the door.

"Thanks again," Ten said, wanting something between him and her, even if it was only words.

"If you have more questions, you're welcome to come back."

Ten closed the door behind him and turned to see Maria waiting. "You think Carney likes me, but he's not flaunting his goods like that woman. I think she wants you to come back and ask more questions. I'm not sure if she cares to see me ever again."

Ten shook his head and walked past Maria toward the stairs. As they met the heaviness of the outside air again, Ten sighed. "She didn't even understand what I meant about calling her kid Punk. She's practically guaranteeing that he's going to be like his dad."

"She's desperate for someone. Anyone, obviously. I think Buddy dodged a bullet."

"Luck of the draw," Ten said.

"All this crazy has made me hungry. Let's say we get a quick lunch. Then I need to go back to the hotel, freshen up, and maybe we can go back to the police station and interview Paton. He might be more forthcoming now that we have the goods on him."

"Sounds like a plan," Ten said. "I just want to stop at a drug store and pick up some extra water for my room."

They found a drugstore and Ten said, "You can wait here. I'll only be a minute." He jumped out and walked inside. He quickly found the handyman section; small, but it had a couple screwdrivers, a tack hammer, and what he was looking for: a pocketknife. Then he found a six-pack of bottled water and walked to the counter, totally focused on getting out of there quickly.

As the attendant rang up his purchases, a hand came around and picked up the pocketknife. He turned to see Maria behind him. She placed the knife in her pocket and patted it with her hand while Ten paid and picked up the water. Outside Maria said, "You've been acting different. I knew something was up."

"Why are you doing this?"

"Why are you? That's the real question. I don't care if you want to reminisce about Amy, but don't punish yourself."

He didn't answer her.

As they drove toward the hotel, neither of them said anything more. It was like they both knew what was going on and neither of them wanted to talk about it. As they rode up in the elevator together, Maria put her arm through his and nudged his shoulder. "I'm going to keep the knife. I'd like to talk about this though. Give me a minute to freshen up and I'll come get you."

"Nothing to talk about."

"I'd like to anyway." She opened her door and went into her room.

Ten opened his door and walked into his room. Jacob sat at the desk across the room. "How'd you get in here?" Ten asked.

"Government business."

"Why are you here? You could have called."

"I do these things in person," he said. "Good to see you, Ten." He held out his hand but Ten didn't take it, so he put it in his pocket.

"Don't take me off the case. Not yet. I'll figure it out. We're getting there," Ten said.

"I'm going to bring Roger in on this."

"Will he even help?" Ten asked. "My understanding is that he doesn't want any part of the government ever again."

"He was very reluctant. I told him I'd gather what information you have and hand it over. He's doing it for you and Maria, not me. That's what he said to tell you. He told me about a dozen times. Anyway, he promised to look through your findings and offer some suggestions. Nothing more. Give me two days and I'll hand this back to you to finish up."

"Two days?"

Jacob nodded. "I don't want to take any of this away but allowing you to work with this Mr. Hobart was my mistake. I was trying to keep out of it, keep ISTI out of it. Roger can help. You know that."

"ISTI is still out of it for the most part. Roger is working independently, I suspect."

"Completely. He doesn't even want to be paid. Wants nothing from us."

Ten said, "I'm sure he can help. I just feel like you don't trust me."

"You don't like letting go of a project. That's why I came here personally. To give you my word that it's only for this small part. You can continue interviewing with Maria about this other situation. The suicide. The perversions. We'll help you make all the arrests. The FBI can help too, if you'd like. Or the local police. It's all up to the two of you." He stopped as though assessing Ten's response. "I don't want to take any control from either of you."

"Does Maria know?"

"Not yet. I knew if I told her, she'd tell you."

About that time, Ten heard the door click and Maria walked in. "Oh, Jacob? Shit. You're not taking us off the case, are you?"

He stepped forward. "I was just telling Ten that I'm bringing Roger in to help with some of the analysis. Give us two days. In the meantime, the two of you can get further along on all the weird shit with the suicide and psychologist and whatever other perverse stuff is going on here. You can talk with Ten. I explained it to him." He tightened his lips. "Sorry I didn't come to you first, but I knew Ten was focused on the technical part and that's what we're taking from you."

"Two days," Ten said.

Jacob wouldn't look him in the eyes. "That's right."

"Then you owe me," Ten said.

"I can live with that," Jacob said. "Once this is over. I'll make it up to you. I promise. Whatever you want." He looked distraught. "I don't think the other escapes are copycats. I think this is bigger than that. I'm afraid if what's been happening were to happen across the US, all hell would break loose. Thousands of prisoners would be free, the public in tremendous danger."

Ten refused to say another word even though Jacob looked at him as though waiting for him to respond.

"Can you email what you have to Roger? Or overnight it?"

"To his house in Seattle?" Maria asked.

Jacob looked at her. "Yeah. Will you make sure it happens?"

"I will. So you think all the sexual stuff is something different," Maria said.

"I talked with Carney. He thinks so too. And some guy from the FBI said this stuff goes on at the prisons. There are three prisons in fairly close proximity. He said he was used to it. Which I'll never understand," Jacob said.

"That was Agent Munson?" Ten asked.

"Yeah. That was his name. But he won't interfere unless you ask him to."

"Just the technical stuff," Maria said.

Jacob nodded and walked around Ten. "Well, I have to go." He stopped to address Maria. "I'm sorry. You have the other investigation under control. Continue with that for two days."

"It's okay, Jacob, we understand," she said.

After Jacob left, Ten turned around. "We don't understand."

"You thought to bring Roger into this in the first place." She smiled at him. "Now, you have Roger's help *and* Jacob owes you. I'd make him pay for dinner when we get back. Make it a nice restaurant and I'll join you."

"It's not funny. He doesn't trust me."

"You don't know that. He's under a huge amount of pressure that we can't even imagine. ISTI was completely shut down and rebuilt around what Jacob believed it could be. That doesn't happen in the government. He's fully responsible and takes that seriously."

"ISTI and the people involved were murdering scientists involved with a government project," Ten said defiantly. "And their families. They had handlers who were supposed to take care of it. I'd say that's a violation on many levels, that's a shit show if I ever saw one."

"That wasn't Jacob. What he's done, how he keeps this together, it's not easy. He has to make hard decisions. It's a totally different operation because of him. If it wasn't, do you think I'd be involved at all?"

"So maybe I leave it to them," Ten said as he sat down at his laptop.

"Stay with me to help figure out who all is involved with the perversions going on. We'll put some people away. Then if you want to leave the rest of the case to Roger and Jacob, we can do that. I still think you'll figure it out though. Roger hasn't jumped into the whole thing like you have. He's coming from the outside. He hasn't talked with anyone involved." She winked at him. "And what if the two cases do overlap? Then we're still moving forward."

"You're saying we keep doing what we're doing. Nothing changes."

"I didn't actually say that." She pointed toward the laptop. "Send whatever Roger needs from you." Ten opened his laptop and started to tap away at the keys. "I'll send Roger a note, then overnight the thumb drives." He glanced her way. "I like the way you think."

"So, our original plan. We'll stop for a sandwich at that sub shop, then talk with Paton," she said.

"We can have the hotel overnight the thumb drives," he said.

"Then we'll get back to it."

"I'll drive."

CHAPTER 29

Ten and Maria walked into the police station together. Chief Carney rushed from his office the moment they stepped through the door. He addressed Maria right away. "Good to see you again."

"It's good to see you too," she said. "We came to talk with Blake Paton if that's okay. Should we go back to your interrogation room?"

He smiled broadly and nodded vehemently. He hesitated before speaking, as though he didn't know what to say or just wanted to look at Maria a little longer. "I'll have him there in a jiffy. You want me to sit in?"

"I don't see why not. Ten tells me you are an integral part of our investigation. The way you handled everything so well with the doctor." She turned to get Ten's approval and he gave her the go-ahead with a slight cock of his head.

Chief Carney bounced away, light on his feet.

As Maria and Ten headed down the hall, she turned her head slightly and whispered, "Don't say one word."

Inside the stark interrogation room, Maria again took the position across the table from where Paton would sit. There were only three chairs at the table when they walked in so Ten pulled another chair to the table on the other side of Maria for Carney, then sat to Maria's left, farthest from the door.

Moments later, Carney brought Paton into the room and sat him down. "He was sniveling most of the night, I hear."

"We were looking over the evidence and didn't hear anything," Maria said.

Carney made a face. "Sniveling quietly, then."

Paton slumped in his chair, eyes down, chin to chest.

"Cuffs?" Carney asked.

"Leave them on," Maria said, once again showing her dislike for what the good doctor's voyeurism represented.

"I didn't do anything wrong," Paton said almost imperceptibly.

"We have photos and video that proves otherwise," Maria said. Her voice didn't sound angry. Disappointed maybe.

"My private life has nothing to do with you," he whispered again, never looking up for a second.

Ten noticed how the man's slack body filled his chair, how fluid. Like a water-filled body balloon. Paton was exhausted, making Ten wonder if he'd slept at all. Was he going over his actions all night? He must have known what he was doing was wrong, yet he still did it. Why? What compelled him?

"You knew what Superintendent Cooke was doing to prisoners and you let it happen. That's a crime," Maria told him.

His chin came up slowly until they were face to face. His bloodshot eyes widened. He didn't speak right away. Then, he said, "Those women need love. They need to know that they're loved. I hear it all the time in sessions. They feel abandoned by everyone. Elizabeth gave them love. She did the right thing."

Ten watched as Maria struggled to maintain eye contact. Her shoulders tightened and hands fisted. For a moment, he thought she was going to hit him.

Her voice was more like a growl. "Love," Maria said, "they may need. Not abuse. Physical abuse isn't love. Sexual abuse isn't love. Sarah Andrews was forced."

"Did she say that? Ask her. In session, she said she liked it."

Maria spit her words at him. "You fool. Did you ever think she was hiding her feelings so she could stay on everyone's good side? So she didn't get beaten by Cooke?"

Paton stood. His chair screeched across the floor. "They like that! They're masochists. It's how they are. They aren't like us. Elizabeth knew that. She was helping them."

Carney got up and walked around the table and put a hand on Paton's shoulder to get him to sit back down. He lingered over him.

"Why'd she commit suicide then? She knew she was wrong. She was afraid she'd get caught and go to prison herself."

Ten leaned toward Maria, getting her attention so he could speak. "In one of the videos. The one in your office. Sarah said she'd 'kill you.' Did she mean you? Or Cooke?"

Paton lowered his eyes again and didn't answer.

In a calm voice, Maria said, "What the two of you did was horrible on so many levels and illegal on a few as well. You are worse than those inmates, thinking that what you were doing was in any way the right thing. You wouldn't know the right thing if it were in front of you."

"I did nothing wrong," Paton said. "I want a lawyer present."

Ten had wondered when it would come to that. Paton had threatened it before. Perhaps fatigue made him vulnerable enough to talk for a few minutes, but he was done now. Maria seemed to know it as well. Rather than take up any more time, she motioned for Chief Carney to take Paton away.

As Carney pulled Paton up, Maria said, "You'll need a lawyer. That is if there's one around that'll work with a pissant like you."

After Carney left the room, shoving Dr. Paton in front of him, Maria sat back in her chair and stretched her legs forward. She let out a long breath of air she'd been holding in and closed her eyes. She was about to cry.

Ten reached out and touched her arm.

She turned her head toward him, eyes still closed. "How can people do that to each other?"

"I don't know. I don't think he could help himself. And I know that explanation doesn't make sense."

She opened her eyes, addressed him directly. "How do you let yourself do what you do?"

Ten shook his head. He didn't want to go there. Not now. Not here. "That's personal. It's nothing like what he's done, or Cooke. I hurt no one but myself. I'm surprised you could suggest it was the same thing." He let her arm go.

"People do things they know are wrong and still do them. You must understand it to break it," she said.

He gritted his teeth. "You think I haven't tried?"

"Am I interrupting?" Carney stood in the doorway.

Maria shook her head. "It's just upsetting is all. This whole investigation. This isn't what we normally have to deal with. We're scientists, not psychologists."

"He's not one either," Carney said. "Not if that's what he does."

Maria nodded and got up.

He stepped forward and took her arm. "You can sit here a bit longer if you want. You look shaken."

Maria patted his hand and let him walk her out of the room and into the hall. "Thank you for understanding."

"What would you like me to do next?" he asked her.

Ten felt invisible standing behind the two of them. He watched as they worked things out.

"I appreciate your concern and your help," she said evenly. "We can handle most of the technical pieces for now. But this has exhausted me, you can tell. If you could interview the other guards, see if anyone else knew about Paton and Cooke; maybe interview other inmates to see what they might have seen, what Sarah might have told them. If you could put it all in a report for me."

Amazed at how effectively Maria let Chief Carney know their relationship was pure business, Ten followed them to the front of the building. It looked like Carney got the message and wasn't bothered by it, had accepted it. At the door, he said, "Our department is here to help in whatever way it can." *Our department*. He accepted the separation gracefully.

Ten was impressed. When they were back in the car, he acknowledged how well she handled the chief without making it obvious or embarrassing him.

"He's a nice man, but I have no interest in him. I couldn't be mean or rude about it. You were right. I hadn't noticed his interest until you said something. I didn't want to hurt his feelings."

"You didn't. Plus, you got him to help out with a lot of the peripheral interrogations."

"Now if I can get you to comply," she said.

Ten ignored her statement and pulled onto the road. "I've been thinking about Paton and what he did. I can't help but think that he knew what he was doing was wrong. He doesn't appear to be stupid. At least at the beginning, he would have known. His interest in Cooke, his own emotions of loneliness and lack of love that he transferred onto the prisoners—all pressured him closer and closer to the edge of his own ability to know right from wrong. Is that how it goes?"

"Like I told the chief, I'm not a psychologist, but your explanation sounds viable. Paton eventually got swallowed up and blinded by his own desires. When she didn't return them, he found a way to be involved with her. The more twisted it became, the more difficult to get out of."

"Before, were you suggesting that in some strange way, I'm going through the same thing? That I'm trying to figure out a way to stay with Amy, when she's not even here any longer? Is that what I'm going through? Some kind of blindness?"

"I don't know if that pit can ever be filled," she said. "But you have to see that there are other things you can focus on that can keep your interest, help you to stay engaged in the world. You don't have to cut yourself to feel, Ten. Trust me. You have more emotions, deeper emotions, than most people I know. You can transfer that away from pain. Turn it around. That's all I'm saying." She shook her head. "I don't know how exactly."

"I'm not sure I can stop at this point."

"I believe you can."

CHAPTER 30

Their next stop was to check in on Nancy and Paul. They called ahead to have an escort assigned and when they arrived, a slender, attractive, middle-aged woman stood near the front of the building, dressed professionally in a navy skirt, light blue blouse, and pumps. As they walked up, the woman held out her hand. "You must be Maria and Ten." She narrowed her eyes toward him. "I got that right, didn't I?"

"You did," he said.

Maria was already shaking the woman's hand.

"I'm Rebecca Lewis. I'll be taking over here for now. If I know this whole operation as well as I think I do, it may be that I'm here permanently." She made a disagreeable face.

"You don't like that idea," Ten said as it was his turn to shake hands with her.

"I live a ways from here and may have to move if I stay." She pointed a finger as though down toward the highway. "About a half hour on the other side of my old job."

Ten noticed that she didn't wear a wedding ring and said, "At least you don't have to move a whole family."

She paused to look at him as though she didn't hear him correctly. Finally, she said, "I'm a single mom. The long drive takes time out from everything else I have to do with two teenagers in school."

"I'm sorry."

Her eyes had steeled slightly. "You didn't know, so you're excused." She turned back to talk with Maria. "Horrible, what happened here. I'll have to interview for a new psychologist, maybe replace more guards. Who knows who's been involved? And that IT girl? I don't know what to do with her."

"She was coerced," Maria said, surprising Ten. After all, Maria wasn't one of Nancy's fans at the beginning.

Rebecca stopped and stared at Maria for a second. "I suppose if you've made an evaluation, I can stand with that." Ten could see that Rebecca might be the right person for the job. Her strong personality didn't get in the way of her listening skills. "Well," she continued to Maria, "I understand you're in charge here." She said it as though shoving it in Ten's face, but he could have been misinterpreting her acknowledgement.

He doubted it though.

"I believe you know where IT is located. Paul is down there. He can help you. I didn't select a guard for you yet. If you do wish to go anywhere else on the campus though, let me know and I'll assign one." She didn't wait for a response. She turned and walked back into the building.

Maria fell in behind her and Ten behind Maria. Once inside, Ten took the lead down the hall and down the stairs as Rebecca walked upstairs. Ten entered the equipment room in front of Maria. "Hey, Paul."

Paul looked up from the computer screen. "Hey, Ten."

"This is Maria. I'm not sure if you've formally met."

"I don't think so." He stood and nodded. "Nice to meet you."

"Likewise." She settled into a side chair. "I'm only accompanying Ten. He wanted to check in."

"Nothing to check in with. I'm testing some interfaces per the manual. After this, I'll be adjusting the wiring harnesses in one of the other buildings."

"Is that where Nancy is?" Ten asked.

"Oh no. Didn't they tell you when you came in? She's at Allenwood helping out today. They're nervous over there, and since Nance and I are ahead of them, well..."

"Why are they so nervous?" Maria asked before Ten got the chance.

Paul glanced at Ten and back to Maria. He shrugged as though she'd asked a dumb question. "The breakouts."

Ten gave him a serious look. "They're installing the same system. The P280."

"Allenwood's a few days, maybe a week behind us. They're worried the same thing might happen to them. They don't want to get into trouble, so they asked Nance to help out."

"I hadn't known any of this," Ten said.

"I'm sorry." It looked like he really meant he was sorry, but his tone indicated he didn't know why it was important.

Ten found that difficult to believe. He motioned for Maria to get up. "I'm sure you have this under control. I'll talk with Nancy when she gets back."

"I'll be checking in with her later. You want me to give her a message?"

Ten shook his head. "Not yet."

Once outside again, Ten squinted in the bright sunlight. "I didn't know they were installing the P280 at Allenwood."

"You'd think Jacob would have told us," she said.

"Maybe he didn't know either. If half his employees are like Paul back there, they only answer the question that's asked. He probably didn't ask about Allenwood."

"What are you thinking we need to do next?"

"I'm thinking we're going to have another breakout if we're not careful. Allenwood, if nowhere else. We'll have to ask Jacob to find out where all the P280s are going in and their schedules. Something we should have known from the beginning. I have Nancy's number. I'll contact her. This does put a bigger crunch on the timing. If they are only a few days behind, then their first test is coming up quickly."

"And we have no answers," she said.

"We don't even have many clues for the most part. And the ones we do seem to point to a few kids on one end or a coerced guard on the other. Basically, then, we know it's happening, but we don't know who's involved or why." He gave Maria a long stare. "A rock and a hard place."

"You're worried."

"Damned straight."

"And copycats? What do you think about that now?"

"Back to one person. Or one group anyway. If they're testing along with the installations, perhaps Jacob was right to be concerned. This could be a huge operation gearing up for a countrywide breakout."

"I can't imagine that many criminals out on the streets at once," she said.

"I don't think I want to."

"What do we do now?"

"Hope that Roger quickly figures something out that Josh and I missed."

"You going to call him?"

"After I have a chat with Nancy. She's closer to this than any of us. I'm going to ask her to wait for Roger's assessment before running her test." He handed Maria his car keys. "Your turn to drive. My turn to talk."

On the way back to the hotel, the sun burned through the windshield. Ten jacked the air conditioner to high and turned the fan to blasting.

Nancy answered her phone right away.

In lieu of a greeting, Ten said, "Two things."

"No hello?" Nancy said jovially.

Ten had to smile. "How's your day going, Nancy?"

"Why wonderful. Thank you for asking." She waited and when he didn't respond, she said, "Now it's your turn. The two things."

Ten appreciated her playfulness. "First thing: can you postpone your first test over there until tomorrow afternoon or so?"

"They're a little behind where they should be, so they won't like that. We were going to try to run the test tonight, in fact. But if it's important, sure."

"It's important."

"Annnnd behind door number two?" she said.

"I've gone through Dr. Paton's office and some things he tried to hide in his house. He wrote some poetry about what Cooke was up to."

"Oh God. He knew?"

"Sorry. I forgot you didn't know. Anyway, it only gets worse. He was in possession of the videos you took. I think they were for him and not for Cooke."

"That's gross, Ten. Are you sure?"

"We have the evidence."

"What's that have to do with me?" she asked warily.

"As I'm getting your reaction, I'm thinking nothing."

"But?"

"He mentions you in one of his poems." He thought he heard her physically gag on the other end of the phone.

When she spoke, her voice cracked. "Oh my God. Oh my God. What did it say?"

"Not important. My question is whether or not either he or Cooke approached you in any way other than to transfer the videos."

"You mean like get involved? Oh God. Please don't tell me that's what they wanted."

"I'm just asking if they approached you in that way."

"Never. Look, I was afraid for my job, but that would have been too far. It's enough to make me sick."

"I'm sorry."

Nancy's voice got serious. "It's not your fault. It's my fault I let it go as far as I did. She scared me. I was afraid she'd do more than fire me. I should have told someone. I'm sorry. I really am. Oh God. Do you think they were videoing me? Following me?"

"No. Nothing like that. He was fantasizing."

"Jesus, Ten. I won't be able to sleep for a week."

"I'm sorry. I know this sounds bad, but if they didn't approach you, then it's okay. You're okay. Thank you for answering."

She didn't talk for a moment, as though trying to get her thoughts together. "I'll have them hold off on the test run until you give me the go-ahead." She hung up.

"That didn't sound good," Maria said.

"I don't think she knows what to do with any of this."

"Truthfully," Maria said, "neither do I."

CHAPTER 31

That evening, Ten stood staring out the window of the hotel room. Clouds accumulated in the west, but the forecast predicted no rain for the next day or two. He and Maria had eaten early, and he'd been in his room for two hours just staring, trying to recall what it was like to love. And be loved by someone you were in love with. An interrupted continuation from the time he stared at Amy's photos. He hadn't taken out Amy's photos again though. Instead, he tried to associate his thoughts with the case of Paton and Cooke. Tried to wrap his head around it. Was it love that Paton felt? The juxtaposition and simultaneous comingling of those two sets of thoughts might have seemed odd to another person, but that's how Ten thought. He made connections where, seemingly, there weren't any. So now, it was Paton and Cooke.

Paton had said that the women inmates wanted love and that what Cooke did—beating them and sexually abusing them—was what they wanted. Ten couldn't help but wonder if he too were a masochist. Perhaps of a different ilk. Was cutting himself supposed to help him feel? Or feel loved? Were love and pain tightly linked like love and hate? He could see that. Physically, it was pleasure and pain, while emotionally, it was love and hate. If all those factors got shuffled, where the physical and emotional were swapped out, then didn't it make sense? Wouldn't that mean that his need for love could be mistaken for pain? Sure, he didn't have others hurt him. He didn't include anyone in his pain but himself. Did Paton and Cooke merely extend their ideas outward?

He rubbed his shoulder. It didn't even hurt anymore, but he could feel the ridges. He knew Maria had seen what he was up to in the drug store. She'd snuck up behind him and confiscated the knife. Was it that easy for her to tell what he was thinking? Then when he tried to explain, she didn't accept the excuse that he couldn't feel. Perhaps she was right. Perhaps he felt too deeply, and pain was his escape. What psychological term was there for that? There must be one.

He leaned his head against the windowpane in front of him. He wanted to cry but couldn't pull the tears out of himself. He scrunched his face, tightened his eyes, but tears wouldn't even begin. What could he do? Scream? He took a deep breath, but his lungs—or his larynx—wouldn't allow it.

A knock came at the door and he popped his head from the window and looked toward the door. He wasn't expecting anyone. And Maria had a key. "Yes?"

"It's Josh Hobart."

Ten let him inside. "Did we set up a meeting?"

"I thought so. Maybe I misinterpreted." He rushed into the room and turned around.

"I could have forgotten. So much going on. I'm not sure what we can do though. My boss—"

"Maria?"

"No. *Our* boss took some of the software work from us and gave it to a friend."

"I barely had time..." Josh's voice trailed off as he looked around as though he'd dropped something. He brought his palms up. They were empty.

"It's not you. I don't think he trusts me."

"But you work for him."

"I'm a consultant. Anyway, that's not important."

"He doesn't trust you, but he brought you in as a consultant." Josh was trying to make sense of the conversation.

"We go way back. It's a long story," Ten said. "Maria needed a partner. I'm an engineer. Anyway, while you're here, let's talk. Maybe some idea will crawl out of our conversation, something we missed."

"You want Maria here too?"

"Sure, why not." Ten walked toward the phone on the desk, then leaned over and banged on the wall. "Wanna visit?"

Josh laughed. "You are a strange man."

"You have no idea. Maybe it comes with the territory." He motioned toward the bed. "Have a seat."

Maria let herself in and stopped when she saw Josh. "Oh."

Ten said, "We're going to go over the case and see if we come up with any new ideas. Josh here is going to bring a new perspective, an outside view of things."

Maria walked around Josh and sat in the stuffed chair on the other side of the bed. Ten took a seat at the desk chair and turned it around. Josh looked nervous and sat quietly.

"Who's first?" Maria asked.

"I'll fill you in," Ten said. He told Josh about the interviews they had with his students, about their concerns Ken might be involved just to show his dad up, about Nancy's work at Allenwood, and, peripherally, about Cooke and Paton. No details. As he spoke, Ten focused on Josh, watching for a sign, any sign, that illustrated a lie or doubt.

"Holy shit. You wouldn't think in a small town..." Josh looked surprised.

"Can you imagine how much of this goes on in a big town?" Maria said.

Josh got serious. "Personally, I don't think it's Ken, or any of my students for that matter. And I'm not just protecting them. I mean it. Valeria might have the biggest motive, but she's a good kid and probably the least likely."

"I agree with you there," Maria said. "I liked her and her mom. What about her sister?"

"Juana has no interest in computers at all. She's more the English lit type."

"Why not Ken?" Ten wanted to know.

"He scares easily. I know his old man is a tyrant, but Ken, deep down, isn't the type to test the odds again. He tried, he failed, and he'll stop. At least that's my take."

"Even under pressure from his friends?" Ten asked.

"You met his friends. That's my point about them. They're more apt to protect each other. They'd try to sway Ken away from trouble. Especial Craig."

"The Black kid," Ten said. "He's clean. I feel for him though. Small town. Country. So few Black families. I get it. I did my best to assure him and his dad that they weren't to worry."

"Consider Valeria and her family then. Same dynamic, only they picked her dad up. I don't know a lot about it. I try to stay out of their personal lives, but it sounds like you have the skinny," Josh said.

Ten continued to stare. The man didn't hesitate, shift his eyes, or wring his hands. Ten was starting to believe him.

"Not that family, but what about Valeria's uncle, Philippe?" Maria asked.

Josh shrugged. The first sign of doubt.

Ten agreed. "We should talk with him. And the next time we're at the police station during the day, we should talk with her cousin."

"Ana," Maria said.

"I had a thought," Josh said. "Late last night."

"And?"

"What if I hacked into Line-Tech to see if the test portion of their system has been hacked and from where?"

"You can do that?"

"Depends on the skill of the hacker, but I could try."

"If not, Roger might be able to," Maria said.

Josh perked up. "Roger. The guy who your boss called in?"

"Ten thinks he's a genius," Maria said.

"He is a genius. That's not why Jacob called him in though. It's because he doesn't trust me."

"He's running scared, Ten, and you know it," Maria said. "It has nothing to do with trust."

"Either way, it sounds over my pay grade," Josh said.

Ten gave him a look. "Don't sell yourself short. I think we should try this. See if you can find anything. Especially tonight."

"Why is that?" Josh asked.

Ten glanced at Maria. "According to Nancy Wilmoth, they were supposed to test Allenwood tonight. Maybe now's the time to be in there downloading shit that doesn't belong."

"We can try, but like I said, it depends on how skilled the hacker is," Josh offered as a disclaimer again.

Ten opened his laptop, punched in his password, stood, and opened his hand in invitation for Josh to sit in his desk chair.

"If anyone asks, I wasn't in on this conversation," Maria said.

"Deal," Ten said.

Josh sat down and began to work. While he worked, Ten called Roger.

"Hey, Ten. I've been looking over the things you emailed, hacked Line-Tech, and poked around. I'm eager to see what the thumb drives have, but it's probably nothing I couldn't get online. They keep an archive. So how are you doing?"

"Doing well," Ten said. Maria lifted her head and squinted her eyes in disagreement. Ten waved her off and turned his head. "So, nothing?"

"Not from what I went through earlier. They haven't upgraded their security software for a while though, which made it easy to get in. Typical idiot company shit. Budget over brains is what I like to label it."

Ten laughed. "Happens in a lot of businesses."

"ISTI isn't all that secure either, but don't tell Jacob I said that."

"Your secret is good with me. Although maybe we should tell him."

The phone got quiet for a moment. "You know I'm doing this for you."

"I know, Roger."

"You and Maria. How's she doing?"

"She's doing well too." Ten looked at her, and she shook her raised hand to tell him she didn't want to talk.

"It's late there," Roger said.

"Late there too," Ten said, recognizing neither of them knew quite what to talk about and the unemotional electronics standing between them—the cell phones— didn't make their interaction very intimate. "We'll have to make it a point to get together."

"I'm in DC sometimes for conferences," Roger said.

"Send me an email and we'll coordinate."

"Great to hear from you."

"The same." Ten lowered the phone after hanging up.

"You can't really talk with friends over a phone," Josh said while his face was still plastered to the screen.

"So true," Ten said. "If Roger didn't find anything..."

"Hmm," Josh said.

"What's that about?" Ten asked. "Don't tell me you found something."

"Timing," Josh said. "There might be someone in there right now. Software people have signatures." He shrugged. "Nuances."

"You found something going on."

"Looks like something Valeria might do. It can't be her, but..."

"Her uncle," Maria mentioned for the second time.

Ten leaned over Josh's shoulder. "I suspect you can check for IP addresses, hack the ISP, and get a pretty close location?"

"Something like that." Josh smiled. "Sounds like you could do this."

"Let's just say I've been around this stuff and picked up some language."

Josh looked at Ten over his shoulder. "Yeah. Let's just say that."

Ten turned to Maria. "Call Carney." To Josh, he said, "Let's locate that computer."

Josh gave Ten a panicked look. "You think it's her uncle, then? You expect it to be local."

"I do. But we'll find out for sure soon enough." Ten called Roger back. After their greetings, he said, "I need a favor. There's more than one person hacking into the Line-Tech site as we speak. Can you capture movements we can verify at a later date? In court if we have to?" He didn't wait for Roger to answer. He handed the phone to Josh. In a few minutes, Roger had what he needed. Josh had found an address, and then Maria, Ten, and Josh were following Carney down the road.

CHAPTER 32

The front of the house was dark. It appeared that no one was awake. All the front window curtains were closed. Carney motioned for them to stay where they were as he walked to the side of the house, then around to the back door. No one waited. Ten, Maria, and Josh followed.

"There's a light in the kitchen," Ten noted.

As they approached, Josh said, "That's not a light. It's the glow from a computer screen."

Chief Carney approached carefully. Blinds were closed. He knocked at the kitchen's back door. They heard miscellaneous noises and the scraping of a chair across the floor. Carney waited and when no one came to the door, he reached down to the knob and turned it. Unlocked. He glanced behind him before walking in with Ten, Maria, and Josh following.

A Mexican-American man stood there in shorts and a t-shirt. He had dark, messy hair with light streaks of gray along his ears. A small mustache covered his upper lip. "What's this about?" He glanced toward the kitchen counter where Valeria leaned, her eyes wide, her hands shaking. "It's okay," he said. "I got this."

"We have reason to believe that someone from this location was just hacking into a company computer," Carney said.

The man looked surprised, then settled his gaze on Carney. "I don't know about that. I was doing some work, and something went screwy. Someone may have taken over my computer. Malware. Or I made a mistake. It's late. I'm tired. I don't know about any company." Carney glanced over at Valeria. "She's visiting. She was reading while I worked. She was just about to go home."

A woman in a bath robe came to the kitchen doorway behind her husband. "Philippe, is everything all right?"

"Something happened while I was working. I'll get it all straightened out."

"Is that possible?" Carney asked no one in particular.

"It is *possible*," Josh said as he walked over to Valeria. "You're out late."

She shook her head and was about to say something when Philippe said, "She had an argument with her mom. I told her she could hang out here for a while."

Philippe's wife started to say something. When he put his hand out to take hers, she stopped.

Carney reached toward Philippe. "We'd like to talk with you at the station if you don't mind."

Philippe said, "I'll answer anything you need to know. Really, I didn't know what was happening. Trying a few things out." He looked at Josh. "Can you make sure she gets home?"

"We'll do that," Josh said.

Maria walked over to Josh and Valeria and put her arm around the girl, who kept her head down.

"You'll come with me," Carney said.

"Of course," Phillipe said. "Let me put on another shirt."

In a matter of moments, the kitchen was cleared, the door locked, and Philippe's computer confiscated. His wife stood at the back door looking worried.

As Ten drove, Josh gave him directions, and Maria sat with Valeria in the back seat. It wasn't far. She could have walked. Ten heard Maria and Valeria whispering but couldn't make out any of their conversation.

They dropped Valeria off at home. Her mom came to the door. "Did you get your homework done?" she asked.

Valeria nodded and ducked inside quickly.

Valeria's mom was right behind her, rattling off questions in Spanish.

"Her uncle," Josh said when they were back in the car. This time he sat in the back seat. Maria was up front. "His brother's in Allenwood. It makes sense."

"We can't be sure it was him," Ten said. "The girl was in the house with him." He glanced at Maria. "You did tell her we'd need a statement?"

"She knows we'll be talking with her again. She was pretty upset. Can we give it a day or two? Now that we have Philippe."

"Her mom didn't seem like they were arguing," Ten said.

Maria glanced into the back seat toward Josh then looked at Ten. "We caught everyone off guard. I think her uncle tried to keep her out of it and didn't know what to say. He said the first thing that came to mind. I agree with Josh about Valeria. Did you see how scared she was back there? Anyway, it makes sense. Her uncle has motive."

"They both have motive," Ten said.

"She wouldn't do that," Josh said again. He sounded sure of himself.

"Could Philippe's computer be taken over like he said?" Ten asked just to hear the answer again.

Josh let out a long breath. "Absolutely. And it could have happened from anywhere in the world. But you called it. You knew it was close. Unless whoever is doing this knows a lot about the locals; it's likely we have our man."

"Why Sarah Andrews?" Ten asked out loud.

"Coincidence?" Maria suggested. "According to the inmates Carney talked with, a lot more doors were opened, but only a few noticed. They didn't want to make a lot of racket and wake the guard. Andrews said the same thing."

"Bertie, taking her evening nap," Ten said. "I'm not sure I believe in coincidences."

Josh leaned forward. "If it was practice, to see if it could be done, Philippe probably didn't care who got out. I'd say he did it at night because few would notice."

"But someone had to escape or he wouldn't know it even happened," Ten said.

"There are always light sleepers," Josh said.

"All the failures happened at night," Maria reminded Ten. "After normal work hours."

Back at the hotel, Josh took his leave. "My wife will be worried." He checked his phone. "She is worried."

"Call her," Maria said.

"Keep me informed?" Josh asked.

"If we can," Maria said. "And keep this to yourself. I know we don't have to tell you, but you're under strict orders to keep silent."

"I won't even tell Mel what happened. But you've got to know that those kids will spread the word."

"Until then," Maria said. After Josh left, Ten motioned for them to get back into the car. "Where are we going?"

"Dunkin' Donuts. I need coffee."

"They probably won't be open, you know."

"Let's try," he said. "There must be something open twenty-four hours around here."

They found the donut shop and it was closed, then McDonald's was closed. Ten pulled into a parking lot and said, "Okay, how about a mediocre cup of coffee and a stale donut?"

"Beggars," she said.

They got out and walked into the 7-Eleven. Maria wandered straight to the coffee and Ten went to the packaged donuts. He grabbed a package of chocolate-coated mini-donuts and walked up behind Maria, who was fixing both their coffees on the counter in front of her. Sixteen ounces. He held up the package. "More preservatives but less stale."

"Off my diet, but it'll do." She laughed, put lids on their coffees, and walked to the counter. "I'm paying," she said. "It's business."

"Be my guest. But know that Jacob allows me to submit T and E statements too."

"I forgot about that." She paid for their food and they walked back out to the car. They ate and drank as Ten drove.

"Valeria looked scared," Ten said.

"Wouldn't you be if the police barged into the house?"

"Guilty scared," Ten said.

"It's not even her computer. Her uncle said he was working. Do you really think he would let her hack into Line-Tech using his computer? And while in his house."

"His hair looked messed up. Like he was sleeping. What if he didn't know? I'm just saying," Ten said. "She helped Ken."

"Josh read them the riot act," she countered.

"She misses her dad," he said.

"She loves her mom and sister."

Ten laughed. "You have a comeback for every suggestion I make about this, don't you?"

"I just don't believe she did it. Her uncle has the skills, the motive, and the hacking led to his house. What more do you want?" She was quiet for a minute. "If you had seen her face and her mom's while talking about when she was little, you'd see that she was hurt but also that her mother needed her. Valeria knows they can't make it without her. She wouldn't take that chance."

"Pictures. You told me."

"You should have seen them. They were so happy. Seeing that girl's smile while riding around on her dad's back."

"I can imagine. They sound like a nice family."

"It's horrible how ICE separates families unnecessarily."

"When this is over, maybe we can help," Ten suggested.

"I can't imagine how."

"I said maybe." Ten stared into the distance and sipped at his coffee.

Maria leaned forward to see what Ten was looking at. "What is it?"

"I was just thinking. Piggyback," Ten said.

"What about it?"

"I remember those days as a kid."

"Me too," she said dreamily.

"That doesn't happen as often with families anymore, does it? Everyone has a damned phone or computer to stare at. Do kids even play outside? With their parents of all things?"

"They do if they live in the country. At least it appears so."

"Every kid should grow up in the country, then."

"Sounds perfect, but then we still have Paton and Cooke. If they grew up in the country, then, once again, it takes all kinds."

"I don't even want to think about them right now," Ten said.

They pulled into the hotel parking lot and finished their coffees and donuts.

"I'm glad you agreed to work with me," Maria said in a solemn moment. "I wouldn't be able to handle this alone. I'm not sure I can anyway. You're more level-headed about all of this crazy."

"Glad you think so. My acting must be working." He tapped the top of the steering wheel, completing their chat, and stepped out of the car into the humid night air. "Let's call it a night."

They went to their respective rooms. It was early morning. Ten hoped to get a few hours of sleep in. Three or four. He thought about the pocketknife but didn't have the same urge he'd had before. Tired, he thought.

CHAPTER 33

"Jacob said we could stay and hone in on Pervert Paton. Close the gap on that one. Charge him and then pack up and go home." Maria sounded more rested than Ten felt.

"He thinks we're done with the breakout case."

"Appears that way," she said. "The FBI is involved in the copycat cases across the country."

"Why'd he get us involved at all?"

She smiled and raised her eyebrows. "You know why. It's a tech job."

"But if the FBI can handle it, he's thinking they should. Since they handled Ken Hemming."

"At first Jacob thought it was a bigger problem than it has turned out to be."

Ten could understand that. "And he thinks the Paton and Cooke thing is open and shut."

"Isn't it?"

"I'm not sure we're finished with any of it. Did anyone say if they found something convincing on Philippe's computer?" Ten held his coffee. They had been sitting for a few minutes and he was hoping the caffeine would kick in soon.

"Traces. Carney thinks that's enough. Josh was there early this morning helping out."

"What about Valeria's cousin? His daughter?"

"Oldest. She can't get involved. It's her dad. Carney gave her the day off."

"I don't know about all this. After sleeping on it, I woke up thinking something wasn't right."

"Care to share?"

"Philippe said that his niece had an argument with her mom, yet her mom asked if she'd finished her homework."

Maria pressed her lips together. "Now that you mention it..."

"Why would they have different stories?"

"I can only guess that Philippe would want to keep Valeria out of it. What if she did her homework earlier that evening using his computer? If he had said that, she'd be under suspicion too. He was protecting her since she had nothing to do with it anyway."

"You're probably right. That's what I would have done. It still bothers me."

"I'm going to have a bagel. You want something?"

They were sitting in the continental breakfast area off the lobby. About half a dozen round tables with chairs were scattered about in the small room. Two other couples sat at tables well away from each other. One, a middle-aged couple, already had their coffees and what looked like bowls of cereal. The other couple, in their late twenties or early thirties, were talking and giggling, holding hands across the table. They got up and walked to the counter. Maria waited for Ten to answer.

"I'll grab some fruit with you." He followed Maria to the food counter and stood with her behind the two lovebirds. He grabbed another cup of coffee, then a second coffee cup that he filled with fruit. Maria smeared cream cheese on a bagel and cut it in half. She put the two halves into a bowl along with a few strawberries. "Ready," she said. "Where to this morning?"

"Can you eat and drive?"

"Who you calling?"

"Everyone."

"Oh?"

"Roger mentioned that Line-Tech kept a log on their site—for each system being installed."

"And?"

"I read through the manuals again early this morning. I didn't see where they did that locally."

"Maybe they don't."

"I thought that too, but then couldn't imagine it. There has to be some sort of record. Somewhere. I'm going to ask Paul to look for it. It could be for the company people only. Liability purposes. But there has to be one."

"Who else you calling?"

"I want to let Nancy know it's okay to go through with the test tomorrow night."

"Why tomorrow? Why not this afternoon?"

"Precaution. I just want to give it another day. Roger will get the thumb drives this morning. I want him to have time to look them over."

"What if Jacob pulled him off the case? Like he's pretty much doing to us." Ten gave her a serious look. "What's that look for?"

"I know Roger. He's like me. He'll look the drives over anyway. Curiosity."

"And we can see if another P280 failure happens," she said.

"You see where I'm going, then."

"I see. I don't agree, but only time will tell. So, again, where am I driving?"

"Let's check in on Paul after I call him. I'll call Carney this morning and see if we can talk with Paton after lunch. Give him time to have his lawyer sitting with him."

"You know how that'll go."

Ten shrugged. "You have other plans?"

They ate as Maria drove. The fields carried a low morning fog with them, a lake of fog with trees sticking up in the gauzy distance. Even the river had a layer of fog, seemingly still, while the current rushed below it. "It's going to get hot." He had just gotten off his third and last call. Carney had agreed to let them talk with Paton around one o'clock.

At the Muncy State Correctional Institution, Ten and Maria approached the administration building. He looked up at the bell tower, wondering what they were trying to portray. He'd always thought of bell towers and churches, maybe the Liberty Bell. What was it supposed to mean here? Before they arrived, he'd contacted Rebecca Lewis's office and let her receptionist know they were coming. They were allowed in and headed to the basement IT rooms. When Ten walked into the equipment room, Paul was sitting in a chair staring at the equipment cabinet as though he'd seen a ghost.

"You okay?" Ten asked.

Paul turned slowly. "Ten. I was just thinking about calling you back. I didn't know you were coming straight here."

"You look worried."

"Nancy is still at Allenwood."

"I talked with her right after you this morning. She's going to download the test payload, and have it run tomorrow night." He saw his message cause a change in Paul's body language and waited for the young man to talk.

"I did what you asked." He blinked and looked away, then back at Ten. He gave Maria a quick grin and looked away again.

"You found something."

"I don't know. Nancy thinks I'm stupid. And I'll admit I'm not nearly as good as she is. Or as good as you, obviously. I would never have thought to look for an archive locally."

"There was one?" Ten stepped closer to him, closing in.

Paul pushed past Ten and sat at the computer. "I've read through the manual and didn't take you seriously. But I started pissing around with the system since that's what you wanted me to do. I was trying to decide to call you right away or start rewiring the cables. That's why I was sitting over there staring. Anyway, I found the log."

"An archive?"

"The system logs all local activities and when they happened, just like you said." He looked up at Ten. "And who." He punched a few keys on the keyboard. "Once I found the log, I went down through the entries looking for the night of the escape. I figured, why not?" He looked up at Ten as he found the log and the entries again. He backed away from the computer.

Ten leaned in and started reading the entries. He looked at Paul.

"Someone going to tell me?" Maria said.

"A direct signal from this control system was sent to open the doors," Ten said.

Paul said, "It's a manual operation. Whoever did this had to be here, in the IT equipment room." Maria gave them both a quizzical look. "The only two people with a key are me and Nancy. While we're working on the new system. You have to login. Nancy was logged in."

"There's no chance that someone else—Superintendent Cooke, Dr. Paton, a janitor—had a key?"

"And her password?" He shook his head. "Besides, all the locks are changed while we're doing the install. Part of the suggested protocol so that the system isn't compromised. Only until the retrofit is completed. To keep the security in place," Paul said. "After that, there are separate keys for the enclosures and the login passwords for the system."

"No one told us about the locks," Maria said.

"No one ever asked," he replied. "It didn't seem important."

"It's not your fault," Ten said, placing a hand on his shoulder.

"But this means—"

"Nancy must have opened the cell doors," Ten finished Paul's sentence. "That's what it has to mean."

"Why would she..."

Ten shook his head toward Maria.

"We let her off the hook," Maria reminded him.

"She's not off the hook now," he said. Paul still looked confused. "We're going to want a statement. First, I want you to close up everything here. Don't talk with Nancy or you'll be an accomplice. Got that?"

Paul nodded several times. "Yes, sir."

"I want you to go to the police station and fill out a statement. Same thing you told me. Then go home. Relax."

Paul nodded again and started to collect his things. "I still can't figure out why."

"A lot you don't know. Sorry we can't divulge any of it right now," Ten said.

"But you have reason to believe what we found was true?" he questioned.

"We do," Maria said.

Ten asked Maria, "Would you mind calling Carney and letting him know to pick Nancy up? Then we'll go upstairs and let the new super know what we're up to."

Maria walked up the stairs with her phone out while Ten took his time so Paul was able to clean up and close everything down.

Ten stopped at the top of the stairs and stood next to Maria, who had just gotten off the phone with Carney. "Your instincts about her were right. Break one moral code, break them all."

"I'm sorry. I know you liked her."

"I was wrong," Ten said.

"You're not wrong often."

"No need to patronize me. I was wrong. At least it looks that way."

"You still want to talk with Paton?"

"More than ever now," Ten said.

Paul came up the stairs and stopped next to them. He reached out to shake Ten's hand. "Thank you. I'll stay available. I'm really sorry."

"I know." Ten shook his hand and let him pass by to go out the door. Ten and Maria watched him bolt down the stairs and into the parking lot.

"Let's make sure someone else doesn't have a key," Maria said.

They walked up the stairs to Rebecca's office. A receptionist used an intercom to let her know they were there.

"Send them in," Rebecca said. She sat behind Elizabeth Cooke's old desk. Papers were spread out everywhere, a red pen in her hand, and a glowing computer screen to her right. "This is important; otherwise, I wouldn't think you'd be in here," she said.

"You look busy," Maria said.

"I am. What have you got to tell me? Or ask me?"

Maria turned to Ten to explain what they'd found. When he was through, Rebecca set down her pen and sat back in her chair. "Well, maybe I do know what I'm going to do with Nancy Wilmoth. I didn't like what I had already heard. Creeped me out if you want to know the truth." She looked across the room for a moment as though gathering her thoughts. "A lot of what goes on in these places creeps me out."

"Then why be here?" Maria asked.

Rebecca's features softened beyond what Ten would have expected. She seemed like such a tough and capable woman. The change surprised him.

"I want to help. Something about all these people. The US has more people in prison than anywhere else in the world. I don't think they all belong here. If I can make it better for just a few of them, well." She took a breath. "People like Elizabeth Cooke, Blake Paton, Nancy Wilmoth... how do they even get into the system?"

"There are as many people who only want to harm others," Maria said. "People who gain a little control or power and want to wield it."

Ten could vouch that Maria knew what she was talking about. Rebecca looked as though she understood too. They had made a connection.

Rebecca gathered herself and before his eyes, she again looked like the strong woman who was meant to do the job. He was glad she was there, even if it was about to disrupt her family.

"Thank you for letting me know. I'll keep everything to myself, of course."

"We know that," Ten said.

She turned her gaze from Maria to Ten. Her eyes softened. They were all there for the same reason—get rid of the bad and do some good.

The morning was short, so they took a drive through the country, stopped at a diner in an adjoining town for lunch, and headed back toward the police station with the intention of arriving by one o'clock. Maria spent some time trying to convince Ten that it was his kindness and good heart that wanted to see good in Nancy.

"I misread her," he said.

"Don't let it disrupt your focus. It happens."

"You know this might prove that the other prison escapes were copycat events. Done by people who actually know how to break through system security. We should let Jacob know."

"I'll wait until he calls me again. He will. He's been calling every day. Then I'll let him know that we have it under control. That we can handle this," she said.

"This may let Philippe off the hook too. He's not planning some big prison break across the country to get his brother free." Ten laughed at the idea. "We've been going in circles," he admitted. "It's nice to stop the spinning for a while. I feel better knowing that Josh's students are clean, that Philippe is innocent, and that we're finally figuring this out."

"Me too. Now we have to figure out why Nancy did what she did."

"Does that even matter at this point?" Ten asked. "Whether she did it to punish Cooke or free Sarah from being abused, she still did it."

"We need to tie things up," Maria said. "What if the breakout was part of the blackmail Cooke was doing with her? If nothing else, it might change the legal outcome. We have to sort it out."

"A lot of options," Ten said.

"Only one is true."

CHAPTER 34

Chief Carney met them on the porch to the station. He leaned against the railing and stood up as they walked up the stairs. His uniform looked starched, right out of the dry cleaners. He was proud of his job and Ten didn't want to mess with that. As they approached, Chief Carney pushed off to stand in front of them. "You might want to know something before going in."

"What's that?" Maria asked.

"Nancy visited Paton last night."

"She did?"

"Yeah. When we went to pick her up this morning, she thought it was about that. She doesn't know that you found those logs you told me about. I didn't tell her either."

"Did she mention why she visited?" Ten asked.

"Said she wanted to yell at him for what he'd written." He scrunched his face in question. "Mentioned some poem."

Ten stood on one of the steps below Carney, looking up at him. "We found her name in one of the poems Paton wrote."

"From the bag in his trunk. Well, she looked pretty mad. Claimed we had no right to arrest her for yelling at him. Said you gave her a pardon and I couldn't do what I was doing. She was not a happy camper."

"She won't be happy once she knows what we found either," Ten said.

He shook his head slowly. "For what it's worth, I thought you did the right thing, surely the kind thing, when you helped her out. Sorry it has turned this way."

"Us too," Maria said. "We're glad we're getting to the bottom of it though."

"One more thing?" Carney said.

"Yeah?"

"Philippe. He's been one hundred percent cooperative. Talk about being kind. I'd like to let him go home. There is still the trail that Josh Hobart found on his computer. But I don't think he's going anywhere."

Maria glanced at Ten for his opinion. "Yeah. I say let him go. I don't think he's involved. Maybe something weird did happen. If that's okay with you, Maria?"

Carney rested his eyes on Maria for the final decision.

"There is still plenty of motive. The fact that his brother is in Allenwood. And he has the skills. Maybe not Muncy, but he could have been a copycat case and figured that he wouldn't get caught while we're looking into who was responsible for Muncy, Texas, et cetera?"

"My two cents?" Ten said. Maria nodded. "Even if that was on his mind and he did hack into Line-Tech, we caught him. He knows we're watching. I don't think he'll take that chance again. We don't know any answers for sure yet anyway. His family must be worried. Traces of something aren't enough. I think we should give him the benefit of the doubt. Of course, I was wrong about Nancy."

Maria turned toward the chief. "Call the bank. Let them know that you picked him up by mistake and that he had nothing to do with anything at all. That he's clean. I wouldn't want this to ruin his job."

"Will do." Chief Carney walked them back to the interrogation room.

"Thank you for clearing that up," Ten said once they sat down. This time there were enough chairs. A tape recorder sat on the table, already running.

"I trust your judgement," Maria said. "And until we know for sure what's going on, there's no reason to ruin his life. Even if it was a temporary bout of bad judgement."

Before Carney brought Paton into the room, an older gentleman with a balding head and bushy eyebrows walked in. He wore a suit even in the hot weather. A different kind of uniform meant to portray a different kind of authority. Extending his hand, he introduced himself in a loud voice. "I'm Chip Watson, legal counsel for Blake Paton."

Ten and Maria both stood. "Nice to meet you," Maria said, even though Chip's eyes were on Ten and his hand extended toward him as well.

Chip cocked his head and swiveled on the balls of his feet to move his hand toward hers. Then he glanced at Ten.

"She's in charge of this investigation," Ten said. "I'm only a consultant on the technical side."

That appeared to satisfy him. He walked around Maria and sat next to Ten while Ten and Maria took their seats again. Chip had a small folder with him and slapped it on the table, placing both hands over it. "Well, Chief Carney will bring him in directly. I asked that he give us a few minutes to get acquainted."

"There's more?" Ten asked.

Chip smiled up at him. "You know I'll recommend that Dr. Paton not say too much, don't you?"

Ten leaned back and let Maria take over. "We're only going to ask questions we know the answers to. And that we have proof of," she explained.

"Then why do it at all?" he asked. "Are you trying to intimidate my client?"

"Not at all. We just want to get the facts straight. Part of what we do," she said.

Chief Carney brought Paton into the room and sat him down across from where Maria normally sat. Once he was seated, she sat down. Carney motioned for Ten to take the other seat.

"Please, take a seat. I plan to stand," Ten said.

"You sit. I'll stand." Carney closed the door and leaned against it.

"I don't have to say anything," Paton said with a quick glimpse at Chip Watson.

Ten figured that Chip told Paton the truth about the situation, that he was in a real jam. Maybe that made Paton cocky or defiant. But Maria didn't seem bothered by the man. She looked over at Chip and back to Paton. "Chip, could you let him know that it's okay to answer yes or no to questions we already have proof of?"

Chip narrowed his eyes in suspicion. "Okay," he said to her before turning back to his client. "Blake, you're allowed to. In fact, I recommend that you cooperate when asked questions they have proof of. But," he added, "only those questions." He smirked at Maria and raised an eyebrow for her to continue.

"Your name is Blake Paton, is that right?"

Now Paton smirked. "Yes."

"You were in possession of photographs and videos of Superintendent Cooke and inmate Sarah Andrews."

"Yes." He glanced at Chip, who nodded.

"You were in love with Elizabeth Cooke—"

Chip interrupted. "That has no bearing on this case."

Maria ignored him and went on. "Your office is equipped with a DVD player and screen."

"Yes."

"You hold sessions in that same office."

"Yes."

"You've worked with Superintendent Cooke for nearly twenty years."

"Yes."

"You know that we are in possession of the poems you wrote about the events happening, and your feelings for Elizabeth."

"Yes."

"You are aware that we've collected evidence from your house and your office."

"Yes."

"You are aware that Nancy is mentioned in one of the poems you wrote."

"Yes."

"You are aware that Nancy was involved with opening the cell doors the night of the escape."

Paton's eyes got big, and he looked at Chip. The lawyer gave a quick shake of his head and shrug of his shoulders. Nuanced. As though no one else might notice.

Chip opened the file in front of him and flipped through a few papers. "That's not here in the documents or the police reports."

"It's coming," Chief Carney said.

"Either way," Chip said, "that has nothing to do with Dr. Paton or his situation. You'll have to talk to Nancy about that."

"We plan to," Maria said. "After we finish here."

"She didn't, did she?" Paton gave Chip an angry look. "That's not true." He sounded incensed. "You don't have proof," he said to Maria. Then he laughed. "You're trying to trick me. If it's not in the file, it didn't happen."

Chip slapped the folder closed and looked flustered. "It's not true until it's in the file, until it's official." He reached toward Paton to get his attention. "It has nothing to do with you."

Chief Carney, from in front of the door, said, "We picked her up this morning. We have proof."

"That bitch," Paton said. "She did all this?"

Maria smiled briefly in a fake way, then got serious. "You did all this, Mr. Paton."

"Doctor!" Paton said.

"Not anymore. Not when we're finished with you."

His eyes filled with tears. The last straw. He began to shake his head slowly back and forth, his eyes dropping.

Chip noticed and leaned forward. "Don't say anything more."

It was like Paton didn't even hear him. He heard only the screaming in his own head. "Elizabeth is dead. Andrews is in confinement. And now you're stripping me of my, of my—"

Chip stood. "We're done here. You're upsetting my client." He picked up his folder. He looked at Carney.

Maria nodded in response. "You're right. We're done here. I'm sure this and a lot more will come out in court."

Carney hauled Paton out of the room. Chip followed without looking at either Ten or Maria. He slammed the door behind him.

"I heard what you did," Ten said after he turned off the tape recorder and they were alone.

"So, what do you think you heard?"

"You verified that he wrote those poems. Possession of photos and DVDs is one thing, but actually writing the poems is another. And the way you worded your question: 'the poems you wrote about the events happening and your feelings for Elizabeth,' the whole thing. The poems can be used as statements now."

She laughed. "To tell the truth, I only thought of it while asking questions. I don't think as far ahead as you do."

"Well, it worked. Those poems are his own words of guilt and I don't think Chip even noticed."

The door opened and Carney walked Nancy into the room. They readied the recorder and uncuffed her. Carney had not even asked about uncuffing Paton.

Nancy was dressed for work in jeans and a tight-fitting pullover blouse that showed her curves in a pleasant way. Her hair was pulled back in a short ponytail to stay out of her way, and she wore a light amount of makeup. She looked a lot better than the last time they were in the same room. She seemed jovial. "Hey, Ten, Maria. Sorry about coming over here last night but after you told me about the poem, I got angry and wanted to face the little weasel." She waited. When no one spoke right away, she looked back and forth between the two of them. "That's it, right?"

"Not quite," Ten said.

Nancy's face got serious. "What's going on?"

Maria sat back in her chair and let Ten handle Nancy.

"The P280 system keeps a log," Ten said.

Her body tensed very little, but Ten noticed. "Not according to the manual," she said.

"I know. I didn't see it mentioned either. Maybe they did that on purpose. I don't know." He thought for a second to mention that Paul actually found it, but then rejected the idea. Why bring him into it unless they had to? "I'll cut to the chase. According to the log, you manually operated the cell doors on that block to allow Sarah Andrews to escape."

"How would I know when to even do that? It was in the middle of the night."

"Video. You saw that she was awake or stirring, and you opened the doors. You probably watched her leave."

"You don't have proof," Nancy said with a slight shiver, as though she got a chill.

"We do. Enough anyway," Ten said.

"Why would I do that?"

"We found a video cued up in Paton's office. A video we know you took because you told us. In that video, you saw what Sarah said into the camera. You saw that she wanted to kill them. Well, one of them. Maybe both."

She sat quietly and took a few breaths, then looked down at her hands in her lap.

"I think they did approach you. When I think back to our conversation, you were a little too grossed out. I think it wasn't the idea but the memory that did that to you. It almost made you sick. I heard you gag."

"He was a pig. She was a monster." Nancy closed her eyes. "I'm glad I did it. I'm glad she's dead. I'm just sorry Sarah didn't have the chance to do it herself. Elizabeth took that chance away from her. I wanted to give her the opportunity. I understood how she felt. I felt the same way toward them." She looked up at Ten. "There!"

"Did they involve you?" he asked.

Maria cocked her head toward Ten in question.

Nancy admitted, "He attacked me once. Grabbed me. Ripped my blouse. He's a weasel. I fought him off and he said he'd get back at me, that he'd tell Elizabeth to fire me. I didn't know what to do. I was up to my neck and they knew it. Once I made that first tape, I couldn't get away. I hated it. I hated myself. He was going to take advantage of the leverage they already had. Just thinking about what he wanted from me, what Elizabeth might do." She looked at Ten. "I'm glad it's over." She lowered her head again and her shoulders shook, but no sound came from her. Though when Carney came over and stood her up, there were no tears in her eyes.

Ten didn't know what to make of it.

CHAPTER 35

The heat of the day slammed into Ten and Maria as they left the police station. Less humidity, more heat. It was only June.

"That was a rough conversation to have," Maria said. "It must have been hard for you to do that."

"Harder for Nancy. In the long run."

"Both of you," Maria said. "You liked her. You believed her."

"I understand wanting to kill those who hurt you. I tried that tactic once, remember? I could be in prison myself if the circumstances weren't exactly aligned in my favor."

"It seems like we're all tied up in one mess or another," she responded.

He knew she understood how he felt. She'd been with him for part of his rampage against the people who had killed the most important people to him: his family. "I appreciate your letting me tell her. I had to make it right, whatever that means."

"You still feel sorry for her. I can see it in your face."

"Maybe that's the favor I ask of Jacob," he said. "Help her out."

"You mean let her go. Completely off the hook."

"She was scared. You do things when you're scared. When you're angry. If not totally off the hook, then at least a lighter sentence. She's young and smart. I hate to see that wasted inside a prison."

She handed Ten the car keys. "We can try talking with Jacob if you want, but please, let's think about it first."

Ten grabbed the keys from her as they walked down the stairs together. "We're clearing things up. Finally. I was thinking. This doesn't mean that the other escapes aren't connected. I know we let Philippe go, and I think that was the right thing to do, but there's still the test taking place at Allenwood. I've got to find out who's in charge over there now that Nancy is completely out of the picture."

"Line-Tech might have to send some people out to finish the jobs."

"That's going to cost the taxpayers," Ten said.

"I'll call Jacob. If I know him, he is going to want us involved until the whole thing is over."

"After taking us off the case?"

"I'll guarantee it. Things have changed. He'll want us here till the bitter end. We may have to fly out of state at some point. Get closer to the problem at other prisons. We're only here because it was the first one. Although, there hasn't been a breakout attempt for a few days."

"Maybe we can keep Roger involved in the test download for Allenwood. Give him a chance to find something we may have missed along the way. If you call Jacob, he's more apt to go along with that."

"You glad Roger's aboard now?"

"Yeah. Roger will make our lives a lot easier. We're operating in his wheelhouse."

"Don't get used to it," she said.

"I won't. The other night on the phone he said he was only doing this for you and me. I believed him. I don't think that offer will ever be extended again. It sounded final even as he was saying it."

"Do you think he's going to discover anything?" she asked.

"I hope not. I'd like to think that Nancy is the answer. I'd like to think that copycats are dumber and are on their way to being caught as we speak."

"Not yet," she said.

"Only a matter of time."

Maria made the call to Jacob. It didn't last long. "Jacob said he would hold tight while we work out the kinks. He said to tell you that he trusts you and he knows you won't stop until it's figured out—regardless of your threats to move on. He also knows you well enough to know that you don't ask for help until it's too late. I think he got nervous, thought it was later than it actually was. This is a big deal. You have to admit that. If it is one person and they let thousands of prisoners loose, well, we've discussed that already. Even if some of the other escapes are copycats, your and Roger's efforts will tell ISTI where to look. Crack one, crack them all. So either way," she said.

"You may be right."

"I am sometimes."

Ten drove haphazardly around the area, partly following the river, partly along patches of woods. They stopped a few times to get out and stretch, to go over what had happened so far. Later, Ten drove out of town and up Route 15 and pulled off on a scenic overlook of the west branch of the Susquehanna River far below and Williamsport in the distance. To his left, sunlight glistened off a wide expanse of water, matching the color of the sky. Farther downstream, he glimpsed an island in the river through the trees growing from the embankment. Fields greened on the other side of the river and stretched toward more trees and hills. The sky was partly cloudy, the sun illuminating the bottoms of cumulous and nimbus clouds. Ten and Maria stood together breathing in the humid air of late afternoon.

"I had to get away from it for a while," Ten admitted. "This is nice. We should come here when it's not a job. I looked it up and there are a few great hiking areas around. Ricketts Glen, Hyner Run, Worlds End."

"We?"

Her comment flustered him. "I didn't mean to suggest—"

She laughed. "I didn't mean to either." She turned back to look out over the vista. "But it might be fun to get away from work, get into the woods, camp."

"I'm sorry. I didn't mean anything. Not from either of my comments. I was just enjoying this, and it came out."

"No need to apologize. You should know that. We're friends. We have history. I'd be glad to hike with you. We do have a standing breakfast date at least once a month. It would be fun to take a casual trip for a change."

"Thanks. You are much more gracious toward me than I deserve."

She swung around to get his attention. Her curly hair shimmered in the sunlight. "You can stop going there. I'm giving you permission. We've been through too much together to be uncomfortable around each other. Both of us. We need to just be ourselves. No expectations. No guarantees. No apologies."

"You're right." He stood back from the railing and stretched his back and arms. "Let's head into Williamsport. It's not far. Just down the other side of the mountain. We can find a place to eat there. The drive back will be pretty."

"Sounds perfect. Get us out of our heads and allow our subconscious to figure all this out, pull the pieces together."

"Wouldn't that be nice."

They drove for another half hour and crossed the Market Street Bridge into Williamsport. Ten took a left onto Fourth Street and drove until it looked like the downtown area ended, took another left on a side street, then another left onto Third Street to go through town again. "A couple of places. Anything strike you?"

Maria pulled out her phone. "Let's try something special tonight. We've been eating poorly." She checked a few things out and said, "Okay, make a left on Market, where we came in and left on Fourth again."

"Did you see something?"

"We didn't go far enough."

When they got close, she said, "Park anywhere; it's on the left up here. The Peter Herdic House."

Ten parked across the street. It was in an old neighborhood with big houses, probably from money when the logging business was going strong in Williamsport. The house was stone along the first floor and brick for the next two, a full porch across the front. It had a castle-like look to it. They walked across the street and under trees that had been planted long ago. There was a foyer inside and then the dining area with round tables and their white tablecloths and comfortable chairs. They were shown to a table for two against one wall. A chandelier of globed lights hung over the center of the room.

"Very nice choice," Ten said as he sat down.

"Well, I thought that since you also had T and E for work..." Maria said.

He laughed. "I get it. You let me put through the big bills."

"We deserve this after last night and today. We'll sleep better."

They ordered wine and toasted. "To our progress so far," Ten said. "I can feel it wrapping up."

They both ordered from the small-plate menu. Ten selected the Shad Herdic which, according to the waiter, was smoked locally and garnished with capers, red onion, house-made pumpernickel and horseradish dill mayonnaise. Maria ordered the grilled shrimp with baby greens, grilled pineapple, pickled sweet onion, and toasted macadamias in a coconut vinaigrette. Neither of them had dessert, even after ogling over crème brûlée and Daisy's bread pudding. They did have coffee though.

Ten leaned onto his elbows and said, "This was a great idea."

"Glad you liked it. Me too. It was just nice to relax and get out of Dodge for a change."

"We're never fully away though, are we?"

"You're going to bring it up. Well, I tried."

"Okay. I'll wait. But if you can drive part of the way back to the hotel, I'll give Josh a quick call and have him talk with Roger again. I still need to get to the guy handling the Allenwood project too."

"You can let Chief Carney do that. He'd appreciate helping. He likes being part of the whole thing. This will make his career worth it."

"Good idea."

"Settled," she said, raising her coffee in a toast.

The rest of the time they talked briefly about Ten going to see Carol, the psychologist, once they were back home. They talked about Maria's other work, and how she was thinking of switching to ISTI on a more regular basis.

"Even though this was not easy?" Ten asked.

She gazed at him across the table. "I feel like I'm actually helping. More than I do at work. This isn't easy, but it feels right for some reason."

"You're looking at me like you want me to do the same," he said.

"I don't expect anything from you. Maybe you can help sometimes. Like you have been." She shrugged. "I'm getting used to your company. The way you think."

"I don't think so," Ten said. "You know how I feel about that."

"You won't always feel that way."

Ten paid for dinner. They left around 8:15. Early evening. "We were in there longer than I'd thought," he said. "Maybe we'll get to see the sun setting along the way."

"Check to see when sunset is supposed to happen. With these clouds, it should be beautiful."

Ten checked and the sun was setting around 8:40. "Give or take a few minutes."

Maria drove while Ten made his first calls. He asked Carney to alert the Allenwood people that Josh and Roger were going to be involved with the scheduled test. He talked with Josh next, about how he and Roger were to work together, and also asked him to go through the P280 archive with PJ early in the morning to see if they noticed any other anomalies. "I'll make sure you get paid for your time." Ten hung up as Maria turned around to enter the scenic turnout. "I'll let Paul know quickly to meet Josh and let him into the IT equipment room."

"You'd better let Rebecca know. Maybe call Carney back and have him take care of the logistics."

"Good idea."

She pulled into the space. Several cars were parked in the lot. Couples lined up along the railing. Already the sky was ablaze with color. They got out, both with their eyes affixed on the sky overlooking the river, the fields, the far mountains. Every color imaginable, from green and blue to yellow and red, and all mixtures and shades shifted and changed as the sun moved down the slope in the back of the Earth's room, which was how Ten thought of it. Something about sunset made Ten recall the space that people occupied in the world. Like a giant room made up of how far one could see in any one direction. No matter where you looked, there was always an end, a horizon. Sometimes he felt closer to it than others. But no matter how large it appeared, it always ended. Like a wall. He felt he was always inside that room, unable to escape. There was no door out, no door in.

Maria nudged his shoulder. "You're falling," she said.

Ten smiled briefly. "Even out here. In this," he waved toward the expanse before them, "I sometimes feel closed in and alone."

She removed the keys from her pocket and handed them to him. "You need to focus on driving. Let go of all that,

Ten. It's not serving you anymore. There are more important things in the world."

Ten felt reprimanded. More importantly, he felt found out.

While driving back to the hotel, he contemplated her words. He had sunk into himself and she had noticed. She was right. It might be time to stop mourning his past and focus on what he was involved with right now.

As though she had heard his thoughts, Maria said, "You don't have to forget Amy or what happened, any of it, to also allow yourself to move on. Don't you think she would have wanted that for you?"

"I do," he said, but the words only reminded him of his wife, not how he should move on.

CHAPTER 36

Ten's emotions had been pulled in all directions over the past few days. From the revelations about Nancy and the disgust with Paton to the wonderful meal and inspirational sunset to the letdown he felt when Jacob removed them from the case—if only for a short while. A crazy few days filled with revelations and juxtapositions. He reviewed those events that morning while sitting on the edge of his bed. Things that should have made him feel better only made him feel worse. Both cases were unravelling, but with the wrong people involved, people he didn't expect. Maybe Jacob was right to question him.

His churned-up emotions brought back the confusion he had been dealing with since his whole life changed. These events had him delving back in to the past. He pulled his shoulder forward to look at the scars. Maria was right to reprimand him. He needed to get over his problems and move on. Intellectually, it made sense. Other people *did* have it worse than he did, and they got through their problems much more smoothly than he had.

Ten got up and washed his face and used the bathroom. He exercised vigorously for fifteen minutes, building a light sweat, then jumped into the shower. He took his clothes with him in case Maria brought coffee early again. He was surprised he hadn't heard from her yet. There was a lot to go through that day. She would want to get started soon, even now that they had help both locally and through ISTI.

The situation for them had definitely changed. Normally, he would be overwhelmed with so many people involved but he was beginning to feel supported. Really, he didn't have to do everything himself and couldn't if he wanted to. It was time to accept the help of specialists.

He dressed and sat down at his laptop. It was almost seven-thirty. Maria was usually up. He knocked on the wall, then sat down. A half hour later, he decided to go get her.

At her door, Ten pressed the key card against the reader and listened for the click. He turned the handle and pushed lightly. "Hey, you in there?"

Nothing.

He pushed his way in and walked past the bathroom half wall to see an unmade bed but no Maria. He looked in the bathroom and stood there for a moment. A damp towel hung on the back of the door and the shower and sink had been used recently. Makeup bottles littered the counter. Her hair dryer sat next to a glass that held her toothbrush and paste, the cord unplugged and curled around the body of the dryer.

He rushed back to his room and grabbed his phone from the nightstand. He selected her number from his favorites, and she picked up on the second ring. "Hi, sleepyhead."

"Where are you?"

"You sound upset. Didn't you see my note?"

"What note?"

"I left a note on the dresser in my room. I thought it would be the first thing you saw. Chief Carney picked me up early this morning. I wanted to talk with Nancy again. Get more details. I didn't want to wake you. After yesterday, you seemed tired. Carney texted me late last night about something one of the other inmates told one of his officers. I had to check it out."

"I didn't see the note, but I'll go get it. I'm ready now." Hearing her voice gave him some relief. She was safe. "I'll grab coffee and head down there."

"Head to the prison. We're done here and I want to see what Paul and Josh found out, if anything."

"Be there when I can." He hung up. His heart raced. What had he expected to be wrong? He wasn't quite over what had happened to him. PTSD. He had to work on that.

He found the note in her room lying on the dresser as she'd said. The pocketknife she had intercepted from him at the drugstore held the note down like a paperweight. The first part of the note was simple: *Had an idea. Went to talk with Nancy. Carney picking me up.* Then there was a line and a second note. *I had no right to take the knife from you. I'm your friend, not your mother. Forgive me.*

He picked up the knife and held it for a few seconds, considering what to do with it. Finally, he threw it into her trash basket along with the note. He rushed back to his room. After gathering his things together, he went downstairs and filled a Styrofoam cup with fruit and poured two coffees for himself. Inside the car, he shoved the coffees into the cup holders and stuffed the fruit cup between his legs. He opened the car windows.

The morning smelled fresh, birds chirped, and the air felt cool. As much as he liked working with Maria, it was nice to be alone. He took his time driving past fields, along the river, past woods and houses. He thought about the knife and double guessed his decision, then settled on it being the right one. He knew he might change his mind once he was back home, but for now, this was the right decision for him. For now, it was a start in making better decisions.

As he walked toward the administration building, Maria and Chief Carney were coming out of the building and down the stairs.

"That was quick," Ten said. "Didn't they find anything?"

"Premeditated," Maria said.

"What?" He stopped on the stairs below her and Carney, looking up at them.

"There were several entries buried. Nancy tried to let Sarah escape several times, both before and after the tests. She planned it. Each attempt happened when Bertie was on guard either alone or with someone else who was on break. We checked with Rebecca about the schedules."

"She was serious."

"That she was," Maria said.

"I sense there's more to it than that. You said you talked with her this morning."

Maria and Carney stepped down and Ten followed them as they walked together toward the parking lot. "Paton did more than grab her and rip her clothes. That was only what happened the first time. She thought that would be the last of it."

"*The first time*. You're going to explain that statement, aren't you?" he said.

"Her reaction the other morning after admitting what she'd done. It bothered me. She shivered but there were no tears. I couldn't figure out if it was because she had no remorse or that her anger was so deep that she felt vindicated for her actions. Or that it was worse than she said."

Ten waited. They stopped by his car.

"He raped her," Maria said. "She was ashamed. It hit her so deeply that she'd lost her sense of emotion, you might say. Her reaction was going to be screaming rage or nothing. It should have been screaming rage. Anger. But it wasn't. She detached."

"Raped," Ten said. "This will change everything for her moving forward, won't it?"

"I think so. I hope so. In a good way for her trial. But she'll need help getting through this. Maybe for years. And I can't see her working here anymore. That would be horrible. I think she held to this because even with everything that happened, her work here was stable. She knew how to do it. It hadn't changed." Maria turned around and smiled at Chief Carney. "Thank you for being there with me this morning."

"My pleasure," he said, his eyes not leaving her for long. She got into the car and gave him a little wave.

Ten joined her, putting the keys in the ignition but not yet starting the car. "I'm sorry. You could have woken me."

"You were so tired. You're not sleeping well. And you spend too much energy in the past."

"You left the knife," he said.

"I didn't have the right to do that. I can't help you unless you ask me to, and I surely can't help by interfering. You need support. You need people who believe in you. That wasn't me. I thought I could fix you. Only you can fix you." She tightened her lips and lowered her head. Her voice broke. "I just want you to feel better."

"I understand. And I do." He started the car. "I threw the knife away. It's in the garbage can in your room. With the note."

"That wasn't because of me. You made that decision."

"I know."

It was only a little after nine, so they decided on a real breakfast and stopped at the diner. Bacon and eggs. Hash browns. And more coffee. "How do you think this evening will go?" Maria asked.

"I think we're finished," Ten said. "We've been all over the map with this, but knowing about Nancy's part in this, I'm starting to believe in copycat cases, which includes what Philippe was trying to do. I'm glad we interrupted him. There's not enough on his computer to convict him and as long as he sticks with his malware defense, I'm sure he's off the hook."

"Valeria?"

"Unlucky that she was there. Lucky it wasn't her computer. I'm giving her the benefit of the doubt. Her life can't be easy. She doesn't need us breathing down her neck."

"So you think she could have been the one trying to break in. After all, Josh said it looked like her signature."

Ten leaned back to think for a moment. "I do. But he believes in those kids. Either way, like I said, not enough evidence. I don't think either one of them would try again. Not after we showed up."

"One more thing. No one has been caught in reference to the other prisons. And you were right: each minor breakout occurred a few days after the test run. They still could be connected." She waited for his reply.

"Could be." He popped the last piece of bacon into his mouth and chased it with coffee.

"You don't think they are now."

"I'm done guessing," Ten admitted. "I'm ready for proof. And I believe Roger and Josh are going to provide that."

That afternoon, Maria and Ten spent time apart, each of them writing reports about what they'd discovered. At some point, they'd go through each report together to be sure they caught everything and weren't too out of joint with each other. Then, once the job was finished, they'd turn them in to Jacob for review and filing. Ten also made a few calls, one to Josh, one to Roger, to discuss how they might work together. He had a plan, even though they were the experts at this point.

Early evening, they called Chief Carney and invited him to dinner at Mulan. He was at a table when they arrived and stood until Maria sat down. "Thank you for inviting me," he said.

"You helped us a lot," Ten said.

"Not with any of the technical stuff," he said.

"You helped where it counts." Maria patted his hand.

"You think we're finished?" he asked. "Almost?"

"Hoping," she said before turning the next part of the conversation over to Ten.

He explained, "After we're through with dinner, you can go with us. We're meeting Josh Hobart at Allenwood, along with the lead over there. A guy named Frank. After

Frank logs in using his secure code, Josh and Roger go to work. They're hooked up somehow and will simultaneously download the test procedure from Line-Tech as it's fed into the P280 system controller."

"What are they looking for?" Carney asked.

"Anything they can find," Ten said. "But I've asked Josh to monitor Line-Tech for interference. That's why he's there." He smiled.

"You have something up your sleeve," Carney said.

"The other night, when we caught Philippe inside Line-Tech—or thought we did—that was the night the download was originally set for. I suspect Line-Tech has a log of that information on their site, a schedule. Anyone clever enough to get into their system would be able to reach that. It's most likely not as secure as the test downloads. I suspect it's updated regularly. It might even be open to anyone installing the P280 system."

Maria said, "And since the download is actually happening tonight... whoever was in there will be back."

"And you'll watch it happen," Carney said.

"Well, Roger will watch it happen. That's our associate at ISTI who's the real expert here," Ten said. "And Josh, of course."

Carney cocked his head and nodded toward Ten. "A leader knows who to pull together to get the job done."

"I appreciate that," Ten said.

After a pleasant dinner and more normal discussion about Muncy, the high school, and the limited crimes that Carney had to deal with regularly, they drove two different cars over to Allenwood, where they met Josh Hobart.

FCI Allenwood was a medium-security federal correctional institution located nearby in White Deer, Pennsylvania. It harbored male offenders, with a population hovering around eleven hundred; a dozen or so inmates were immigrants picked up by ICE and awaiting decisions. Ten knew that one of those men was Ricardo Marin,

Valeria's father and Philippe's brother. He hoped like hell they weren't involved.

The building looked much newer and more modern than the Muncy facility. They met with officials out front and were introduced to Frank and another member of his team, Allan, and followed them to the IT equipment area.

"This must be a big deal," Frank said.

"It is," Maria answered.

Frank, like most of the men they'd met while there, looked surprised that Maria answered. He got over it quickly though. What did he care? "Sorry to hear about Nancy. What did she do anyway? Is she still in custody?"

"All that will come out eventually," Carney told him, shutting down that conversation.

In the equipment room, Josh got on his phone to Roger and sat down at the computer. Frank leaned over for a moment and logged in. He stepped back. "All yours." He looked at Maria. "So, it's been a long day. Allan here is our night guy in case anything goes wrong. Can I go home?"

"We'd like you to stay," Maria said in no uncertain terms. "As you said, if anything should go wrong."

"Yes, ma'am." He sat at another desk while Allan watched what Josh was up to.

"You're pretty slick at this," Allan said.

"Thank you." Josh kept at it. He huffed and turned toward Ten, who stepped forward.

"Find something?"

"I'm shocked at how many people are trying to hack into a system like this all at the same time. It looks like several."

"Can you sort them out?" Ten asked.

"Do you mean are any of them Philippe?" Then he held up his finger to halt the conversation. He wore an earbud and was listening to Roger through his phone. "Roger doesn't see anything wrong yet. He's asking what he's looking for."

Ten glanced at Maria. "Shouldn't he know?"

"He wants a clue," Josh answered. "There are a lot of avenues."

Ten paced away from the desk, his hand to his forehead. "We all want a fucking clue." He walked in a big circle, then raised his eyes toward Maria.

"What?" she said.

"Something you told me. A memory from the pictures."

"Okay?" she questioned.

"Is it possible that one of these hackers is also piggybacking onto the download?"

Josh nodded. "He heard you and is looking. He hadn't thought of that." He laughed.

"What is it?" Maria asked.

"Some kind of mutual admiration society. He just called Ten a genius."

They all laughed at that. Maria took Ten's arm. "He is a genius."

"Found something," Josh relayed.

The whole room lit up with happy faces. "We might be getting there," Ten said.

"We're tracking together." Josh stopped and sat back.

"Did you lose it?"

"It's coming from Philippe's computer again." He shook his head. "I sure hope someone's hacked through his system and it's not him."

"We all do," Maria said.

Carney shifted his weight from one foot to another, then back. "Do we go there again? Tonight?"

"Too late," Josh said. He popped the earbud cord out of his phone and handed it to Ten. "He wants to talk with you."

Ten took the phone and walked out the door away from the others. "Roger?"

"I have the plan and didn't want to relay it through someone who wasn't part of the ISTI team."

"Go on."

"I'm in the middle of this. It won't take much longer. Maybe a half hour. Can I call you later?"

"Sure. I'll wait for your call."

"An hour, hour and a half. I want to doublecheck a few things. And you can tell Josh he can get out now. He can go home. You all can. You're finished there. Go back to your hotel."

"I'll wait for you to touch base later," Ten said.

"I'm not sure what I'm getting and what it might mean. I'll call you."

Ten walked back into the room. All eyes were on him.

"We're finished here." Then he shook his head at all the faces staring at him. He wasn't going to answer any questions. "Wrap it up," he said.

CHAPTER 37

Maria waited with Ten in his hotel room. "That was an ominous message."

"Roger's not usually so cryptic, which makes me wonder what's going on."

"Carney looked disappointed we didn't explain everything to him before disbanding," she said.

"I don't blame him for that. But it's our investigation and at a certain point, we have to hold the cards. You can relay bits of information to him as we decide it's okay to do so." He cut himself off. "Sorry. You're in charge of this. I'm only an onlooker. I don't mean to tell you how to run this."

"Never stopped you before. Besides, you know that's not true," she said. "Regardless how you say things, I know you're providing an opinion. And anyway, I agree with you. If I didn't, you know I'd say so. We'll parse the information out as appropriate."

"Once we get Roger's email, we'll know more."

"You think it's Philippe," she said.

"It's not him," Ten said.

"Who would take over his computer?"

His phone rang. "I hope we're about to find out."

Roger said, "You were right. It took me a while to get it all straight but there was a piggyback instruction set over the standard payload that doesn't kick in for two days." He laughed. "Very ingenious. Pieces of information were scattered to a variety of passive sensors, temperature, pressure, and keyed to fall into place when the program kicked in. That's the short story."

"The two-day wait?"

"You're there. You tell me."

"To give the installation team time to make any final adjustments before putting the system online," Ten said.

"Of course. By the way, the tests came back perfect. Going online will be inevitable. They won't hesitate. And I can guarantee they won't be paying attention because they'll be working on the next section."

"What's the new set of instructions doing?" Ten asked.

"That's what I wanted to talk with you about. I was curious and called Jacob to check to see what they'd found out about the other breakouts."

"And?"

"They're stumped. Nothing is showing up. I'm not surprised. They didn't know what to look for. You figured it out."

"What are you getting at, Roger?" Ten widened his eyes toward Maria.

"Put it on speaker phone," she whispered.

Ten pushed the SPEAKER button and set the phone on the dresser next to the TV. "Maria's here with me."

"Oh, hi, Maria. Did Ten tell you what I told him the other night?"

"He did and that was very nice of you to say. We're thrilled to have you helping." She made an exaggerated shrug with her palms up, expressing the idea of 'what should I do except answer him?'

"I meant it. I wouldn't do this for Jacob, only you two."

"Well, again, thank you. So, what did you find out about the case?"

"Ah, back to business. Yes. Okay." He didn't sound upset and kept going with little hesitation. "Once the instruction set has engaged, it immediately deletes itself. They'll never find out who's involved. At least that's what normally happens. I've been able to find traces in the past but it's really difficult and unlikely. If you have to know, there are organizations that do this for a living. They can help. You probably won't need that. If I know Ten, he's figured this out already."

"What does this all mean?" Ten asked. "Where do we go from here? I need proof. I don't have that if everything is deleted."

"Sorry, guys. I can only supply so much information about where things came from and what the instructions are. If it ties in tightly enough, maybe you can do something with that. You'll still have to catch the people red-handed."

"You must have more information that can help us."

"Oh yeah," Roger said. "That's the interesting part. I keep getting off track. In talking with Jacob, he said that each prison had a different cell block and different set of cells that opened for a short while and then closed. A limited number of people escaped each time, and then only those who heard the doors click open or were already awake. Some prisoners didn't escape even though their doors were open for a short period of time during the night. Apparently, they slept through the opportunity. Which tells you that it's either random or the person doing this doesn't care if the prisoners escape or not."

"Practice runs," Ten said.

"You got it."

"What about Allenwood?"

"Only one cell is opening," Roger said.

Ten again looked at Maria. This time he nodded.

"You there? I expected you to be excited to hear that," Roger asked.

"We're here," Ten said. "And we're very excited to hear that. I guess I should ask, which cell?"

"I'm going to email you the block and cell number along with other information I found in the instructions. You'll want to see who's in that cell. I suspect that will confirm your suspect."

Ten nodded his head. "I think I already know."

"I figured you would. Like I said, I know you. You probably figured it out long ago but didn't want to accept your own determination until you had proof. You're good at this. Hopefully my help just got you a lot closer."

"I can't thank you enough."

"No worries, my friend. My *friends*. This is it though. I'm sorry. I have to walk away, but I owed you."

"Debt paid," Maria said.

"Come see me sometime. Really," Roger said. They talked for a few minutes more while Maria and Roger caught up, then said their goodbyes.

"Now what?" Maria asked.

"We find out who's in that cell," Ten said, sitting down with his laptop.

Maria walked behind him and leaned over his shoulder as he pulled up his email. Roger's email had just arrived. He opened it, wrote down the block and cell number. The additional information Roger included mentioned the time of the operation, a signal to freeze the videos from recording, and subsequently which doors would open sequentially as part of the escape route. "We'll call Allenwood in the morning and find out who's in that cell. In the meantime, let's get a good night's sleep."

Maria gave him a hug before leaving. "I'm proud of you." She didn't have to say why—he knew and it had nothing to do with the case.

Ten took the stairs to the lobby and grabbed a cup of coffee. Once back in his room, he set the coffee cup on the nightstand next to his phone, then stacked pillows at the head of the bed, stripped to his underwear, and leaned against the pillows. He had a hunch—he was sure everyone had the same hunch—about who was in that cell, but until he made any accusations, even to himself, he'd wait until he verified who it was.

He thought through the investigation and everything they had found out while he sat there drinking his coffee. Eventually, he slid down into the bed and turned out the light. He couldn't sleep. He tried. And it wasn't the coffee. He turned on the light and grabbed his phone. It wasn't difficult to find the phone number he needed. When Rebecca answered sleepily, Ten apologized.

She sounded tired but not annoyed. "You're not that sorry or you wouldn't have called. Well, you called for a reason."

"I need a favor."

"About the breakouts or the sex scandal?"

"Breakouts."

"What can I do for you?"

***

The next morning Maria carried coffee, fruit, and Danish to his room like normal. It was sitting on the table and dresser long before Ten got out of the shower. She had yelled through the door once she'd arrived, so he knew she'd be waiting. He ran his hand through his hair before walking out.

"When do you want to check on that cell number?" she asked right away.

"I couldn't help myself."

"What did you do?"

"I called Rebecca late last night. Well, early this morning, for a favor."

"I probably already know. We all do but tell me anyway."

"Ricardo Marin and another guy named Alfonzo Rios."

"Yeah, that's who I thought." Maria hung her head. "What do we do with that information now that we have it?"

"We don't have a choice. We have to catch everyone in the act. So we wait. We let it happen."

"There are too many suspects. Is that part of the reason?"

"Three as I count them," Ten said, opening the possibilities as wide as he could. "For the plan and software, that is. There could be others involved."

"It happens tomorrow night," she said. "Who else do we let get involved?"

"We can't say anything to anyone. I asked Rebecca to keep it quiet too."

"Carney?"

Ten thought for a moment. "Ultimately, that's your call. You're in charge."

"You don't suggest it?"

"I know you'd like him to know, but I worry about how he might participate. I think we have to finish this on our own."

"He'd rush in with guns blazing, ready to arrest everyone," she said, understanding Ten's reluctance. "I'll talk with him and let him know we have a plan in place without letting him know the details about what's going to happen. I'll let him know we'll be working the case alone for the next few days. He may not like it, but he'll understand."

"As long as it comes from you."

She smiled sheepishly. "He's a nice man."

"And he's been helpful. Never pushed his way in. Very respectful. We owe him a call. Tell him we'll explain when it's over."

"Maybe I'll wait and call him later."

Ten nodded, already thinking about how he might approach the pending situation and having no real idea where to start. He didn't like the feeling. It made him feel vulnerable.

That day, Ten and Maria went through their collective notes and each report they had written, doublechecking their deductions for both cases. Writing and going through their reports meant they stuck around the hotel, which allowed them to relax much of the day. They did take some time to have a brief conversation with Ana, Philippe's daughter who worked in IT for the police station. Carney didn't complain when they asked him to step outside. Ana answered all their questions without hesitation. Afterward, they had a quiet dinner together and got a good night's sleep. The calm before the storm. They both knew it.

The day of the event, Ten and Maria decided to drive the forty-five minutes it took to get to Ricketts Glen State Park. They wanted to explore the area before they were finished with the case and had to drive back home. They hiked for several hours that afternoon. On their way back toward the car, Maria broke the silence they had carried with them most of the day. "Should we consider following each of the suspects? Or pick up Ricardo once he's out?"

"I don't think this will be that difficult once he's escaped. I can only guess though. Like I said before, there may be more than one person involved and we'll want to catch them all, including if someone picks him up, where they take him, and who all is there when he arrives. He won't be able to stay home, so maybe they're planning to go back to Mexico."

"Or go to another state," she suggested.

"I'm not sure I'd try that."

"You expect there are more people involved?"

"I don't expect anything in particular, but I was thinking, while we were hiking, there might be other friends of his who we don't know about who are helping. His mechanic buddies. We haven't talked with any of them. His family will have to know eventually. I get the sense that they're not all onboard yet. We'll see."

"Should we call Carney at the last minute? As backup? Especially if there are a lot of people involved. And if not him, then those FBI agents?"

"We can do this," Ten said. "I expect everyone involved to be in the same room at some point. They'll have to be. Like you suggested before, Carney will get in the way."

"You expect Ricardo to be at his brother's house eventually."

"You're digging," he said.

"Well, you haven't announced who you think is involved. And logic has it that since Philippe's computer appeared to be used both times Josh traced the hacker, Ricardo would end up there."

He stopped walking. They were almost to the car. "I don't know why I'm being so mysterious. Maybe it's caution. Maybe I'm not completely positive I know who's doing the hacking."

"You can tell me. I won't hold it against you if you're wrong."

"I know," he said. "I just want to be sure."

Once they were in the car, Maria asked, "Are you sure now?" She smiled at him.

"Okay, okay. You know I don't think it's Philippe."

"Ana?"

"Valeria," Ten said.

Maria pursed her lips and looked through the window at the path they had just left. "The piggyback thing."

"Yeah. That has stuck with me more than anything else."

"Why not Philippe?"

"I don't think Philippe would do it. He'd be putting his family in jeopardy. He's seen what it's done to Ricardo's family. He wouldn't do that to his own."

"And Ana?"

"You were there. She's been so out of the picture. She lives in a small apartment on her own, has her own boyfriend, her own life. She seemed shocked when we brought her dad in a few days ago. No. I don't think she's ever been involved." He pulled from the parking lot. "She could be a good liar though."

"We'll find out tonight," Maria said. "Tonight."

CHAPTER 38

Allenwood was not alerted about the breakout. If they were going to catch anyone, everything had to go as planned. That meant waiting it out. Ten and Maria took a short nap early in the evening and met at two a.m.—the time Roger emailed that the sequence would start. They took their time, getting themselves together, grabbing their guns, going downstairs, stopping in the foyer near the front desk for two coffees.

"I can practically hear that first door open," Ten said.

Yes, there would be a guard, more than one, but they wouldn't be looking for any problems. And according to Roger's analysis, the cameras would be looped in sequence, showing empty hallways. If all was timed properly, and there was no reason to think otherwise, no inside help would be needed. Ricardo—and his lucky roommate—would walk out as though he had the keys to the place. It sounded insane, but it wasn't.

Ten and Maria sat in the car, made sure they had what they needed, and left the parking lot toward Valeria's house. They arrived a half hour later, and parked down and across the street. When the clock hit an hour after the escape should have happened, Ten got nervous.

"Maybe someone should have followed them as they escaped," Maria suggested.

"They have to regroup somewhere. And I'm sure I know where."

"What if they picked him up and drove off?"

"They wouldn't do that. They're family. They'll come together for a reunion first. At least that's what I thought. But I don't know now. I had it all figured out."

"You could still be right. Maybe he's already here. If the escape went smoothly enough and someone waited for him, picked him up, he could be here."

"Let's take a look."

They left the car and walked around to the back of the house. Ten had his Glock in his hand just in case he'd need it. Lights were on in the kitchen, faded behind the blinds. It could have been a stove light left on as a nightlight or it could be just enough light for them to gather in the kitchen early in the morning. "That has to be them," Ten whispered as he walked up and knocked on the back door.

"I don't hear anything," Maria said.

Ten tried the knob, but the door was locked. He knocked again. He looked at Maria. "Go to the front and make sure he doesn't go out that way."

She shook her head at him. "We could have asked for help."

"Carney would have brought a team and broken in, disrupted everyone in the neighborhood."

Maria walked toward the front of the house and Ten was about to knock again when a woman's voice yelled through the door. "Who is it? And what do you want?"

"Mrs. Marin, I'm Tempest Nesbit from ISTI. You talked with my associate, Maria."

"What do you want? It's too early."

"We suspect your husband has escaped and is coming here."

"The door unlocked and opened." Mrs. Marin backed from the door, staring at Ten's Glock.

He shoved it into the back of his pants.

"How would you know that? Did you hear something?" She wore a bath robe tightly around her, arms crossed over the front, her eyes penetrating his. "Where is your friend?

The woman I met?" Her eyes darted behind him, looking for Maria as though she didn't believe Ten.

"I'm here," Maria came into the kitchen from inside the house.

Mrs. Marin swung around, surprised to see her.

Valeria, dressed in shorts and a wrinkled t-shirt, stood next to Maria. "I saw her at the front door and let her in."

Ten shot Maria a look. "He's not here," she said.

Ten shook his head. He looked at Mrs. Marin and Valeria. "This is highly critical government business. If you tell anyone we were here, you can be arrested and go to prison for the rest of your life." He looked at each of them. "You understand?"

"Yes," Mrs. Marin said, "but what's this about?"

Ten looked at Valeria.

"Yes. I understand," she said.

"I'll explain later. We have to go." Maria followed him out the back door and around the house, right behind him as he ran to the car, got in, and pulled onto the street. "I was wrong. You were right. It's Philippe. I don't know how I was so off the mark."

"It's okay," she said.

"No, it's not. It may be too late. If I fucked up and he got away... Shit."

The drive was short. Philippe's house was as dark as Valeria's when they arrived. Ten rushed to the front door and knocked hard and loud and continually.

Philippe yelled from inside the house, clomped down the hall, and opened the door in shorts and a t-shirt. "You again. What can I help you with this time? And why do you work late at night always?"

"Your brother. A software download was supposed to open his cell door tonight. For him to escape."

Philippe got a confused look on his face. "He's free?"

Maria stepped forward. "We don't actually know for sure. But it was supposed to happen over an hour ago."

"You don't know, but you think he's here?"

"Can we look around really quick?" Maria asked.

"Yes." Philippe backed away from the door for them to enter. It was a small house, and in a few minutes, they had been through every room and out the door again, apologizing about the interruption.

"Look," Ten started, then realized how stupid he'd been, "we're sorry." He turned away with his head down. "Why am I so wrong about this." The door clicked behind them.

"Maybe it *was* Ana?"

"Or the mechanics we never talked with. Jesus. I wouldn't expect any one of them to be a software guy though. So what did I miss? This is not what I do well. I don't even know where to go to next. I thought I knew. It all made perfect sense in my head." He sat in the car and started it but didn't put it in gear. "Call Carney," he said reluctantly. "We need help. This has been a massive failure. I may have allowed the escape. What was I thinking?" Maria pulled her phone from her pocket. "Call that guy from the FBI too, Agent Munson." Ten felt the adrenaline pulsing now. "Ask Carney to deal with the mechanics. He probably knows them already. The FBI can chase down the other students. They are familiar with them."

"And us?"

"It'll be morning in a few hours." He closed his eyes and shook his head, trying to clear up the muddy pool it had become.

Maria shuffled in her seat. The phone was ringing. Before Carney picked up, she said, "I think we should call to be sure the escape actually took place. We've been all around this. What if they aborted? If they're waiting for us to get out of here?"

Ten laughed in despair. "God. Wouldn't that be so utterly fucked up?" He nodded. "Of course. Anyone who was inside the Line-Tech system while Roger and Josh were there might also have made a new plan. I feel like I missed something so crucial yet have no idea what it would be."

Maria talked with Chief Carney for a brief time and hung up. She answered Ten. "If you missed it, you wouldn't know," she said. "Get out. I'll drive. You think. I know it's in there somewhere. Roger does too."

"I missed the whole thing. I don't know where to look anymore."

Maria jumped out of the car and so did Ten. They switched places. "I'll call Munson. You call Rebecca and see if Ricardo escaped."

"Yes, ma'am."

In a few minutes, Maria hung up from her call to Agent Munson's house. "He wasn't happy that I called him at home. Wondered how we got his number at first, then it dawned on him that we have the same resources he does. How about Ricardo? Are we on a wild goose chase?"

"Don't know yet. I have to say, Rebecca seems to take all this in stride. Either that or she's getting used to me calling in the middle of the night. Anyway, she said she'd call me back."

They sat together for a short while when Ten cocked his head and stared out the window for a moment before turning swiftly toward Maria.

"What?" His demeanor had changed.

"Josh Hobart."

"Seriously. What motive would he have?"

"He loves those kids. Maybe he didn't want to watch Valeria suffer without a father. Wouldn't that be enough of a motive? We know nothing of his background. He could have been in foster care for all we know. Or abandoned. Anything."

"Let's head to Josh's house. Worst case, we find out on the way that Ricardo never escaped, and we don't have to wake him this early in the morning. Then at least someone gets a break," Maria said as she drove.

A few minutes later, Rebecca called. "You were right. He's gone. They had no idea. Didn't find out until I called and asked about him. I requested that they wait for my call back before telling the police, but they refused. I couldn't prove who I was, and they have protocols to administer. Sorry. This just opened up bigger than you probably wanted. I thought you'd want to know."

"Alfonzo?"

"Interesting you should ask. The guard on duty happened to be there the night Ricardo got beaten and had to be taken to the hospital. Assholes put him right back in with the guy who did it."

"Alfonzo didn't escape with Ricardo, then."

"Ricardo knocked him out before leaving. They found Alfonzo alone in the cell. A big lump on his head."

"Thank you," Ten said. "You've gone beyond the call."

"It is my calling," she said.

Ten hung up and said, "I like her more every time we talk."

"She'll be good for those women over there." Maria was almost to Josh Hobart's house. A light haze from the rising morning sun crested the eastern hills. "Getting close to sunrise. Josh might be up already anyway."

"We'll wake him if he's not. But if he's involved, he'll be up."

"And perhaps not here," she said.

"Or they'll both be here. He helped us. Who would suspect him? This might be the safest place to hole up for a short while. Let things settle down, then head out of town."

Maria parked down the street. Ten had his Glock with him again. Maria had her gun in her side holster. Ten knocked at Josh's front door.

Josh took a few minutes but answered the door dressed in jeans and a t-shirt. The Who, Ten noticed. "Hey."

"Can we come in?"

"You have your gun out. Am I under arrest for something?"

"Not yet."

A woman stepped into the hallway from a back bedroom. "What's going on, Josh?"

"I don't know yet. But I'm guessing it's serious." He backed away from the door. "Come in. And you can put that away. I'm not going anywhere."

"I'll get dressed," the woman said.

Josh led them into the kitchen. "That was my wife, Mel. She'll be here in a second. Forgive me if I don't look worried, but the FBI has shown up on my doorstep several times lately and now you guys. I must be getting used to it."

Mel walked into the kitchen and Josh introduced her to Ten and Maria. After they shook hands, she walked to the cabinet. "Coffee?"

"Absolutely," Josh said.

She turned from the counter. "You guys look like you've been up all night."

"Coffee would be great," Maria said.

"What happened?" Josh asked as he sat down and motioned for them to do the same. "Did Ricardo escape?" When no one spoke, he said, "Isn't that what all this is about. That's why we went to Philippe's house the other night. Did you pick him up?" His head moved back and forth between them, confused.

The drip coffeemaker spit in the background. Mel clanked cups as she pulled them from the cabinet and placed them onto the counter. The refrigerator seal popped with a hush of air as she opened it to get half-and-half from the shelf.

Ten stared for a moment. "Something isn't right," he said.

"I'm not following any of this," Josh said.

Ten heard all the clanking and rustling, observed how calm Josh and Mel were, and didn't know what to make of it.

Were they totally innocent or totally guilty? "Ricardo Marin escaped from prison late last night or early this morning."

"Expected," Josh said.

Mel stopped what she was doing and turned around to listen. "Valeria's dad?"

"Yeah," Josh answered his wife but kept his eyes on Ten. "I never told her about the other night. Figured it was to be kept discrete." He narrowed his eyes and cocked his head. "You think Valeria's involved, don't you?"

"I did originally, but we were there earlier this morning. We woke the whole house up," Ten said.

"No one had even been awake," Maria said.

"So you thought it was me?" Josh asked with a nervous laugh.

"Or one of the other students, perhaps. You might have a clue," Ten said, finally coming back to reality.

Josh turned in his chair and looked around at Mel. She said, "Ken?"

Josh's forehead wrinkled. "I doubt it, but I don't know now. I thought it was Philippe, to be honest. He has plenty of reasons."

"It could be any one of the students," Ten said.

Maria's phone rang and she pulled it from her pocket. Then she stood and walked away. "Sorry, I have to get this."

"Uh oh," Josh said. He turned to his wife. "Can you make those coffees to go? I have a feeling things have changed."

Maria walked back into the kitchen. "That was Chief Carney. He just got a call from Mrs. Marin. Valeria was missing when she went to rouse her this morning."

Ten looked at Josh for a reaction.

The man sat back in his chair, shaking his head. "I can't believe that. It's not like her."

Maria said, "Ten, I think you may have been right after all."

"But now we've lost her. She could be anywhere."

Josh stood. "Those coffees done, honey?" He turned to Ten and Maria. "I think I know where she is."

CHAPTER 39

The sun crested the mountains as they arrived at the park. The grass leading to the woods soaked Ten's tennis shoes long before they reached the woods path. No other cars were in the parking lot this early in the morning. Josh took the lead. He held a finger to his lips and slowed as he led them deeper into the woods, then parted some brush and walked off-path. Ten and Maria were right behind him. The woods opened to a clearing.

Valeria let out a tiny scream and jumped in front of Ricardo. She shot an accusing glare at Josh Hobart, daggers straight from her eyes. "How could you? I should never have brought you here."

He shook his head as though he had nothing to say, or nothing he could think to say. His downturned eyes displayed how sorry he was. He stepped aside as Ten walked forward, his Glock in his hand and raised. "Mr. Marin, I have to take you in."

Valeria had her arms stretched to her sides and stood in front of him. "Take me. I did it. I let him out. They'll beat him again if he goes back in."

"Who told you about that?" Maria asked.

"I'm not stupid!" Valeria yelled. "Mom tries to protect us, but I know."

"And Juana?"

"I didn't tell her. She would worry. She already cries at night." Valeria looked comfortable in loose sweatpants and a hooded sweatshirt.

"Your mom. Does she know about this?" Maria asked.

Valeria shook her head. "No one knows. Not even Uncle Philippe."

"He must," Ten said. "You were using his computer that night."

"He thought I was doing homework. Mom did too. I told them my internet access was broken. Mom wouldn't know, and Uncle Philippe believed me."

"There must be someone else. Where are you going? How will you get there?" Ten asked.

"It doesn't matter. Take me. Please." She began to cry.

Ricardo pushed her arms down and wrapped his arms around her. He looked at Ten. His eyes were soft, kind, compassionate. "I told her not to, but then wanted to see my children one last time," he said. "And my wife."

Ten felt Ricardo's words harder than any words he'd ever heard. He would have liked to have seen Amy one last time. But he was at a bar for a friend's fake birthday, a friend who had turned out to be his handler, the man who was supposed to kill him. A blur. His whole past blurred before him carried by Ricardo's heartfelt pronouncement. Ten shook his head and waved the gun. "Sit," he said. "I have to think."

Maria stepped toward Valeria to hold her but stopped mid-stride as Ricardo pulled her closer.

Then they heard a rustling from the path. Before Ten could react, Josh yelled, "Over here!"

Mrs. Marin and Juana burst through the underbrush and ran to Ricardo. "I knew you would be here!" Mrs. Marin yelled as she hugged and kissed her husband. Juana wailed as she threw her arms around her sister, mom, and dad.

Maria reached out to touch Ten's arm. He didn't even turn to look at her. He didn't want to see the look on her face. He could guess.

Before anyone said anything, while they were all just watching the reunion, Chief Carney and four of his officers burst through the underbrush.

Again, Valeria let go of her family and stood in front of them with her arms out. "I did it!" she screamed. "It's my fault! Take me."

Mrs. Marin reached for Valeria and yelled, "No!" She was in tears with worry for her daughter, for seeing and touching her husband, for the confusion, the overwhelming fear of what would happen next. It all displayed in her eyes.

Chief Carney must have seen Ten's reluctance to move and stepped forward. "We'll take care of it from here."

Maria said, "Mrs. Marin and Juana didn't know. Valeria is telling the truth."

"And Mr. Hobart?" Carney asked. "What's he doing here."

"He led us here," she said.

"Then he knew too?"

Josh didn't say a word.

"No. It's not like that—" she tried to explain.

Carney cut her off. "Doesn't matter. We're taking them all in. We'll sort it out once everyone is under custody."

"But we know," Maria said.

"At the station," Chief Carney said as the four officers escorted the sobbing family out of the clearing. Josh followed as though in shock but made no attempt to say anything. The chief turned to Maria and Ten.

"You followed us," Maria said.

"It's my job," Carney said apologetically. Then he nodded to them both and walked after his men.

Ten said nothing. He stood there, detached from the activity but not the emotions, which washed over him like an ocean wave, toppling him to the ground, soaking him.

He let a tear drop from his eye. If Maria saw it, she said nothing, allowing him the dignity to have that moment. He brushed his eyes with the back of his hand. "We'd better go."

"Are you going to be okay?"

"I have a favor to cash in."

Maria thought she knew what it was. She drove slowly toward the police station.

"Give them time to get everyone settled," Ten said. "Take the scenic route while I make the call."

Maria drove. She listened to Ten's half of the conversation. She couldn't hear Jacob speaking, but caught the gist of the conversation.

Once Ten finished, he stared out the window. Maria didn't say a word, which he appreciated. She let him be in his own world and he knew it. She was like that.

He hardly saw the scenery as it went by, his mind elsewhere. His hopes elsewhere. Jacob had made no promises. In fact, he seemed annoyed during the whole conversation. But Ten was relentless, demanding, pleading. And eventually felt as though he got through. Jacob wouldn't—couldn't—understand where Ten was coming from. But he listened. As they approached Muncy, Ten turned to Maria. "There has to be some semblance of justice in the world."

"Regardless of what happens, you have to know that you did the right thing."

"Tried to," he said.

"Your hunch was right from the start. I don't have to tell you that."

"Lucky guess."

"Never," she said. "You knew."

They pulled up outside the police station. Carney met them on the porch. He didn't look happy. His mouth sagged into a deep frown. "I'm sorry," he said as they approached.

"You're just doing your job," Ten said.

"We picked up a buddy of Ricardo's from the shop. He was out of his car and headed down the path when we arrived. I had two other guys chase him down." He shook his head. "This is a mess. One I wish we didn't have. I feel for the family. Usually, we capture the escapees and take them back to prison. I'm going to hold them as long as I can so they can be together." He lowered his eyes and shook his head. "I think you're right; the mom and sister didn't know. I don't know what will happen about Valeria."

"What about the buddy?" Maria asked.

"Accomplice."

"Hobart?"

"We'll let him go. You'll have to make a statement, but he said you came to him and he just happened to know where they were because Valeria took him there one time to talk. His story seems legit. I'll get a statement about the whole thing before he leaves though."

"Can we talk with them?" Maria asked.

"Sure," Carney turned for them to follow.

Ten said, "I'll be in. I have one more call to make."

***

The next morning, Carney sat across from Maria. Ten sat off to the side, the consultant. "I don't know how you did this," Carney said.

"Let's just say my consultant friend here cashed in on a huge favor." She nodded her head toward Ten. "He's probably going to owe *several* favors to make up for this."

"I can't speak for you, but I think it was worth it," Chief Carney said as he shifted his attention toward Ten. "How you got the paperwork to be backdated a month, that must have taken some doing. A few people got into trouble at the prison, I heard, but nothing they won't get over. No one got fired. So because of the mix up, Ricardo is now free. His immigration paperwork has been fully approved. I haven't told them yet. I wanted to let you know first."

"Is that why you called us in?" Maria asked.

"I thought you'd want to tell them," he said to her. He smiled at Ten then. "Or maybe the guy who called in the favor."

"No favor," Ten said. "Regardless of what Maria told you, this was all done beforehand. Somehow the paperwork got slowed up going through the system."

"If that's the story I'm supposed to tell," Carney said.

"That's the one."

"His friend from the repair shop was just going there to take him home. A friendly visit to help out a friend from what I understand. That's what your ISTI group, who called this morning, explained anyway." Carney glanced between them, back and forth. "You tied up all the ends. So who wants to tell the family?"

Ten turned to Maria. "You tell them. I need to walk outside for a minute. Get some air."

Maria stood. "Shall we, Chief?"

"You should really start calling me Jake."

"Jake, it is," she said.

Ten walked out the front of the building. He called Jacob to thank him.

The second Jacob answered the phone, no hello, no how are you, just "you owe me."

"I thought that might be the case."

Jacob laughed. "Do you have any idea how fucking hard you make my job?"

"I may have an idea."

Then Jacob got quiet. "This was important to you."

"Yes, it was."

"We used up our connection with Roger."

"I know that." Ten took a breath. "You don't have to pay me."

Jacob laughed. "Don't be ridiculous. We're paying you. You're not getting off that easily. I'm collecting too. You bet your ass that's going to happen."

Ten had to laugh. Only part of their conversation was funny though. He knew he was on the hook and Jacob was the type of person who would collect.

***

Later that month, Maria sat across from Ten. His favorite meal. Breakfast. Maria drove. They sat at a window table inside the Denny's closest to his apartment. "It looks like a plea bargain got Blake Paton off. He'll never practice again, so maybe that's punishment enough," Maria said.

"I don't think he had any marketable skills. He wasn't the type of person who knew how to use his hands for anything," Ten said.

"Gross."

"Oh God, I didn't mean that. I'm sorry."

"Nancy was right. He was a weasel. Which reminds me. I wasn't aware of you getting Ricardo's friend off the hook, or Nancy for that matter. Why didn't you tell me?"

"I wasn't sure my request for Nancy would go through. I told Jacob that Valeria and her dad were priority one. I don't know why, but I threw Nancy in at the end of the conversation. Honestly, I think he did that for himself."

"Himself?"

"Nancy is a techie."

"And now that Roger is off the books."

"Exactly. And the other guy, Ricardo's friend, I think that was mostly Carney's idea. He made up the story about the guy finding out and going to give Ricardo a ride home. Jacob said that it worked for him. Why not take advantage of the paperwork story?"

"Anyone mention how Ricardo got from the prison to the park?" she asked.

Ten grinned at her.

Their breakfast came. Ten downed his coffee and asked for a refill before the waitress walked away.

Maria reached over and lifted his shirt sleeve. "Are things getting better?"

"What Valeria and her sister and mother went through was worse than what I'm going through. I don't always think so. But for the most part, I know my ending. Ricardo had already been beaten once. They were in constant fear of the unknown, whether he'd live another day or not. And they couldn't do anything about it. At least I know. I don't like it, but I know. Some people do have it worse than I do."

"Is Carol helping with therapy?"

"I'm still going."

She nodded. "Glad to hear that. So you know the next job is going to be worse than this one," Maria said. "Jacob will be sure of that."

"I'll be ready."

"We'll be ready," she said.

***

AUTHOR'S NOTE

First of all, any mistakes you might find in this novel are mine and I take full responsibility for them. But also note, I took a lot of liberties about prison layouts, building layouts, and street names and numbers. I had some friends look over the software and hardware sections to be sure I wasn't pushing things too far. I spoke with several people in the computer security business and can't mention their names here, but thank you, thank you, thank you. Where I've stretched what's actually possible or feasible, forgive me. But also, let me tell you that some things you think are impossible? Aren't. Just so you know.

THE KILLING MACHINE

TERRY PERSUN

WILD BLUE PRESS

WildBluePress.com